"Gus is a rescue. I promise to keep a better eye on him," Nicole said.

Holly ran up to them, catching the end of the conversation. "Daddy knows all about animals. He's a vetnerian."

Confused, Nicole met Ethan's gaze. Ethan's lips quivered.

"I'm a veterinarian."

"Oh. Gotcha."

"And I'm sorry if I came off too strong. You can always bring Gus by the clinic if you need some pointers."

Her previous ire vanished. "Thanks. I'm still working on the commands I recently learned in obedience class."

Ethan eyed Gus and chuckled. "I can see it's working."

"He can be a handful to deal with."

As Holly and Gus played, Ethan glanced over her shoulder. "The cottage?"

"That's right. I'm renting for the next month."

"You're not settling down?"

"No," she blurted with more emphasis than necessary.

Nicole didn't stay anywhere long-term.

Dear Reader,

Welcome to more romances set in Golden, Georgia, with new characters to meet and a chance to check in on old friends. And since this is Golden, you never know what the people in town have tucked up their troublemaking sleeves.

As I was plotting this new series, I kept returning to one theme: sisterhood. Something to be valued, unless family dynamics have caused an estrangement that seems insurmountable. This is the dilemma for the Connelly sisters, who have grown apart. But Nicole, Addie, Briana and Taylor will discover that forgiveness is possible through love. In my life I don't have sisters, but the idea of exploring these relationships had me looking forward to seeing how their stories would turn out.

In their journeys, they'll meet the men who will change their lives forever. The healing process will let them fall in love, but not without a few ups and downs along the way.

Nicole Connelly hasn't lived in Golden for years, but a job lands her in town, renting a cottage next door to the handsome town veterinarian, Ethan Price. Right from their first meeting there are undeniable fireworks. If you delight in a meet-cute, sit back and watch their relationship unfold. Then throw a feisty golden retriever and an adorable five-year-old girl into the mix!

Thanks for taking another trip to Golden with me. I hope you enjoy your escape to the mountain town I have fallen in love with. Let romance capture your heart.

Tara

THE SURPRISE NEXT DOOR

TARA RANDEL

Harlequin

HEARTWARMING

Harlequin®
HEARTWARMING™

Recycling programs
for this product may
not exist in your area.

ISBN-13: 978-1-335-05153-0

The Surprise Next Door

Copyright © 2025 by Tara Spicer

 Harlequin Enterprises ULC
22 Adelaide St. West, 41st Floor
Toronto, Ontario M5H 4E3, Canada
www.Harlequin.com

Printed in Lithuania

MIX
Paper | Supporting
responsible forestry
FSC® C021394

Tara Randel is an award-winning, *USA TODAY* bestselling author. Family values, a bit of mystery and, of course, love and romance are her favorite themes because she believes love is the greatest gift of all. Tara lives on the west coast of Florida, where gorgeous sunsets inspire the creation of heartwarming stories. Tara has received the Heart of Excellence Readers' Choice Award and the National Excellence in Romance Fiction Award. For more information about her books, visit Tara at tararandel.com and like her on Facebook at tararandelbooks.

Books by Tara Randel

Harlequin Heartwarming

The Golden Matchmakers Club

Stealing Her Best Friend's Heart
Her Christmastime Family
His Small Town Dream
Her Surprise Hometown Match

Meet Me at the Altar

Always the One
Trusting Her Heart
His Honor, Her Family
The Lawman's Secret Vow

Visit the Author Profile page
at Harlequin.com for more titles.

To my mother, Dorothy, for all your encouragement
when I'm in the writing process and the happiness
you share when a new book is released.
Thanks for being there for me.

CHAPTER ONE

NICOLE CONNELLY DRAGGED out the last box of work supplies from the storage space located in the rear of her green Jeep and hauled it inside the rental cottage. Balancing the box against an upraised knee while opening the door, she stumbled inside to deposit the items on the desk located in the corner, nearly tripping over her furry roommate in the process. Her current project for Sanders Entertainment, a company offering large event staging and conference or trade show setup services, had her staying in Golden for a month to decorate the town to be photographed for a magazine spread. As a senior manager in charge of designing and staging scheduled events, she traveled often to oversee each project. "So far, so good," she announced to Gus, the new addition in her life. The golden retriever barked, then sat back and watched her.

"What?"

Gus blinked.

"We're only staying a few weeks, so don't get comfortable."

After a big yawn, Gus wandered off to inspect

the other boxes she'd lugged inside. Blowing out a breath, she rolled her heavy suitcase into the cozy bedroom and tossed it on the bed. They'd arrived in the dark last night, so she'd yet to explore the cottage her mother had arranged for her to rent for her stay in Golden.

The mattress had been top-notch and once she'd fallen into bed, Nicole slept soundly. A nice change, since she'd been plagued with nerves after being assigned this job in her old hometown.

What was she thinking, coming back to Golden? She should have gotten a colleague to head the project instead. If her mother hadn't pleaded with her, Nicole would have refused. After all Mom had been through, Nicole couldn't tell her no. And besides that, she was a bit curious about her hometown these days.

The last time she'd set foot in town had been six months ago, after their father had died. Once the memorial service ended, she'd hightailed it back to Savannah like her feet were on fire. Yes, she felt bad for taking off so soon, but what was she going to do? Make small talk with her sisters, the three women whom she'd become estranged from ever since their father's infidelity had come to light? The family dynamics had eroded to the point that Nicole left Golden as soon as she graduated from high school.

It wouldn't hurt to stick around after the service. Find out what your sisters are up to.

The hurt and regret in her mother's eyes when she'd said those words had been too much, so Nicole did what she did best. She ran. Now, she wanted to make up for causing her mom the unnecessary pain. The sister issues were for Nicole to deal with later.

Shaking off the guilt, Nicole ventured into the living room. The owner had great taste in decorating, making the cottage much homier than her condo. The walls were painted a mellow yellow shade, and combined with the wide windows that ushered in a lot of natural light, made for a very bright space. A large brown sofa featured bright patterned pillows, and a colorful patchwork quilt in earth-tone shades with pops of peach to soften the effect was draped across the back. The matching armchair, this with a crocheted throw on the arm, also came with an ottoman covered in a checkered print. At home, the walls of her condo were still construction-grade white. She'd managed to assemble a couch she bought at a big-box store that sat in the middle of her living room, facing a television she hadn't found a stand for. In this space, the TV was mounted on the wall above a beautiful fireplace trimmed with colorful mosaic tiles, the surrounding bricks and hearth painted a creamy white, making it the focal point of the room.

She frowned. Maybe once she stopped traveling so frequently, she could spend more time making her place a home.

In the corner, Gus nudged his nose against the plastic box storing his food and other pet supplies. Yeah, Gus wouldn't mind it if she stayed in one place for a while.

"It's not time for lunch, buddy."

At his hangdog expression, Nicole chuckled. The fluffball was nothing if not serious about his food. Seems like being talked into bringing a rescue dog home from the shelter was going to be more of an adventure than she'd first anticipated. To pacify him, she opened the container and began removing his toys, tossing them on the floor. Gus ran over to pick out his favorite. "Give me a couple minutes and I'll feed you."

He huffed in response, a mangled toy—a stuffy in the shape of a giraffe that squeaked—hanging from his mouth. He'd made a big deal about that particular toy when they'd wandered through the pet store, so she bought it for him when he was getting acclimated to living with her. Happy now, he wandered off to plop down on his bed.

Once she inspected the kitchen, she'd find a place to keep his bowls and a high storage space for a bag of kibble. In the meantime, she needed to finish unpacking and review her plans.

Her gaze fell on the box from the office. Despite her at-odds emotions about being back in the small mountain town, she had to admit, she was excited about staging Golden for a *Holidays in Small Town Georgia* magazine spread—a first in her career—though it didn't come without its challenges. Her timeline was short, and she'd be working solo since this job wasn't labor extensive, but she'd have to simultaneously decorate sections of town in different holiday themes in order for the photographer to capture the essence of a festive Golden. Her mother had been persuasive to the point of begging when the topic came up, so Nicole had given in, despite her personal reservations and took the job head on.

"Nope. Get organized first," she said out loud as she moved back to the calming bedroom, decorated in shades of soft blue and gray, and unzipped her suitcase. She'd just flipped open the lid when she heard a noise that sounded suspiciously like the back door slamming. She'd shut it securely after Gus's early morning walk, hadn't she? Rushing into the kitchen, sure enough, she found the room empty. The back door hung open a crack.

"He did not…"

After grabbing the leash off the hook by the door, she ran out to the concrete patio, dodging outdoor furniture like a pro football player making a run to the goal line, just in time to glimpse a flash of deep yellow streaking across the backyard, heading straight to the next-door neighbor's house. This morning, when she'd taken him out early to do his business, he'd wanted to wander, but she hadn't let him, promising to take him exploring later. Apparently, the escape artist had other ideas.

"Gus," she yelled, but he paid her no mind. She took off after him, catching sight of his fluffy tail as he rounded the corner of the two-story home.

In flip-flops, she skidded on the damp grass, nearly wiping out before finally discovering her errant dog sitting in front of a kneeling girl, lapping up her attention.

"You have got to be kidding me," Nicole muttered under her breath, slowing her pace so as not to startle the little girl. If it hadn't been for Gus invading her space, the girl might not have even noticed her.

"Hi, there!" Nicole called out. "I see you've met Gus."

The little girl rose, a delighted smile on her face. "He likes me."

Nicole strolled up to them. "He does. He likes everyone. He's a very friendly dog and loves kids."

"I'm a kid."

Nicole bit back a chuckle. "Yes, you are." She stopped to frown at Gus, who merely smiled up at her, then focused on her new neighbor. "My name is Nicole. What's yours?"

"Holly."

"Nice to meet you, Holly. Gus and I just moved in next door. Looks like we're going to be neighbors."

"Oh, good. I've been wanting someone to play with. I don't have school today."

Nicole glanced around the spacious, neatly maintained yard. A playset with swings and a slide sat in one corner, a shed in the other. Her gaze traveled back to Holly. She hadn't been around children much, but if she had to guess, she'd put her age at five. Why was she outside all alone?

"Where is your mom or dad? Do you have any brothers of sisters?"

"No. Just me and Daddy."

Hmm. Where was this daddy and why did he let his daughter go out into the yard where anyone could come over and talk to her? Was her mother not home? Gus walked over and nudged his wet nose against her knee. Nicole patted his head. "Okay, buddy, we should head home."

She grabbed his collar to hook the leash when a door slammed behind her. Heavy footsteps pounded on the wooden deck. With a yelp, she jumped and spun around to find a tall, dark-haired man, panic reflected in his eyes.

"What are you doing in my backyard with my daughter?"

"You startled me." With a hand over her beating heart, Nicole nearly asked him why he left Holly alone in the first place.

"Much the way I felt when I spotted my daughter talking to a stranger."

"She's not a stranger, Daddy. She's Nicole." Holly came up beside her. "And this is Gus."

"Sorry to cause a fuss. My dog escaped. I was chasing after him," Nicole explained, hooking her thumb over her shoulder in the direction of the cottage. "New neighbor."

"I have a new friend, Daddy." Holly hugged Gus, who ate up the attention by falling on his back to get tummy rubs. "Can he stay and play?"

Nicole tried not to roll her eyes over Gus's antics. Then she read the indecision on the man's face. "He's safe," she assured him, also noting the love shimmering in the depths of his dark eyes. The earthy scent of his cologne—sandalwood, maybe?—tickled her senses.

"For a minute, while I talk to…"

Nicole moved to the steps and held out her hand, wishing she had put on a cute sundress instead of a baggy T-shirt and shorts. "Nicole Connelly."

He stepped down to the ground, taking her hand in his. "Ethan Price."

When his skin touched hers, a tingle shot up her arm. Her gaze flew up to meet his, catching the surprise that matched hers. He quickly masked his response while she removed her hand from his to tuck her thick, short hair behind one ear, and she wondered again where his wife was. She attempted what she hoped was a sneak peek at his ring finger, finding it bare, which was good in light of her reaction to his touch. Still, no ring didn't mean no wife…

"Again, sorry," she said, trying to recover from the jolt of awareness. "I haven't had Gus for very long so we're still training. His behavior is usually pretty good, but he is very friendly. Honestly, if the shelter hadn't already named him, I'd have christened him EA."

A questioning frown formed over gorgeous eyes. *Gorgeous? Wait. What?*

"EA?"

"Escape Artist," she explained. "Or Dash. Either sums up his tendency to take off willy-nilly."

Then she noticed the tiniest twitch move the corners of his lips and her interest rose.

She cleared her throat.

"He's been like this since I met him. Gus, I mean."

She cleared her throat again. "An animal rescue worker lives in my condo complex and introduced us at a fundraiser. Gus is good with people so Holly will be fine. He just likes to see what's around the next corner. It's funny really, since I don't know what kind of home he originally came from, but we're working on his manners. Hopefully the folks in Golden won't mind a dog who would rather lick you than bark at you."

At Ethan's raised eyebrow, she clamped her mouth shut. Where was the calm, cool, professional woman Nicole usually presented to the world? Ditched by the woman inside who admired his handsome face.

Temporarily moving back to Golden was clearly messing with her head.

Feeling suddenly awkward, she wanted to wrangle Gus home, but he raced across the grass with Holly in hot pursuit. "Again, I'm sorry if we upset you."

Ethan's focus on her remained steadfast. "Is this going to be a problem?"

She tilted her head to regard him more closely. "This?"

"You and your dog?"

Her shoulders squared. What did he mean by that question?

"Do you want it to be a problem?" she asked with a kick of sass.

He frowned.

"Do you have something against pets?" Nicole queried. "Maybe I should check with your wife."

His expression closed. "I'm divorced."

"Oh, my gosh, I'm sorry."

He sent her a brusque nod.

"To explain, Gus is a rescue. We're still getting used to each other, so there might be times he comes for a visit."

She wanted to be offended by this direction of the conversation, but it was clear by the intense expression on Ethan's face that his only intention was to protect his daughter. "I promise to keep a better eye on him."

Holly ran up to them, catching the end of the conversation. "Daddy knows all about animals. He's a venterian."

Confused, Nicole met Ethan's gaze. Ethan's lips quivered.

"I'm a veterinarian."

"Oh. Gotcha."

"And I'm sorry if I came off too strong. You can always bring Gus by the clinic if you need some pointers."

Her previous ire vanished. "Thanks. I'm still trying out the commands I recently learned in obedience class."

Ethan eyed Gus and chuckled. "I can see it's having an effect."

"He can be a handful to deal with."

As Holly and Gus played, Ethan glanced over her shoulder. "The cottage?"

"That's right. I'm renting for the next month."

"You're not settling down?"

"No!" she blurted with more emphasis than necessary.

Nicole didn't stay anywhere long-term. She didn't believe in it anymore. Not since her father's lengthy indiscretion was revealed and had torn the family apart. Angry and embarrassed, she'd escaped the drama and gossip in Golden for good and had kept on going. If it hadn't been for her mom and talks of a promotion before she left Savannah, she wouldn't have accepted this project. Who knew where she'd be next, once this job was complete. She would need to seriously consider her boss's offer of a more senior post, as well as learning if he was interested in her idea of forming a new boutique-party division within the company.

"What will you be doing here?" Ethan asked.

She pulled her scattered thoughts together. "The chamber of commerce hired the company I work for to decorate Golden, from one end to the other, highlighting different holidays throughout the year. It's for a great magazine layout."

"Travelers Quarterly?"

"That's the one." She paused. "Wait. How did you know?"

Tone wry, he said, "Golden is a small town."

Right. She should have guessed.

"So, you're going to decorate Golden in four different seasons in the middle of April?"

She shrugged. "In order to get Golden in the last issue of this year, we need photos taken now. This way tourists can see and then decide which holiday they'll visit a decked-out Golden. It's good for tourism."

Ethan nodded. "I see."

"It'll be fun. I've never seen Golden decorated for Christmas this early." She counted off on her fingers. "Or Easter, Fourth of July, or Thanksgiving." She stopped babbling. "You get the gist."

Interest lit his eyes. "You're from Golden?"

"Originally. Haven't lived here in a long time."

Not that she planned on living here again. But her mother and the chamber of commerce's chief marketing director, Carrie Mitchell, were relentless when promoting Golden, so a month it would be.

"I guess that means we'll be bumping into each other around town," Ethan said, his gravelly voice causing another tingle to wash over her.

It was then she really took notice of him. Tanned skin, warm brown eyes flecked with gold and dark hair, cut short, so effortless a style it was clear he didn't have time to worry about messing with mousse or spray every morning. A neatly trimmed beard added to his allure—she did have a thing for beards. Broad shoulders stretched his button-down shirt and his long legs filled out neatly pressed khakis.

She swallowed hard. "Right. I'm sure we'll see each other." She clapped her hands together to get her wayward pet's attention, then Gus ran over with Holly at his heels.

"C'mon, buddy. We need to get home. It's feeding time."

Gus danced around her. Holly's sweet laughter filled the air. Nicole turned her attention to Ethan. Wow. He was gorgeous.

"We should get inside," he told his daughter, holding out his hand. Holly placed her tiny hand in his and the sight stirred Nicole's heart.

"'Bye." Holly waved with her free hand. Ethan nodded in Nicole's direction before they walked up the steps to the deck that ran the length of the house.

Nicole took hold of the leash, dragging Gus home.

What was wrong with her? At thirty-two years old, she never tingled over a guy. Never committed to a long-term relationship. She was too busy. On the go, with a job that took her all over the southern US. If she happened to meet a man who caught her attention, she enjoyed dating, was always up front about her situation, until she moved on again.

But most of all, she didn't want any guy to have all the power. Especially not after what her father had done to her mother and his family. So, she kept on the go, never planting roots, perpetuating her vagabond lifestyle.

She took one last glimpse over her shoulder. The little family had disappeared inside their house. She pictured them eating lunch, Holly talking a mile a minute, Ethan, with his serious expression, listening to every word.

Serious. That was okay—serious never bothered her. But bumping into her neighbor while she was in Golden? That might pose a bit of a challenge due to her unintended interest in the guy. But, hey, when had she ever let obstacles get in her way?

"Never," she told Gus once the cottage came into view and he started to jog. "This won't be a problem at all."

She had a job to do. She prided herself on her work ethic and this important photo shoot in Golden was no exception. And she was good at juggling, so maybe her next-door neighbor would be a welcome distraction as she navigated her dealings with her family. Because those unresolved issues were coming to a head, she could feel it.

Once inside, she released the leash and kneeled before Gus, ruffling his fur. "You have to vow not to escape again." He cocked his head. "Don't give me that," she muttered, knowing that innocent expression was just a ploy.

"I LIKE HER," Holly said in between bites of her PB&J. As soon as they'd come indoors, she'd beelined for the table to dig into her lunch. Ethan joined her, carrying a cutting board to the table with a red delicious apple on top. Seemed his five-year-old daughter had made up her mind about the mystery woman, which didn't surprise him. For such a young age, she was quite opinionated.

Ethan chuckled. "You do, do you?"

Holly sent him a sideways glance. "What do you think?"

He paused cutting apple slices. What did he think? He'd been making lunch when he heard voices outside. Peering through the window, he'd been taken aback by a stranger talking to his daughter in their yard. He hadn't even noticed the dog, and had jumped into protective mode as he always did when it came to Holly. Before he realized it, he'd been out the door confronting his new neighbor.

"She seems nice," Ethan said.

Holly accepted a slice of apple. "And pretty."

True. Ethan reluctantly admitted that Nicole's sapphire-blue eyes were hard to erase from his memory. Her chin-length, wavy blond hair in a blunt cut was in messy disarray, but it suited her, the dark roots evident as the sun emphasized the highlighted shades that softened the effect. Obviously, she'd been after her dog, who'd sniffed Ethan before he'd realized Gus was there.

"Maybe you could be friends," Holly suggested as she took a bite of her sandwich.

Ethan met her gaze but stayed quiet. The little buzz of…something he'd felt when he shook Nicole's hand had caught him off guard. While the sensation was pleasant and unexpected, he didn't want to get Holly's hopes up because the answer was most likely no. After his divorce, he wasn't actively seeking out female friends. He didn't want Holly to get hurt again, even if the outgoing neighbor with an adorable dog, who was sure to steal his daughter's heart, meant well.

As Holly chatted about Gus, Ethan laid down the knife and rested against the high-backed chair. Crossing his arms over his chest, he listened, but her suggestion of being friends with a new woman echoed in his head. True, he'd been so busy getting used to the full-time veterinarian practice, making much-needed updates to the clinic he'd taken over, that he hadn't gone out of his way to start a friend pool. Was it out of habit? He and his wife, April, had traveled for her job in the beginning years of their marriage, so he didn't form attachments easily. Then, after Holly was born and he wanted permanent roots, the marriage fell apart. The opportunity to come to Golden had been perfect and he couldn't pass it up. He was only thirty-five. They'd been here for six months. Surely, he should have a social life by now.

"I think Gus will come visit me every day," Holly asserted.

Ethan wasn't sure how he felt about that. Also, he wasn't sure he wanted to dwell on Nicole either. She was intriguing, but by her own admission, she'd only be in Golden for a month. He didn't want Holly to get attached.

Changing the topic, he asked, "Want to come to the clinic with me this afternoon?" Today had been a teacher-planning day, giving them a long weekend, so Ethan had taken advantage of the time off from school to spend it with Holly. There were no patients scheduled this afternoon, but he had some business to catch up on.

Holly's face lit up. "Yay! Can I play with the puppies?"

"You can," he promised. There was nothing like

the lure of puppies to motivate a child. "Why don't you finish up your sandwich and apple slices, then brush your teeth."

"I will, Daddy."

He cleaned up while she finished every crumb on her plate, then dashed from the kitchen to run upstairs to get ready for their jaunt to town.

His chest tightened uncomfortably. Spending long hours at the Golden Veterinary Clinic was necessary, but it also meant that he'd been away from Holly too often. Since the divorce and move to a new town, his daughter had been clingy. Going to school had helped, and thankfully, he had a great babysitter in Mrs. Johnson, who lived two doors down the street. She watched Holly some days after school, or he'd pick up Holly and she'd come to the clinic, content to sit in his office and draw pictures for the animals currently recovering overnight. He didn't want separation from Holly to become a habit. They'd moved to this small town for stability and a grounded future. No more moving around to catch April's next big opportunity. It bothered Ethan that his ex-wife had put her job first, but he couldn't be sorry he'd made the decision to leave the marriage. To consider his daughter's needs before his own. This was home, now and for years to come, all for Holly's sake.

"Daddy, where are my sneakers?" Holly yelled from the foyer.

Shaking off shadows of the past, Ethan wiped down the counter, then found Holly rummaging in a shoe basket he kept by the front door. She'd tossed every item, big or small, on the floor. Of course, the pair she was searching for was on the bottom.

She held them up for Ethan to see. "Found them."

With a sigh, he picked up what resembled the remnants of a shoe store on sale day. Holly waited for him in the living room, her feet swinging from the couch. "Lace me up, Daddy."

"With pleasure, princess."

His nickname elicited a giggle. "I'm not a princess."

He leaned down to kiss the top of her head, his lips brushing the soft brown curls. "You are to me."

Her little arms hugged him, reminding him that she was the best thing that had ever happened to him. Seeing her happy and content made every decision he'd made on her behalf worthwhile.

"How about we stop at the park before going to the clinic? We haven't done that in a while."

Holly pumped her hand in the air. "Can I go on the swings?"

"I think that can be arranged."

After locking the front door, they started down the sidewalk, her tiny hand in his as she skipped to keep pace. His gaze strayed to the cottage next door. All was still. At odds from the woman residing there.

He really needed to stop thinking about her.

They were only a quarter mile from downtown. The bright sunshine on this warm spring day made the stroll worthwhile. He loved being outdoors, loved the mountain town of Golden. He and Holly had already hiked up to Bailey's Point, a popular tourist destination. The leaf-strewn path in the heavily wooded landscape and the scent of pine surrounding them made him feel alive. At Bailey's Point, they could just make out downtown but it offered a full view of Golden Lake. Holly had been thrilled when they'd made it to the higher altitude, but he'd had to carry her halfway down the dirt trail on the return trip. There were other locations he wanted to discover with her as soon as he had his practice at a place where he could take off a few hours a week.

Listening to Holly's animated conversation made the walk go quickly. When they entered Gold Dust Park, his daughter slipped her hand from his, running to the playground as she called out to her classmates. For a Friday afternoon, the area was crowded with parents and children, along with older residents, also out enjoying the nice day.

Once he made sure Holly was fine, talking to a few of the kids from her class, Ethan stood on the sideline in silent vigil. It didn't take long before one of the moms noticed him.

"Dr. Price. How nice to see you." The pretty woman approaching had a sleeping baby resting on her chest, swaddled in a wrap carrier.

"Mrs. Donovan."

"Faith, please. We don't stand on ceremony here."

He nodded, already having learned that tidbit about the people of Golden. The fact that he'd taken over the clinic had immediately made him part of the community.

"How's Rocky?" he asked.

He tended to remember dogs and their owners as a pair.

"Growing like crazy," Faith said. "Thanks for suggesting obedience classes. They're working like a charm."

"Most animals just need love and discipline."

"Love, he's got plenty of. Now that Roan has taken over the role as disciplinarian, things are almost calm at our house." She kissed the head of the baby nestled against her. "How are you and Holly settling in?"

"Great. We're figuring out life in Golden as we go."

Faith chuckled. "There's never a dull moment in this town."

He sent her a smile. "I've heard."

"You and Holly should come by for dinner sometime. The kids would love to play together. Also, I make a mean pot of chili. Or Roan could fire up the grill and we could cook burgers and hot dogs."

If Ethan remembered correctly, two of Faith's children were ahead of Holly in elementary school. He glanced in his daughter's direction to see her playing with the Donovan children.

The silent reminder that he needed to make more friends had him agreeing to her invite. "I'd like that."

"Can I contact you at the office to set up a date?"

She motioned to the baby. "My cell phone is in my bag and as you can see, I've got my hands full right now."

"That works."

"Great. We'll be looking forward to it."

"And, please. Let me know what I can bring."

"I will." She tilted her head. "You know, there's a group of—"

"Mama," one of the children shouted. "Lacey needs you."

Faith shook her head. "Duty calls."

"Need help?"

"No. That wasn't a panicked yell for Mama, that was my-sister-is-annoying-me tone."

He nodded. "Good to know."

She took a step, then turned back. "Fair warning. The fans are amassing." She winked and hurried off to the play area.

It was then that Ethan noticed folks making their way toward him. First came Mrs. Patterson, a sixty-something woman whom he'd seen at the clinic multiple times since he arrived.

"Dr. Price. Thanks so much for making Mittens feel better. He has a new lease on life."

Before he could answer, her companion, Mrs. Hurd, joined in.

"And the way you took care of Buster, I can't believe the change in him."

Ethan smiled and asked after each of the pets, getting updates. Once the women moved on, he checked his watch. Time to get to the clinic.

"Holly!" he called.

She stopped at the top of the slide, waved and swished down before her tiny feet were firmly planted on the ground. Then she yelled, "'Bye" over her shoulder and ran to him.

Seems his daughter was doing a better job of making friends than he was. Maybe Faith's invitation would be the beginning of solving that problem.

"Let's go, Daddy. I want to pet the puppies."

"Right. Puppies."

She skipped ahead of him as they exited the park. The clinic was located two blocks off Main Street, in its own building across the street from the busy town hall. With the traffic heavier in this area, he made sure to take Holly's hand again, leading her safely down the sidewalk. Once the long, sandstone-colored, one-story building with a variety of animals painted on the side came into view, Holly's pace picked up.

"Do you think the puppies will remember me?"

This week, a French bulldog mother had been brought in. It was clear she was in labor but having difficulty, which happened frequently with that breed. The dog owner and Ethan had stayed by the mother's side, doing what they could to make the delivery safe, until three little puppies were born. He'd suggested keeping them at the clinic, to make sure mama and babies were doing okay, before sending them home.

"They're only a few days old. Their eyes haven't

opened yet, so they aren't aware of what's around them. Mostly they're eating and sleeping."

"But I petted them the other day."

"You did. And you were very gentle."

Her chest puffed up. "I remembered what you told me. And the mother dog was nice to me."

Ethan grinned. Being able to introduce Holly to the beauty of animals brought him almost as much joy as keeping his patients healthy. From the time he was a boy he knew he'd wanted to be a vet and that desire had never wavered.

They'd just crossed the street when Holly asked, "Will Gus be okay if I'm not home?"

Just as he'd guessed. Holly was already bonding with the neighbor's dog.

"I'm sure he's happy to be with Nicole."

"But he ran away to see me."

"He did, but he'll be happy wherever she takes him."

"Can we ask Nicole over for a playdate?"

How to answer? He didn't want to let Holly down, but he wasn't sure if spending time with the woman who was going to leave town after completing her project was wise. Moving to Golden had been good for his daughter. They had a house, a backyard for Holly to run around in, a new school and the clinic, where he could practice for many years to come. There were so many positives, including friends who would come in and out of their lives.

"What do you say we take each day at a time.

If Gus is around, you can play. If he's with Nicole, you'll have to be patient."

"Gus likes me."

"He does, but remember, he and Nicole are only in town for her job. He is going to leave when she's finished."

"Not if we make them really, really good friends."

Oh, to have the optimism of a child.

"Just remember, princess, he can be a friend for a while but after he leaves, we'll find you another friend."

When she met his gaze, he read the sly determination in her eyes. He could imagine the wheels turning in her head.

"Like my very own pet?"

He sighed. She'd been on the pet kick for a while now, understandable for a little girl who was frequently around other people's animals. And while he wasn't against it, he'd been putting it off until he got a handle on the vet practice.

"How about we have that discussion when Gus leaves?"

"Okay, Daddy, but I think Gus is going to stay."

He remained quiet, not wanting to shatter his daughter's confidence. He pictured Nicole again, her laughing eyes and the way she'd been so friendly with Holly when he'd discovered them in the yard.

To his own chagrin, he reluctantly added Nicole to the list of positives of living in Golden, even if he hoped he didn't regret it.

CHAPTER TWO

"NICOLE, SWEETIE, are you home?"

"In the kitchen, Mom."

Nicole closed the cabinet door after storing the kibble bag out of Gus's reach. As she turned, her mother, Linda Connelly, entered the kitchen and deposited a large paper grocery bag, printed with the logo of Linda's General Store, on the small table. Her blue eyes, the hue similar to her daughters', sparkled with joy. She'd cut her shoulder-length graying blond hair shorter than the last time Nicole had seen her. Her skin had a healthy glow, like she'd been spending time out in the sun. It pleased Nicole to see her mother so happy.

After her parents' divorce, her mother purchased the old general store and turned it into a very successful business. Not only did she stock grocery items, but through the years she'd also added goods from local vendors, anything ranging from jams and jellies, homemade baked goods, natural soaps and candles, to, more recently, pottery and jewelry. Over time, the store had become a tourist stop and her mother had capitalized on the boom of Golden's rising popularity.

"What's all this?' Nicole asked, watching her mother reach into the bag.

Her mother pulled out a sack of apples. "Since you got in late last night, I figured you didn't have time to stop by the store. I brought a few things over to get you started."

"I have coffee, that's all I really needed this morning."

Her mother sent her a stern frown. "You need real food."

"Like?" Nicole placed a finger at the edge of the paper bag and tugged to peek inside. Her mouth watered at the pastries she glimpsed inside. "Are those from the bakery?"

Her mother tapped Nicole's hand away as she reached in for a chocolate-drizzled croissant. "It's for later."

"I didn't have lunch yet," Nicole pouted.

"Whyever not?"

"Because of Gus."

At the sound of his name, the big fluffball bounded over to nudge her mother's leg.

"Hey there, sweet boy."

Nicole snorted. "Sweet? Hardly."

"What did he do?"

"Escaped. Right into the neighbor's yard. I don't think he was pleased."

Her mom's eyebrows rose. "He? You mean Dr. Price?"

"That's the one." Nicole took an apple from the bag, then washed it before taking a bite. The sweet, tart taste reminded her of summer. She chewed, enjoying the burst of flavor.

"Huh," her mother continued. "That doesn't sound like him."

"To be fair, I was talking to his daughter and since he doesn't know me, he went all superdad mode."

"He does love Holly."

"Clearly."

"He's doing a great job raising his daughter alone." Her mother met her gaze. "He's divorced."

"I heard."

Her mother tilted her head. "But…?"

"But nothing. It ended okay. Holly wants to see Gus, so when I have time, I'll make it happen."

Her mother's face lit up. "Speaking of time, are you ready to make Golden holly jolly?"

Nicole placed her hands on her hips, puffed out her chest and deepened her voice. "As in 'ho, ho, ho'?"

Her mother chuckled as she took a loaf of bread and a package of lunch meat from the bag, then opened the refrigerator door to place them inside. "It will be your main focus."

"Believe it or not, I am looking forward to this. I enjoy decorating for different holidays as much as the next person. This will just be on a bigger scale."

Her mother slowed, removing a package of cooked chicken and some vegetables to add to the fridge. "It's not too much?"

"Mom, this is what I do."

"Since I only see you a few times a year," her mother sniffed, "how do I even know what you do?"

"I send you pictures."

"Not the same thing."

Nicole refrained from sighing. Her mother wasn't wrong, but memories of the past always made Nicole reluctant to return. "Now, you get to see me in action. Nicole Connolly, event-staging manager, enchanting Golden."

"The chamber of commerce made the right call to contact Sanders Entertainment."

"They could have called me directly, you know," Nicole said in a dry tone. "Instead of going straight to my boss."

"Carrie at the chamber thought it best we keep this project professional from start to finish."

"Until she asked for me by name. Then Mr. Sanders called me to the office to ask what was up. It's normal operating procedure for my team to book the event, plan logistics, and then for me to go on location and supervise the job. The CEO has bigger concerns."

"That would have been Mrs. M.'s input. You know she always aims right for the top."

Which made her a lovable meddler. Everyone in Golden knew that if Helen Masterson-Carmichael had you in her sights, nothing would stop her from getting results. From what Nicole understood from her mother, a few of the newly married couples in town could chalk up their wedded bliss to Mrs. M.'s interfering. She and her group of dedicated match-makers had made their mark on almost all the single people in town. The wily woman had even managed to snag a very distinguished gentleman and gotten married herself.

Mrs. M. was a legend, a force of nature, with a thriving Golden tourist economy as her ultimate goal. That's why so many of the people Nicole had grown up with were now happily hitched, residing in Golden and running businesses that lured tourists to the once-sleepy mountain town for their weekend trips or yearly vacations.

"Well, securing a spread in *Travelers Quarterly* is quite a coup," Nicole said. "I know some people who work at the magazine, and let me say, they are pretty picky about the locations they choose to highlight."

"As soon as we got word from the magazine, we knew we wanted you to handle the entire photo shoot."

"We?"

Her mother preened. "I'm on the volunteer support committee now."

Surprised pleasure shot through Nicole. "Since when?"

"Last year."

And her mother hadn't said anything. This was a big deal, especially with the aftermath of the divorce and the rumors that had swirled around the Connelly family for years. That her mother was truly part of the community thrilled her to no end.

But still, Nicole tried not to let the fact smart that she had been left out of the loop. She'd chosen not to reside in Golden, therefore missing out on most of the big news.

"So, that's why you were so adamant I take the job?"

Her mother wasn't one iota guilty. "What can I say? It was a sure way to get you to Golden for more than a few hours."

Nicole narrowed her eyes. "When did you become so sneaky?"

"When did my daughter refuse to see reason?"

Her mom had her there. Her ruse had worked.

"Anyway," Mom continued, "once we decided to contact your company, Mrs. M. started making calls."

Nicole picked up the remaining items that needed refrigeration and put them away. "And here I am, back in my hometown."

Her mother folded the bag and held it against her chest. "I couldn't be more thrilled. And you can visit with your sisters."

Her sisters. A whole other sticky wicket.

"I thought that after the funeral you'd stay for a bit," her mother commented in a neutral tone.

"You know why I didn't."

The last time she'd spoken to her father hadn't been pretty. Guilt, blame and asking for forgiveness had been thrown around, but Nicole had stood firm in her viewpoint. And then, he died. Now, she couldn't deny the remorse she felt after the final conversation she'd had with him, and her part in it.

Her mother tucked the bag into the pantry. "Nicole, it's been a long time."

Right. Her sisters. "And in that time, we've grown apart."

"That's why I'm so excited about you being in Golden for more than a few days. You can reconnect."

"Do they want to, Mom?"

It was an honest question. One she wasn't sure she deserved the answer to.

When Nicole left Golden all those years ago, she'd severed contact with all but her mother. On purpose, at first, since she and her sisters had differing opinions and ways of dealing with their father's actions. Then she got busy with her job and time flew by.

"Actually, Briana lives the next block over."

Nicole wasn't surprised. She couldn't see her oldest sister leaving town since she was an officer for the Golden PD.

Her mother's brow wrinkled. "You've met Cami, right?"

"Just once."

"She's a darling and Briana is a proud mama."

Nicole tried to dredge up a mental picture of her independent sister adopting a daughter and being a single mom, but somehow it worked.

"Addie and Jacob live on the other side of Main.

Not a far walk from here. You should see your nephew, he's sprouting up. And Taylor—"

"Mom, I don't want to talk about Taylor."

A rare touch of steel infused her mother's tone. "Well, you're going to have to. She's an innocent party in all your father did, just like the rest of us."

Nicole knew better than to argue. Her mother had made it known for a few years now that she wanted her family intact. Nicole's trip was just the vehicle for her mom to start making noises about the girls getting together.

"On another topic," her mother said, "did you get a call from the lawyer taking care of your father's affairs?"

She swallowed a groan. "Yes. He needs to meet with us on Wednesday afternoon." Us, meaning all the sisters. Not that she wanted to be included. She didn't really want anything from her father.

Her mother nodded. "At the old Sinclair building."

"That's the one." Very deliberately changing the subject, Nicole asked, "How did you manage to rent this place on such short notice?"

Her mother's gaze moved over the room. "This cottage is one of Mrs. M.'s properties."

"Of course, it is." The woman, along with most of the Masterson family, owned a large percentage of the real estate in Golden.

With a smile, Nicole walked to her mom and placed a kiss on the woman's soft cheek. Her signature floral scent, one Nicole remembered from when she was a little girl, enveloped her. "It's perfect. I'm really going to be comfortable."

Her mom hugged her, holding on a few beats longer than was necessary. Nicole soaked it up.

"I've missed you, sweetie."

"I know, Mom," she whispered. "I've missed you too."

They parted, both wiping their eyes.

"Enough of that," her mother said. "Are you all settled in?"

"I am. In fact, I was going to take Gus for a run around town. Get the lay of the land before I jump into making Golden holiday central."

"I don't want to keep you. I need to get back to the store." Her mom snapped her fingers. "Oh, did you let the post office know you'd be forwarding your mail?"

Since the project would take a month, Nicole had decided to have her mail sent here. "Yes, Mom. I remembered."

"Hey, you had a lot to accomplish before you left Savannah. Just lending a helping hand."

"Which I always appreciate," Nicole said. "Let me walk you outside."

Grabbing the leash, she hooked it to Gus's collar and led him from the cottage. The scent of freshly mowed grass brought a sense of nostalgia. Nicole had cut the grass at her mother's house when she was a kid, using the exercise to deal with the family stress. Now, she lived in a complex where a lawn crew took care of the grounds.

Nicole stopped short. "You're driving the delivery van?"

"All part of the service from Linda's General Store."

Nicole frowned. "Yeah, but why are you driving it?"

"My car is in the shop. I told Alyssa that I'd make a few stops while I was out."

"I thought you had employees to do that stuff?"

"What can I say? You haven't met Alyssa yet. She's my manager and runs a tight ship."

"Because you're busy building your dynasty?"

Her mother beamed. "I love that you think so, but it's just a general store."

"One you really put on the map."

"True." Her mother's face lit up. "Will you decorate the outside of the store for a few pictures? Maybe the magazine will choose one or two."

Since her mom had been instrumental in getting her this gig, Nicole had thought ahead. "It's on my list."

Her mother clapped her hands. "This is so exciting!"

Nicole chuckled. It may seem exciting, but for Nicole it would be hard work.

Her mother walked to the van, slowing to nod at the compact four-door Jeep, more SUV than off-road, that was parked ahead of her on the driveway. "How in the world did you get suitcases, boxes, pet food and Gus all in that vehicle?"

"Practice, Mom. I've been packing and unpacking every time I travel to work at a different location."

Her mom frowned. "Seems like an awful lot of fuss when you can just remain in one place."

Nicole held back an eye roll but understood her mother's perspective. Even though she hadn't mentioned her promotion to anyone, or the expansion proposal she'd floated by her boss, she wondered if she'd be able to stay in one location for long. Savanah was beautiful, but did she want to be cooped up in the office every day? Thankfully, she had an entire month to decide her future.

Her mom opened the van door. "Plan for family dinner Wednesday night after your meeting with the lawyer." She pointed at Nicole. "You will be there."

Not a request, more a command.

"I will. And thanks for the food."

"Not that I expect you to cook, but at least you have something in the house."

"You know me too well."

"I do." Her mother started to climb into the van but stopped. "I almost forgot." She fished her fingers in her front jeans pocket. "Here's the key to one of the town's storage units. Number twenty-three. There are plenty of decorations you can use so you don't have to order brand-new items."

"That's great. It'll keep my budget down."

"The collection spans a few years, so you should have luck finding what you need."

She moved back into the van, started the engine

and backed up. Nicole waved then brought Gus inside. "How about a run?"

Gus barked in agreement. She made a quick change into running shorts and a tank top, laced up her running shoes and secured her phone in the band wrapped around her upper arm, then collected her dog. On the sidewalk, she stretched before heading out in the opposite direction from Ethan's house, pausing at the shrubs delineating the line between her cottage and the white Craftsman house with red trim next door. It had been dark last night, and she hadn't checked out the neighborhood yet, so she took the time to study her surroundings, realizing the house seemed familiar. The curtains fluttered in the window. Nicole squinted. Waited a few moments. When there was no more movement, she put in her earbuds and got going.

She'd made it three houses down when she realized that the house she'd stopped in front of before was the home of her childhood best friend's grandmother. Well, best friend was stretching it. Nicole hadn't seen Kimmy since she left town and they'd grown apart. Nicole didn't think her old friend lived nearby any longer.

A wave of sadness swept over Nicole, which surprised her. Not an emotion she usually attributed to recollections of Golden. She brushed it away as quickly as it popped into her mind.

She reached Main Street, then headed toward Golden's greater downtown. Six tree-lined blocks built on an increasing incline that showcased gift shops, restaurants, lodging and a few professional offices. The buildings were painted in vivid colors. Old-fashioned, ornate cast-iron lampposts lined the street, supporting large planters overflowing with sunny yellow chrysanthemums.

The town had been established after a gold vein was discovered in the surrounding mountains. Folks had trekked to this beautiful spot of land, hoping to make a fortune, and establishing Golden in the process.

She slowed her pace, smiling at the canvas she would transform into a year's worth of holidays for the magazine spread. From what she'd remembered, the town had always been decorated in a mishmash of themes. In advance of the project, Nicole and her team had collected a slew of great images to help her form a cohesive strategy.

To start with, she'd decided on a winter wonderland on the west side of Main Street, which would be nostalgic and welcoming. Trees covered with faux snow outside the shops, pine garlands hung on doors and windows. The idea of a Victorian-themed Christmas in the shop windows kept returning.

On the east side of Main, she'd pick strategic spots to highlight other seasons during the following weeks. For spring, she'd stage baskets overflowing with flower blossoms. Elsewhere, she'd feature autumn with cornstalks, hay bales, scarecrows and the like. She'd have the photographer capture scenes from the lake for summer, and for the Fourth of July, she'd add patriotic decorations at the courthouse, which also housed city hall.

She pulled her phone from the band on her arm and started dictating.

"Main Street. Talk to store owners. Prevailing theme of a Victorian Christmas? Costumes and all?" Even though Golden played up its gold-discovery history, Nicole wanted to showcase the downtown so it would appeal to folks who wanted to travel to this vacation spot to experience a special holiday season, no matter which time of year it fell.

She had a list of people who were to be featured in the article. She'd stop and speak to each one when she was ready to make contact, but not today. Right now, she wanted to get a feel for the job at hand, see how much the town had changed, with no distractions. She snapped pictures as she went, knowing she'd need them later when she planned the staging of each scene. She might even add a few surprises as inspiration struck.

Gus barked, drawing her from her thoughts.

"Sorry, buddy. Let's keep going."

Creative ideas were popping into Nicole's head faster than she could dictate them into her phone. They ran to Gold Dust Park, making a wide swath of the grassy area. She passed the tall, bronze statue on a raised concrete platform showcasing a pickaxe and large golden nugget, a nod to the history of this mountain town.

Once they left the park, she made her way past Smitty's Pub, a popular hangout for the locals, and her mother's store, where she crossed Main Street before jogging down the other side of the street, taking more photos to get a visual layout of the rest of the businesses. All the while she pictured how she was going to transform the town.

For her last stop, she ducked into the chamber of commerce office to introduce herself to the staff. She spent twenty minutes with Carrie Mitchell, her point person, and discovered that the woman was a marketing wiz. The Sanders Entertainment brand was in good hands with Carrie.

After that, she and Gus traveled to the end of the district, heading toward the courthouse, knowing the stately Federal-style, redbrick building would be a key component in the magazine layout. A huge flag would hang over the portico, with swags of red, white and blue bunting over the white door and black shutters. Somehow, she had to introduce spar-klers into the scene. She would even…

Gus tugged on the leash, jerking Nicole toward the side street.

"Gus, what are you—"

As Nicole tried to control her wayward pet in vain, he headed directly toward a tall, broad-shouldered man walking down the sidewalk in front of them. A man she recognized from earlier that morning.

"Gus, no."

The man halted at her shout and turned around just in time for Nicole to barrel directly into him.

BEFORE ETHAN COULD brace himself, his lovely new neighbor crashed into him. Thankfully he had the presence of mind to grip her upper arms and catch her before she took a tumble. "Whoa there."

"Thanks," she said, eyes wide. When their gazes met, that funny sizzle of energy seized him again. They both paused for an elongated beat before Nicole pulled back. Once she did, Gus took her place, jumping up to put his paws on Ethan's chest.

"Gus!" Nicole tugged on the leash.

"Trust me," Ethan assured her, "this is a daily occurrence."

"Right, because you're a veterinarian."

He ruffled Gus's head. "Comes with the territory."

Once he'd had enough attention, Gus dropped down and moved away to sniff the sidewalk around them.

Nicole tucked her hair behind her ear. She'd done it when they'd met earlier today. Was she as affected by this chance meeting as he was? "I'm sorry."

"For meeting again under circumstances surrounding your dog?"

"He has a way of taking off unexpectantly." She tightened her grip on the leash. "Seems he's stronger than I thought."

Ethan pointed at the collar. "Can I make a suggestion?"

"About Gus?"

"Yes."

She shrugged. "You're the professional."

"When out running, try using a harness instead of hooking the leash to the collar. You'll have better control that way."

"I hadn't thought of that."

"You said you're a new pet owner, right?"

She nodded, her forehead wrinkling.

"There are a few tricks that'll make your life easier."

She blew out a sigh. "As I keep learning."

He chuckled. "I suggest you take a class. It never hurts to be the best dog mom you can be."

She sent an affectionate smile Gus's way. "He is a keeper."

"Learning as much as you can about your pet will go a long way with discipline and overall health." He shoved his hands in his pants pockets. Did he sound stuffy? Coming off like he was a know-it-all? He hoped not. "Out for a run?"

"Yes. It's been a while since I've spent any length of time in Golden, so I wanted to scout the territory before I get to work."

"Smart."

She tapped her temple. "That I am."

He chuckled.

"I don't want to keep you. I need to get back home to make notes."

"Until we meet again," he said, then inwardly cringed.

She tilted her head, met his gaze again, then she and Gus took off. He watched as they turned the corner, then disappeared farther down the street. It felt like she'd taken all the energy in the atmosphere with her.

"'Til we meet again," he muttered to himself.

He was batting zero right now. "What were you thinking?"

With a shake of his head, Ethan continued his walk back to the clinic. As he entered by the side door, he could hear barking in the doggy day-care section of the building. He'd implemented the service since taking over and it had become a big hit. One of the many updates he hoped would secure his and Holly's future, once the sale of the practice was finalized.

He walked down the hallway leading to the reception desk. His two clinic employees, Sandra Nixon, a fiftysomething wonder who kept the office organized, and Jossie Alvarez, a twenty-five-year-old vet tech, had been more than happy to remain in their jobs when Ethan took over. Both were dressed in matching navy scrubs.

Sandra pushed her glasses higher on her nose as he approached. Her light blond hair, with strands of gray, was weaved back in a complicated style. Never one to beat about the bush, she asked, "What did your lawyer say?"

He tried to swallow his frustration. So far, the previous doctor was dragging his feet in returning the final paperwork.

"Dr. Andrews hasn't signed the contract."

Sandra's eyebrows angled as she frowned. "I'm not surprised. He was wavering about the sale to begin with. His wife was the driving force behind it."

Ethan knew this. Still, he'd feel more secure having everything formalized and in place. "I fulfilled my end. It's frustrating, but Dean said he'd call Dr. Andrews's attorney again and find out what the holdup is."

"Dean knows what he's doing."

Ethan sent her a grin. "You say that because he's your son."

"And a good lawyer."

Jossie let out a long, infatuated sigh as she rested her elbows on the counter, her long brunette ponytail swishing over her shoulder. "And cute."

Sandra sent her coworker a stern frown. "Don't get any ideas. Dean is still establishing himself in Royce Stevens and Grace Harper Matthews's practice, so no distractions."

"Not that he notices me, anyway," Jossie huffed.

This was an area Ethan was not diving into. "Where's Holly?"

Jossie's expression brightened, making her caramel-brown skin glow. "Still with the puppies. They're exploring their surroundings with more confidence now."

Ethan shook his head. "I know for sure she's going to want one from the litter."

Sandra placed her hands on her hips. "And that's a problem?"

"It wasn't until she made friends with a new neighbor's dog. I'm sure the can-I-have-a-pet discussion will pick up in full force."

"Why wait?" Jossie asked. "You love animals."

"I do, but I wanted Holly to get settled before introducing anything new into our lives."

"She's been around animals all her life," Sandra interjected. "It's not like she'd have to make a big adjustment. Besides, she seems to be doing well, all things considered."

True. If Ethan was being honest, he was the one who needed more time adjusting. A signed contract proving he owned the clinic would go a long way to making this entire move more secure.

Sandra picked up a file, then paused. "Who moved in next door?"

"A woman named Nicole Connelly."

Sandra and Jossie exchanged glances.

"What was that?"

"We haven't seen Nicole in forever," Jossie quickly said.

He'd relied on his staff to help him navigate information about the residents of Golden. Both women were natives and had the 411 on most folks. Ethan had never lived in a small town and wasn't sure if he found their local knowledge comforting or terrifying.

"I didn't really know her well," Jossie continued. "She was friends with my older sister. There were stories going around town about her parents' divorce and a half sister and how Nicole didn't handle her father's decisions well."

He watched Sandra as she opened a filing cabinet to place the file inside. "Do I need to worry?"

"No," Sandra assured him. "Nicole was troubled, but since leaving Golden, she's done well for herself."

Jossie snapped her fingers. "She's staging Golden for the magazine layout."

"She mentioned something about that," Ethan admitted.

"It'll be great for Golden," Sandra said, then tapped the keyboard to wake up the computer screen. "Good for the clinic if more folks move to town."

"Speaking of the clinic, do you have the schedule for next week?" Ethan asked in his doctor tone.

"I can print it out."

"Just forward it to the computer in my office."

"Will do."

"And I'll check on Holly," Jossie offered.

Ethan strode to his office. As he took a seat at his desk, his gaze fell on the thick file dead center. What was taking Dr. Andrews so long to finalize the deal?

Ethan hoped the doctor wasn't thinking about backing out. He'd sensed that Dr. Andrews was dragging his feet, but Ethan had gone through all the necessary steps to make the clinic his own. The older man had agreed to let Ethan take over even before they'd signed the papers, so care for their patients wouldn't be interrupted. Never imagining there'd be a holdup, Ethan had agreed to the terms. Now, he wished he'd waited for all the paperwork to be completed.

His phone buzzed. He pressed a button and heard Sandra's voice.

"Faith Donovan on one."

"Thanks."

He pressed another button.

"Hi, Dr. Price—"

"Ethan," he corrected.

"Ethan. I haven't talked to Roan yet about a date to get together, but my hands are free so I wanted to get your cell number if that's okay."

"Of course." Ethan rattled off the number.

"I'll get back to you soon," Faith said before signing off.

Ethan replaced the receiver. Holly would be thrilled to visit new friends, even though she also wanted a playdate with Nicole and Gus.

"Not right now," he muttered, opening the file in front of him. He had to focus on the clinic, not his temporary neighbor, which was difficult after literally running into her on the sidewalk. He'd clasped her firm arms to keep her from falling, drawing close enough to inhale the lemony scent that now lingered in his memory. That close, his heart rate had spiked. What was it about the woman that caused such an intense reaction? Shaking his head, he took the papers from the file to read again.

Until the sale was finalized, he wouldn't go to the expense of updating the computer system or utilizing new techniques the older doctor hadn't implemented. Sure, he was seeing patients, which gave Ethan purpose, but until the papers were signed, he couldn't deny the worry sitting heavily on his shoulders.

"Daddy, the littlest puppy licked my hand," Holly said as she ran into his office. "I named him Tickles."

Oh, yeah, they were going to have the pet discussion tonight.

"That's great."

She rushed around his desk and climbed into his lap. "The mama licked me too. I think she knows I like the family."

"She knows you care about her and the puppies."

"Just like you showed me, Daddy."

When she laid her head on his chest, Ethan rested his chin on the top of her head. Drank in the scent of bubblegum-scented shampoo. This was why planting roots in Golden was so important to him. He wanted security and a sense of home for Holly. Wanted her to never doubt that she was loved. Nothing would stop him from fulfilling that life for her.

"I was going to stay longer, but the puppies fell asleep. Jossie said she'd take me to the day care, but I wanted to come see you."

Ethan hugged her. "You passed up a chance to see more dogs so you could be with your old dad?"

"You're not old."

He chuckled. "Thanks."

Silence enveloped the room. Ethan felt Holly relax and waited for her to fall asleep like the puppies, but she lifted her head and met his gaze.

"Can we invite Gus and Nicole over for dinner?"

He blinked, not surprised at the request.

"I hadn't thought about it."

"They just moved in. Maybe they don't have any food yet."

"I saw Nicole when I walked back from the lawyer's office. She mentioned that she needs to get ready for her new job."

Disappointment shone in Holly's chocolate-brown eyes.

Much like the same emotion careening through him. He hadn't expected such a strong reaction toward his new neighbor. The way his pulse quickened, and his breath stilled when he was close to her. This attraction was unanticipated, although not unwelcome, and certainly problematic. He hadn't thought much about dating, and right now, it wasn't a priority. He had too much on his plate. After the divorce, he hadn't been ready to wade into that particular pond. But his reaction to Nicole sort of snuck up on him and he wasn't sure how he was going to deal with it.

"But we can ask her another time?" Holly persisted.

"I'll check with her."

Her daughter beamed at him.

"But in the meantime, I talked to Mrs. Donovan in the park. She's going to have us over for dinner."

Holly's eyes went wide. "I get to play with John and Emmie and Lacey?"

"You bet."

"But not the baby. Miss Faith needs to take care of Finn. He's small, like the puppies."

Ethan grinned. "He is."

Holly nodded her head. "Okay. We'll have dinner with them, but don't forget about Nicole and Gus."

Seems like forgetting about his neighbor was not an option, especially if Holly had anything to say about it. Which meant he was going to have to see Nicole again, whether he was ready to or not.

CHAPTER THREE

FIRST THING TUESDAY MORNING, Nicole made calls to local merchants to confirm that she would decorate outside their establishments, and put a check mark next to each call. This way she wouldn't over order the larger supplies she needed.

She'd taken the weekend to sketch out her final plan for the town's transformation. She and Gus had jogged downtown a few more times to nail several specific details. Since the west side of Main would be predominantly Christmas-themed, top of her list were white string lights, red bows, artificial pine boughs and strands of holly berries, most of which she was told were available in a storage unit that she had a key to, thanks to her mother. Combined with the pictures she'd already taken and the image of the final staging in her head, decorating Golden was a go.

Perusing the list one final time, she smiled. She was most excited about a new idea that had taken shape after scouring the internet. On a whim, she'd ordered the items she'd need and couldn't wait for them to arrive.

"Now," she said out loud, "what's next?" She rustled through her notes.

"Permit from town hall. Inventory of storage unit." She glanced over at Gus, who was sprawled at her feet. "Care to go for a ride?"

His head lifted and his excited, brown-eyed gaze met hers.

"I'll take that as a yes."

After closing her laptop, Nicole changed into a blue-and-white-striped top and navy shorts. She chose a comfy pair of sneakers too. After adding a splash of makeup and running a brush through her hair, she was ready to go.

Lastly, she grabbed Gus's leash and secured it to his brand-new harness. Ethan was right, this setup felt much more secure when she took Gus outside. She grabbed her keys and backpack, locked up the cottage and ventured out to the Jeep. Well, she walked. Gus strained at the leash, his direction clear. He wanted to go next door.

A vision of a happy little girl and her handsome father filled Nicole's mind. The instant attraction she'd felt when first meeting Ethan had intensified after their literal run-in on the sidewalk.

"This way, buddy." She steered him toward the Jeep. "We have errands."

She was in Golden to work, not to daydream about the town veterinarian.

She opened the driver's door and tossed her backpack inside, then moved out of the way. Gus placed his front paws on the seat, then stared up at her.

"Really? We're going to go through this again?"

He waited patiently. Nicole lifted his hind end and nudged him forward. When his back paws made purchase, he scampered across to the passenger seat.

"Every time," Nicole muttered under her breath, but reached over to affectionately ruffle the dog's fur.

After a short drive, she parked in the busy lot of the courthouse and led Gus toward the stately building, envisioning it decorated in patriotic splendor. It didn't take her long to find the permit office, located upstairs in city hall, to place her request.

A gray-haired woman who was seated behind a tall counter, and wearing glasses hooked to a multicolored beaded chain around her neck, greeted Nicole. "May I help you?"

"I'm here to apply for a permit to decorate Golden."

The woman's face lit up. "You're the young lady who is going to up our holiday game."

"That's the plan," she replied, keeping a side-eye on Gus, who was getting antsy.

The woman glanced around, then leaned toward Nicole, her voice pitched low. "I'll get this permit expedited," she said in a conspiratorial tone. "I have connections."

Not sure how to respond, Nicole nodded. Who knew permitting was clandestine? Especially since her mother had insisted that she get the formal approval so there wouldn't be any problems if she had to close a street or block off a section of the park for photos.

After filling out the paperwork, Nicole passed

it back over the counter. The woman read over the form and nodded with satisfaction. "I'll call you just as soon as it is approved. If you have any questions, just ask for Dot."

"Thanks." Nicole tugged Gus toward the door.

"One last thing," Dot called out.

Nicole turned.

"Are you going to dress up the courthouse? We'd love to be in the magazine."

Nicole grinned at the woman's eager expression. "Because you've been so helpful, I'll go all out on the decorations and make sure we take plenty of pictures."

Dot's wide smile spread across her face.

Job done, Nicole was walking to the exit when she heard rapid bootheels echoing on the marble floors. She turned, a smile tickling her lips. "Why, Police Chief Brady Davis, imagine meeting you here, of all places."

His brown eyes twinkled. "Seems to me the last time we saw each other you were in trouble."

"Me? We were both in hot water. And you didn't have the authority to arrest me back then."

"No, but Mrs. Allen sure had it out for us."

Nicole chuckled. "How is Mrs. Allen?"

He ran a hand through his already tousled hair. "Still insists I can't be the chief because I'm a criminal."

"For failing to hot-wire her car? It never even left the driveway."

"The woman has a long memory."

Nicole sent him a warm smile. "Well, I'm glad to see you didn't fall victim to the dark side."

"Back at you."

"Has my sister taken over the department yet?"

"Hey, I'm still in charge. Briana answers to me."

Nicole snorted. "Are you sure?"

Brady chuckled. "Fair." Then his tone turned wry. "But there is an issue right now."

What could she have possibly done in the fifteen minutes she'd been inside city hall? "What's wrong?"

He nodded to Gus. "Only service dogs are allowed inside the building."

"You mean Gus?" She glanced down at the dog's innocent eyes and up again. "Oh, gosh, I'm sorry. Being a pet owner is brand-new to me."

"I'll let you go with a warning."

Her lips quivered. "Thanks."

"And a suggestion."

"I'll take it."

"Across the street is the Golden Veterinary Clinic. They have a day care that might solve the problem of what to do with Gus in these situations."

The vet clinic. Ethan's domain. Guess she'd be seeing him sooner rather than later. And why didn't that bother her all that much despite her silent vow to not let thoughts of the man distract her from her duties?

"Mostly my job will be outdoors," she told Brady. "I suppose there will be times when Gus can't be underfoot, so good idea. I'll check out the day care."

"I also want you to know," he said in what she thought might be his in-my-capacity-as-chief voice, "if you need anything while working in Golden, please let me know."

"Party line?"

"Direct orders from the chamber of commerce. Not surprisingly, they hold more weight than the mayor among local merchants."

"I met the marketing genius at the chamber, so I can see that."

"Now that my duty is done, let me say, welcome back to Golden."

She shrugged. "It's just until the job is finished."

"You might want to stick around." He paused for a moment, then his lips curved into a crooked smile. "The place has changed since we were kids. You might like it."

Nicole doubted she'd ever feel that way, but said, "I'll consider it."

Brady nodded. "Now, I need to get back to the station."

"Be safe out there," she said with a jaunty salute.

Brady chuckled. "Some things never change."

Soon she had Gus down the wide marble stairs, through the foyer and back outside. Gus wagged his tail, as if sensing an adventure. For him, perhaps. For the sake of her job, she'd have to check into lodging for Gus when he couldn't be with her.

As she drew close to the clinic she slowed her pace, finding herself strangely hesitant. Because of her heated response to Ethan? It was just a misunderstanding in his yard. Shouldn't be a big deal. But the way she'd gotten all shivery later when she collided with him on this very sidewalk, well...she wasn't sure she wanted to risk seeing him today.

Thankfully, two entrances were on opposite ends of the building. One to the day care, the other to the clinic at the far end. Since Ethan was the doctor, what were the odds he'd be in the day care? She could get in and out without running into him. Feeling good about her theory, she made the decision to go inside to inquire about the services and walked right into a conversation between Ethan and a young woman in tan shorts and a black T-shirt bearing the clinic name, a clipboard and pen in her hand.

She slowed her steps to study him. His dark hair was styled, his beard neatly trimmed. Broad shoulders filled his navy button-down shirt, which was covered by a white lab coat. His khakis were pressed, his loafers shiny. Was this his usual workday attire? Good grief, why did that matter?

What was with this strong reaction to Ethan? Sure, she dated, but never got serious. This time shouldn't be any different, but it was, and she didn't understand why.

She had to face the fact that since the moment they shook hands, everything about the man intrigued her.

She nearly let out a groan but caught herself in time.

"I told Mrs. Aims that we'd make sure to keep an eye on Layla while she's here. I don't expect any issues, but to be on the safe side, keep an eye on her skin. Her allergies have been acting up."

"Got it," said the woman taking notes.

"I think that's it for now, Andrea."

"Thanks, Doctor."

His day-care manager opened a door to move into another room echoing with loud barking. Ethan noticed her as Nicole stood just inside the threshold. Their eyes met, unspoken questions in his brown depths. Gus scampered Ethan's way, dragging Nicole with him.

"Nicole. What're you doing here? Is Gus okay?" He leaned down to give Gus a good scratch behind his ears.

"He's fine, but it's been brought to my attention that I won't be able to bring Gus everywhere I need to be for this project. I want to inquire about your day-care facilities."

He raised a dark eyebrow. "You didn't have this figured out before arriving in town?"

She blew out her breath, her cheeks heating at his logical question. "I haven't been a pet owner for very long. I just took Gus home and made him happy."

There was no criticism in his voice when he said, "That's a good start, but a lot more goes into being a pet owner."

She should have known that and felt foolish now. But in her defense, she'd been busy, then this job popped up and she couldn't resist Gus's eyes when he gave her that woe-is-me expression. The dog was a master manipulator.

"Let's come over here," Ethan said, leading an adoring Gus to a corner of the small foyer. He sank down on his heels to peer more closely into Gus's face. Taking it as a game, Gus inched closer and licked Ethan's face.

"He certainly likes people," Ethan said in a wry tone.

"Actually, he didn't seem to be all that social at the shelter. That's one of the reasons I was drawn to him."

Ethan rose. "As a foster?"

"No. I adopted him."

Ethan nodded then asked, "What's his history?"

Nicole loosened her hold on the leash as Gus began to explore his surroundings.

"He's a rescue. Not sure of his entire story, but he was wary when I was first introduced to him." She sent him a rueful smile. "Since he has a habit of escaping whenever possible, something must have happened to make him skittish."

"Abused?"

"The shelter thought so. And since he liked to run off, he was kept in the kennel a lot. I felt sorry for him."

Ethan studied Gus for a drawn-out moment. "He seems to be happy now."

"Ever since we came to Golden, I've seen a new side of him."

"Environment is important."

"I'm learning."

His lips quirked at the corners. He'd done that the day they'd met in his yard, and she had to admit, the gesture made her tummy flutter.

Unaware of her reaction, he kept up with the questions. "Did you want a pet?"

Brushing aside her curious response to Ethan, she said, "I mentioned that my neighbor works with a rescue group. He'd been trying to get me to come see the animals, but I was always working. One weekend, his group held a fundraiser that I attended. Gus approached me and they were shocked. From then on, the group made it their mission to get me to take him. He's four years old and they wanted to get him into a good home. I kind of decided to take him on impulse."

"Not the best way to make a decision."

"No."

But she couldn't deny that she liked having him around when she got home from work. The empty apartment got to her sometimes and she'd grown accustomed to his company. What did that say about the current state of her life? She lived alone. Didn't make time to go out with friends because she worked all the time. And the thought of being in the office full-time if she got the promotion wigged her out.

Her gaze traveled to Gus. Ever since Mr. Sanders had brought up the possibility of promoting Nicole at work, the question of what she wanted in her career had been front and center. How would her decision affect Gus? And to top off her concerns, this job in Golden, the one place she swore she'd never spend any amount of time in, brought Gus out of his shell. Was she cut out to be a dog mom?

"Nicole? What's wrong?"

Her gaze jerked up to meet his. Were her reservations that obvious? Surely, Ethan had dealt with lots of pet parents. Maybe confiding in him wouldn't be so bad. More like a professional service.

Yeah, she'd go with that.

"Do you think Gus is happy with me?"

Ethan rubbed Gus when he came to sit beside her feet, gazing up at her.

"Yeah, I'd say so," Ethan replied confidently, which made her heart swell.

Relief poured over her because she'd fallen in love with Gus. Ethan's positive response made her feel like she was doing the right thing keeping the big dog in her life. But she knew going forward she would have to make lifestyle changes to accommodate him.

Ethan frowned, a wrinkle creasing his forehead. "Weren't you concerned about your traveling keeping you away from him?"

"I was, but my neighbor kept him for me while I was on the road. And my boss isn't opposed to me bringing Gus to the office if we aren't meeting with potential clients.

"It's worked out so far, but to be honest, I feel bad that he's indoors all the time. You saw how happy he was running around your yard with Holly." Regret washed over her. "I thought since I'd be outdoors for most of this work trip, he'd be okay, but it makes sense that he can't go everywhere I need to be."

He ran a hand over his beard. "So, you decided to check out the day-care services."

"Exactly."

"When were you thinking of starting?"

She bit her lower lip. When Ethan's gaze moved in that direction, her stomach got all shaky again.

"Now?"

Amusement creased the corners of his eyes. "That can be arranged."

"Good, because I have to make a trip to a storage unit to do inventory today, and while I love Gus being with me, I might regret him being underfoot."

"That's right, the volunteer support committee."

"I have no clue what I'm about to uncover."

"We moved to Golden near the end of last year. I did notice lots of decorations around the downtown streets. Very festive."

She tried not to let out a groan. "That's what I was afraid of."

"And you're going alone?"

"I don't have a team with me for this job, so, yes."

A door opened and the woman, Andrea, returned. She smiled when she saw Nicole and let out a laugh when Gus barreled in her direction. "Who have we here?"

"A new friend," Ethan said, then turned to Nicole. "Andrea is my day-care manager. She'll give you the details about the services we offer."

"Thanks. I appreciate it."

He glanced at his watch. "I have one more patient before lunch. I need to get back to the clinic."

"Of course. I didn't mean to keep you."

"Don't worry. He'll be in good hands." He rubbed

Gus's head. His hand paused in the fur. "I see you got a harness."

"I never turn down advice from an expert."

Ethan sent her a professional nod then disappeared down a hallway, leaving Nicole to go over details, fees and payment with Andrea, when all she could think about was Ethan's gorgeous eyes and smile. "There's a large pet room, so Gus will have room to move around. We also have a big outdoor space the dogs love…"

Nicole's gaze drifted to the hallway, and she wished Ethan would return. Silly. They both had jobs. They were busy people. Still, he'd put her doubts of being a pet owner at ease. Made her think that maybe the time spent in Golden wouldn't be so emotionally charged with him as her neighbor. Since he hadn't been a part of her past, she could let down her barriers. Something she hadn't done with another person in a very long time.

ETHAN STRODE TO the reception area of the clinic to see if his next patient had arrived. The area was silent, which was a relief after his hectic morning.

"Where have you been?" Sandra asked, moving to the checkout counter that separated the front office area from reception. "I buzzed your office, but you didn't answer."

"I had instructions for Andrea. Then I talked to a pet owner about signing her dog up for day care."

"Her?" Interest flashed across Sandra's face. "May I ask who it is?"

Ethan coughed, then cleared his throat. He was still getting used to the curiosity of small-town folks who wanted to know every little detail of other people's lives, his included.

"Nicole. My neighbor."

Sandra went still for a moment, then a small smile crept over her lips. A smile that made him very nervous.

"Nicole came here?"

"All she said was that our services were suggested to her."

"Hmm." Sandra tapped a finger against the counter. "And you assured her that her dog would be well taken care of?"

"Yes." His patience was starting to unravel. "What else would I be doing?"

Her eyes twinkled. "You don't usually assist folks wanting information about the doggy day care."

"Andrea had stepped into the large pet room, and I was in the foyer. It would have been rude if I walked away."

Not that he would have been able to. Once he glimpsed Nicole, he wanted to remain exactly where he was.

He hadn't felt this way since the divorce. Before, really, when the marriage was falling apart, and the relationship was changing. In a way, his out-of-the-blue response to Nicole reassured him that he could still notice a woman. But he'd reserved all his love for his daughter and the intensity he experienced around Nicole made him wary. Moving forward hadn't included getting involved with a woman. Not yet, anyway.

She isn't staying.

Did that make her safer?

Sandra tilted her head. "I thought all the decorating was outside? Can't she take…?"

"Gus."

"Gus with her?"

"It's mainly at specific locations. Like today, she's doing inventory at the committee's storage unit and didn't want Gus getting into mischief."

His employee's eyes went wide. "Alone?"

Her alarm startled him. "Yes, why?"

"It isn't one unit. There are two combined large spaces. I know because my aunt is on the committee." She placed a hand on her hip. "It'll take Nicole forever if she does the inventory solo."

"Sandra, I'm sure she knows what she's in for. This is her job."

"And I can guarantee you that the committee didn't tell her what a big task that would be." She frowned. "They're cagey that way. And they wanted Nicole's company to do the magazine staging, so they probably didn't mention that little detail."

"Nicole will figure it out."

Sandra went quiet for a moment, then her steady gaze met his. "You need to help her."

"What?" The back of his neck prickled in warning. The calculating gleam in Sandra's eyes made him anxious. "I can't. I have a patient."

"I was calling to let you know the appointment

was canceled. You're free until two o'clock this afternoon."

"I have paperwork to catch up on." It was as good an excuse as any.

"You can do that later. You need to go with Nicole. It's your civic duty."

"That's a stretch."

Sandra sent him a determined glare.

He tried again. "I doubt she'd want me."

Would she? He was pretty sure she felt the same attraction he did. But what if he was wrong?

"Doesn't matter. This is Golden, Dr. Price. We help folks around here."

At the use of his professional title instead of just "Doc," Ethan knew she was serious. And not about to let up.

"She probably left already," he asserted.

Sandra came out from behind the counter, took hold of his arm and turned him around. With a push, she said, "Only one way to find out."

And this is how Ethan found himself walking back down the hallway to find the woman who stirred a great deal of interest in him still in the building.

He wasn't sure if he was happy or nervous to find her at the counter, signing a form.

"You haven't gone."

Nicole looked up at his voice. "Just finishing up."

"I'm glad I caught you."

Her eyes narrowed. "Why?"

At her suspicious response, he had to wonder if

she would find it so outlandish that he would volunteer his help.

"I had a cancellation, so I thought I'd give you a hand at the storage unit."

Her eyebrows rose.

"You know, to chip in for the good of Golden."

She grinned. "Right. For the good of Golden." She stared him down.

"Okay, my office administrator firmly told me that it is my civic duty to join you. She claims there are two units."

"Two?" Exasperation filled her tone.

At Nicole's wide-eyed reaction, he said, "Really, I don't mind tagging along." He wanted to learn more about the woman who had barged into his life.

Also, didn't he want balance in his life? Friends, along with Holly and work?

She seemed to think about his offer for a moment. "Why not? It'll be nice to have company. I've gotten used to talking to Gus, but if you're with me, I won't be talking to myself."

"Thanks, I think."

She waved him to the door. "My Jeep is parked across the street."

Before long, they were on their way across town. With the windows down, the warm breeze brushed Ethan's cheeks. Blooming wildflowers scented the air. Or was it Nicole's fragrance? He enjoyed the ride and the presence of the woman next to him.

He tried not to make his covert study of her obvious. Her hair blew in all directions in the wind, but she didn't seem to mind. In fact, since she'd started driving, the smile hadn't left her lips. She slowed to exit onto a side road, crushed gravel crunching under her tires as she slowly navigated the pine-tree-lined lane until reaching a huge, metal industrial structure. At the midpoint of a long building, she stopped to read the sign pointing out the direction of the unit numbers.

"Twenty-three," she said, then turned the wheel to the left.

When they found the correct unit, she parked. Ethan stepped out of the vehicle, assessing the serene surroundings. Birds sang in the trees while hopping between branches. The occasional vehicle passed on the main road. The jingle of keys drew his attention back to Nicole.

"Here we go."

She unlocked the door, paused to find a light switch, flipped it on, then moved inside. Ethan nearly crashed into her when she stopped short.

"Oh, wow."

Was she commenting about the way they'd come into close proximity again? No, he realized as he followed the direction of her gaze. It was the size and volume of boxes and decorations in the double unit.

"This is a lot," she said.

Was that astonishment or resignation he heard in her voice?

He put a little space between them. "You aren't kidding," he said, a little disappointed that she wasn't more upset about their collision than with the job ahead. Being this close to her took his breath away.

He soon realized that Sandra had been right. The room was the size of two combined units, one side filled with all kinds of Christmas paraphernalia, the other with assorted holiday displays. How many years had it taken the committee to accumulate such a collection? After Nicole opened one of the rolling garage doors, natural light flooded the space. Her citrusy perfume trailed behind her as he followed.

She wandered to the first section of artificial trees.

"How many?" he asked, clearing his throat.

She lifted her hand and pointed as she counted. "Twenty."

"Is that enough for your purposes?"

"Should be." She pulled her phone from the back pocket of her shorts to show him a picture. "For downtown, I want the trees outside of the shops, covered with lights and snow." She lowered the device. "Some of the trees already have white flocking. That'll help with my snow vision."

Her blue eyes shone brightly. Instead of being overwhelmed, she seemed…energized.

He rolled up his shirtsleeves. "What do you want me to do?"

She shouldered off her backpack, opened it and pulled out a tablet. "I'll tell you what I find, you record."

"Yes, ma'am."

She quirked an eyebrow.

"Hey, I can be as easygoing as the next guy."

"Remind me of that when Gus gets loose and runs into your backyard again."

"I did ask if that was going to be a problem."

She shot him a smile. "I think you know the answer to that question."

Yeah, he did. But Gus's visits meant Nicole wouldn't be too far behind.

She further surprised him by removing a red elf hat from the backpack and adjusted it on her head. When she noticed the direction of his gaze, she said, "Hey, I'm getting into the spirit."

Remarkably, so was he.

"Let's start here," she suggested. They walked down the first aisle, Ethan making notes of the items in plastic bins lined up against the wall. "Ornaments. Six containers' worth."

"Got it."

She opened a few of the containers. "Some solid color, others with stripes or designs."

It went on like this as they uncovered garland, wreaths, a box of pine cones—the list went on. When they reached the back wall, Nicole laughed.

"What?"

She stepped aside to reveal a full-size, red sleigh.

He reached out to touch the black metal runner connected to the wooden body. "Actually, this is pretty cool. Think you'll use it?"

"It would be great in the park. It's got the Victorian vibe I'm going for. I could trim it out with greenery and tiny white lights."

"Holly is going to love this. Christmas is a big deal to her."

A hint of a smile showed on Nicole's face. "Because you named her Holly?"

"Yes. She was born on Christmas Day."

He remembered the day like it was yesterday. She was the greatest gift he'd ever received, regardless of the demise of his marriage.

"Doesn't it bug her that she has to share her birthday with the holiday?"

He let out a chuckle. "No, she thinks sharing Christmas makes her special. I don't disagree with her."

Nicole turned back to the sleigh. "Where's her mom, if you don't mind my asking?"

He hesitated, not sure if he wanted to go down this road. The truth wasn't a secret, but he still had regrets and didn't like to dwell on them. "She works in New York."

"Holly must miss her."

"She has her moments."

It seemed that Holly asked about April less and less often now that they were living in Golden, which was a relief. Ethan kept Holly busy enough, so her mind didn't dwell on the distance from her mother. He also didn't shy away from the tough topics if Holly brought them up. To see his daughter happy and grounded assured him that all the turmoil and moving from one home to another had been a sound decision.

Nicole held his gaze. "How about you?"

He drew back. "Me?"

Emotion shimmered in her eyes. "Divorce can be tough."

"Are you…?"

"Oh, no. Never been married." She waved a hand. "My parents were divorced when I was twelve so I kind of understand."

"I see." He lingered an extralong beat. "Boyfriend?"

"Too busy."

"I hear you."

A silence fell over them, a bit charged after the personal aspect of the conversation, then Nicole said, "Next row."

She folded her arms over her chest as she spied another aisle crammed with decorations. "Good grief. Do they put all this out every year?"

"You'll have to ask the committee."

Letting out a puff of air that tousled her hair, she continued until they made it to the end of the row, then turned into the next aisle.

Curious about the woman who had shown up out of the blue in his backyard, he tried to think of some nonintrusive questions. They'd already gotten the elephant in the room—their marital status—out of the way, so anything else they talked about should be simple. "So, what is it you do, exactly?"

"I stage major events."

"Like?"

"Trade shows and conventions, for one. We have contracts with malls to do holiday decorating, outdoor events like corporate picnics or holiday parties, local fairs, that sort of thing."

"You said you travel a lot?"

"That's the nature of the business. I also design the events, as well."

"Like the seasonal theme for Golden?"

Her smile brightened. "Yes. Because I'm familiar with the town, I already had ideas going into the preliminary plans."

"How did you get into the business?"

She inspected another set of containers overflowing with red-and-white-striped plastic candy canes as she talked. "After I left Golden, I worked for a small event-planning company called Lila's Parties. We arranged local birthday or anniversary parties and even some weddings, but on a small scale. I built up the company's brand and one day Sanders Entertainment got in touch with an offer to buy the entire business. Lila wanted to retire, so she took the money. I went on to work for Mr. Sanders and made my way up the company ladder."

"Is this your passion? Why you left Golden?"

Nicole went stiff and he felt a wall come up. She angled away from him. "Long, uninteresting story."

"I get it." He wasn't a fan of discussing how his marriage had fallen apart or the subsequent divorce.

She sent him a sideways glance, as if to see if he was telling the truth.

"Anyway, I sort of fell into the business." She returned to the topic of her job. "Just last month I planned a corporate retreat. I went from throwing kid's birthday parties just a few years ago to corporate cookouts for two thousand employees."

"Sounds like a lot of work."

"It is, but it's where I love to be."

"You don't miss the smaller parties?"

She lifted the lid of another box to peer inside. "Sometimes. The big events aren't as personal. I spend a lot of time with the executives." She paused. "Add autumn wreaths to the list."

He dutifully typed it in.

Sounding a little unsure, she said, "I've been offered a promotion, after I finish this job."

"Congrats."

They moved to the end of the aisle and started along the wall to finish their inventory.

"It'll mean lots of office time. Not sure how that will affect Gus."

"You have good instincts. He'll be fine."

She rolled her lips inward, like she wasn't sure.

"How about you?" he persisted. "How will the office work affect you since you're used to traveling?"

With a shrug of her shoulders, she answered, "Guess I'll find out."

He noted a distinct lack of passion in her tone.

"Where are your headquarters?"

"Savannah. I live there."

And the place she'd return to after she completed this project. When he found himself trying to mentally come up with the distance between Golden and Savannah, he stopped himself short. Golden was home for now and in the future. He intended on keeping it that way.

"Look at these wooden rocking horses," she said, a thankful reprieve from his thoughts. Yeah, he was attracted to Nicole, but that was all it could be. And it wouldn't go any further.

"Think you can use them?" he asked, focusing on the conversation.

"I'm going to try."

They reached the open door. Ethan handed her the tablet. Their fingers brushed and once again that buzz of attraction arced between them.

Nicole cleared her voice and pulled away. "Now that I know what I have to work with, I can get started once I get the permit."

"I can't wait to see Golden dressed up, especially all four seasons decorated at one time."

"Trust me, when I'm finished, you won't know what time of year it is. Well, maybe because it'll read eighty degrees on the thermometer, but otherwise, you'll be transported."

"Tall order."

A confident smile lifted the corners of her lips. "I'm good at what I do."

Their gazes locked and he felt as if he'd been hit by a wagon full of bricks. His heart knocked against his chest, and he found himself leaning toward her, then stopped himself. What was he thinking? They'd only met last week.

Still, there was no denying the fascination that

had wrapped itself around him so tightly that his breath was shaky.

Nicole tucked her hair behind her ear. "I should get you back to the clinic."

Glancing at his watch, Ethan was amazed at how fast the time had flown by. "I need to grab some lunch before my first afternoon appointment."

"And I want to take Gus home."

He rolled down the door. Nicole locked up after them. They were back on the road and all too soon, she parked behind the clinic. "Thanks for your help."

He stepped out of the Jeep. "My pleasure. I know you're going to make Golden proud."

A flicker of hesitation crossed her features, but she quickly smiled as she joined him. "That's the plan."

They parted once they entered the clinic, he to his appointment, she to the day care. He went to his office to retrieve his lab coat, reflecting on the time spent with Nicole. He liked her. Her sunny personality. Her confidence. The tug of attraction that reminded him that while he might be a father, he was also a man. Then he shifted gears, thinking that he needed to focus on Holly, Golden and the clinic. He didn't need a possible romance throwing him off track. Especially if it was with the alluring event planner who one day would be off to big and better things in Savannah.

CHAPTER FOUR

THE SUN WAS shining late Wednesday morning when Celeste Johnson strode into Linda's General Store, inhaling the scent of baked goods that not only tickled her nose, but also her sweet tooth.

Moderation echoed in her head, sounding much like her doctor, as the hardwood floor creaked under her feet.

There were a few customers browsing in the grocery aisle while others, tourists most likely, gathered around the specialty displays. Happy to see the store busy, Celeste made her way to the back of the building, where she was sure to find Linda Connelly at work in her office. The door was open, but Celeste knocked on the doorframe to alert Linda to her presence.

Linda lowered a paper she was reading, a smile breaking across her pretty face. "Miss Celeste. What's going on?"

"We need to talk."

At her serious tone, Linda pulled a chair from the corner to a right angle beside her desk. "Is everything okay?"

"Your daughter moved in next door to me," Celeste said as she sat.

"I know. I rented the cottage for her."

"I saw her outside my window."

Linda frowned. "Is there a problem?"

Celeste planted her purse on the desk. "No. It's a challenge."

"Come again?"

"Do you recall the day I stopped into the store, and you were lamenting the fact that Nicole was so touchy when it came to your family or returning to Golden?"

An amused smile creased Linda's face. "I do, but to be fair, I always talk about wanting Nicole home. What's your point?"

Celeste tapped her temple with a finger. "We must put our heads together."

Linda frowned. "Heads together?"

"We need a plan to make Nicole see that Golden is her home."

Sadness washed over Linda's features. "You know I've tried. I'm afraid she's stubborn on the matter."

"I remember that trait from when she was a little girl. When she and Kimmy used to pal around, they got into more scrapes because Nicole wouldn't back down. She managed to find a willing partner in my granddaughter."

Shaking her head, Linda cringed. "I dreaded the phone calls from school."

Celeste sighed. "She wasn't out of control, just… misguided."

"Depends on who you talked to."

"Those folks didn't see the hurt little girl behind her hijinks."

But Celeste had. She'd tried to draw Nicole into conversations, but the girl was shut tight.

Linda straightened her desktop, not meeting Celeste's gaze. "I'm afraid that the mess of the marriage Kenneth left behind had repercussions. All of which he chose to walk away from."

"But you didn't. You were there for the girls, Linda. All of them."

The year the Connelly divorce made big news was also the year Celeste's husband, Reginald, had died. She'd missed most of the drama and, thankfully, the rumors. Once the haze of grief had lifted, Celeste realized how much the Connelly girls had suffered from Kenneth's decisions.

"He should have stood up for his family."

Her papers aligned in a neat pile, Linda picked up a pen and tapped it against the wood desktop. "I suppose the surprise success of his electronic business, plus the money that came with it, went to his head."

"As well as destroying his reputation as a committed family man and loyal employer. Not only did he hurt you and the girls, but also the employees of Connelly Electronics who thought Kenneth put them before the bottom dollar."

"Which he always did, until the contract with the auto manufacturer to make a new vehicle component changed everything. The small warehouse we worked out of wasn't enough. Moving the operation south to a larger facility made sense at the time."

Except for the fact that many of his local employees couldn't just pick up and move. The hours-long commute didn't make sense, so folks had to find other jobs. The blowback had been huge. Kenneth had dodged the fallout, abandoning Linda and the Connelly sisters, leaving them to face the brunt of people's anger.

The pen tapping stopped and Linda stared across the room. "If I'd gone with him instead of staying here…"

The unspoken thought—*he wouldn't have had an affair*—hung in the air.

"You did it for the girls. Put them first."

"Did I?" She shook her head. "I knew Kenneth and I were growing apart but…" Linda waved her hand before tapping the pen again. "It's all in the past. What's done is done."

It wasn't until Kimmy had brought Nicole around that Celeste realized just how deeply the family had been impacted. Nicole put up a strong front, but to anyone searching below the surface, it was clear that she was devastated. Celeste had tried to help Nicole the best she could, but the damage had been inflicted.

Through the years, Linda had been a strong mom, but she also had to work. There'd been teenage mischief to one degree or another, but the sisters loved their mother and Celeste meant to take full advantage of that fact.

"Agreed. We need to focus on Nicole while we have this window of opportunity."

Celeste had a chance to make up for not being on the ball. Nicole was right next door, and if she could, Celeste was going to do her darndest to get the girl to see how much her mother missed her.

"How long is Nicole staying in Golden?" she asked.

"Four weeks. I suppose that may vary depending upon how long it takes her to get the job done."

"Then we need a plan."

Linda tossed the pen onto her desk. "About trying to get my daughter, who doesn't like roots, by the way, to stick around?"

"Exactly."

Linda's expression turned doubtful. "And how do you propose we do that?"

"Love."

"Love?"

"It's a strong motivator. Once Nicole spends time with you, her sisters and the townsfolk, there's no way she can turn her back on Golden again."

"I don't know. That's asking a lot." Linda's voice grew thick. "She's been gone for so long."

Celeste waited a beat, then said, "Perhaps, but I can be persuasive when I want something."

"And you want Nicole to stay?"

"I do. Kimmy and her family have a life up north. My son-in-law accepted that job down in Atlanta for a few years, so my daughter isn't right around the corner." Celeste understood how Linda's heart missed her daughter. Even though the other sisters were in town, they were still estranged. Getting through to Nicole could be the first step in the family healing.

"Then they took my driver's license away—"

Linda made a choking sound, then asked, "They?"

"Those know-it-alls at the police department. Just because I rolled through a few stop signs doesn't mean I'm a menace."

"I think they had every reason to be concerned."

Celeste waved her hand as if erasing the incident. "I made sure to check that the intersection was clear before going through. I never caused an accident, did I?"

Linda pressed her quivering lips together.

"Fine. I was wrong, but the punishment was severe."

Still no agreement from Linda.

"Since I can't drive, I need someone to get me from point A to point B."

A light shone in Linda's eyes. "Nicole?"

"She is right next door." Celeste opened her purse and removed a sheet of paper. "I didn't have a plan before, but I do now."

She handed the paper to Linda.

After reading it, Linda handed it back. "Very comprehensive."

"I can't sit by and do nothing."

With her family gone, Celeste missed noisy dinners and the great grandkids running around. Sure, she had local friends to visit, but what she really needed was a mission.

Linda's uncertainty was visible. "You're sure about this?"

"Only if you're on board."

"I would like my daughter to come home…"

Celeste waited, hoping Linda was hooked on her proposal. When she met Celeste's gaze, determination shone in the blue depths.

"I want my daughter to come home," she declared.

"Then we have work to do."

LATE WEDNESDAY AFTERNOON, Nicole squinted against the sun to block out the glare. "This is what Dad left us?" The old Sinclair building looked just that—old. The paint had faded, and the windows were dirty. There was an unkempt air about the once distinguished structure.

"You each have an equal share," Royce Stevens, their father's attorney, answered. He was their parents' age, a tall man with light brown hair and hazel eyes that didn't miss a thing. If Nicole remembered correctly, he was a native of Golden.

Nicole covertly studied her sisters to gauge their responses to the inheritance. The women had varying shades of blond hair, except for Taylor's darker shade. She resembled her mother, who was not Linda Connelly.

"You know, I could convert the ground level into a fitness club," Addie, her younger sister, mused. As she turned to the oldest, Briana, her braided ponytail swung over her shoulder. Nicole noticed that they had an easier, warm relationship. Because they both had kids? "It would be perfect. Centrally located." She walked up to the large window, placed a hand over her eyes and peered through the grimy glass. "There's plenty of room for equipment and classes. Plus, we could rent out the office space upstairs for extra income."

"Fitness center?" Nicole asked.

Addie struggled with a convincing smile. "I've been toying with the idea of opening a center here in town. I'm a certified personal trainer and could offer one-on-one workout plans and classes."

"Right now, the only place to work out is at Mountain Spa Center. We need a gym for the locals," Briana said.

Addie's gaze moved to each sister. "If you all agree, that is."

Since Nicole didn't care one way or another, she shrugged. "Fine by me."

"I have the store," Taylor, their half sister, added. "I don't need the space."

Briana tapped a finger against her chin. "It's a definite possibility, a fitness center, but we'll need to have it inspected. No need rushing ahead until we know the condition of the building."

"After your father's passing," Mr. Stevens interjected, "per his request, I had the building professionally inspected and appraised. It's structurally sound and I have the current value for you." He handed them each a sheet of paper.

Nicole hid her surprise at the large number. She studied the structure again. Run-down for sure, but then, maybe a good coat of paint would change that impression.

"He'd planned on making upgrades and had put aside a healthy account, which is now yours to use. You can find the number further down the document."

Nicole's eyes went wide at all the zeros. Not shabby.

"Once you're all in agreement on what you want to do going forward, you'll each have to sign off," the attorney instructed. "We can set up a time that works for all of you to come to my office."

"We're going to Mom's for dinner tonight," Addie told him. "We'll let you know what we decide."

Mr. Stevens nodded, then opened his soft-sided leather briefcase. "There's one more thing. I have something else for you from your father." He removed envelopes, handing them out as he read the name written in cursive on the outside of each one. "A final farewell."

When he came up empty-handed for Nicole, his gaze turned sympathetic.

Her chest squeezed tight. What was she expecting? That her father would leave her something like he had her sisters? After the harsh words she'd hurled at him when they'd parted ways the last time she saw him? It shouldn't matter, and it didn't matter, she told herself, but the pain that infiltrated her heart was proof that his actions hurt. Again.

Mr. Stevens said goodbye and left the women alone.

Thankfully, her sisters were all preoccupied with the last piece of business. None moved to open their envelopes. They were probably just as conflicted about the contents as Nicole was about not receiving a letter.

Addie stuffed her envelope into her tote bag. "I need to pick up Jacob from school. I'll see you all at Mom's house."

Without waiting for a reply, she strode away.

Taylor dropped hers into her purse. "I need to get back to the store. I'll see you later." She turned on her heel and headed to the crosswalk to return to her clothing shop, which was located on the other side of Main Street.

Briana met and held Nicole's gaze. Growing up, the two had been inseparable. But when their father admitted his affair, Briana had tried to give him the benefit of the doubt. Nicole had not, and a schism formed between them.

"You're coming to Mom's?" was all Briana said.

"I'll be there," Nicole replied, her throat tight. "I need to go home and get Gus."

"Gus?"

"My dog."

Briana let out a laugh, not sarcastic, more like the kind they'd shared when they were kids. It made Nicole's heart hurt even more.

"You have a pet?"

Nicole's defenses rose. "Yes."

"Good for you. Mom is always worried because you live alone."

Nicole's hackles went up. "You live with a small child."

"Yes, but I'm a police officer and I have an attack cat. Trust me, no one messes with Cami and me, especially on my own turf. Mr. Darcy makes sure of it."

Nicole blinked. "That's the name of your attack cat?"

Briana's shoulders rose. "You'll understand if you ever meet him."

Which Nicole was almost positive would never happen.

"I need to go," she said, leaving Briana behind and increasing her pace to get home to Gus. Suddenly, she wanted to hug the fluffy guy and allow the tears she kept blinking away to roll into his fur.

Before making it to the cottage, images of the night her father had come clean with her mother about his affair flashed in her mind. The argument she hadn't meant to eavesdrop on, but had been caught doing so.

"What are you doing here?" her father had asked Nicole, his face red with anger.

Her mother hurried to Nicole's side. *"Leave her alone."*

"So she can tattle to her sisters? She's already said too much. This is between us, Linda."

"Not anymore. I want you out. Now."

His angry gaze fell on Nicole. *"This is all your fault."*

"Don't blame her," her mother said. "It's all you, Kenneth. You and your selfishness."

He stormed through the house and slammed the front door on the way out, leaving Nicole shivering in her mother's arms.

Nicole stopped, her face hot, her breath short. She bent over, placing her hands on her thighs as she sucked in fresh air. That night still had the power to bring her to her knees. But just as soon as the vision receded, another followed right on its heels.

"I'd like to talk to you, Nicole."

She saw her father, shocked to find him at the trade-show staging she'd been overseeing. His gait was hesitant, his expression wary. It had been years since she'd seen him. His dark hair had thinned and grayed, his face an unhealthy pale shade.

"Dad? Why are you here?"

"I only need a minute of your time."

"I'm busy."

"Please."

The conviction in his tone got to her. She told her assistant she'd be right back and led him into the vestibule of the convention center.

She kept her tone tight. "What are you doing here?" she repeated.

He took a breath. Coughed. A watery sound that made her heart pound. Was he sick?

"I owe you an apology."

She stared at him in disbelief. "An apology?"

"Yes. I made a mess of things with your mother. With you girls."

Concern slowly welled to anger. An apology now, after all the blame he'd heaped on her? "And you just expect me to say 'okay'? After the way you hurt Mom? I can't forgive you for that."

"Please. I know it will take time, but I want the chance to make it up to you. Start over."

"You didn't hear her cry at night after you left her with the humiliation of your affair." *Nicole would never forget the long hours she'd lain awake listening to the aching sobs from her mother's bedroom.* "The way we were all talked about behind our backs because you left us. Kenneth Connelly, the renowned family man."

"I was wrong, Nicole. I came to explain."

"After blaming me?"

He ran a shaky hand over his face. "I was wrong. I never meant..."

A taut silence fell between them. "Why now?" *Nicole asked.*

"Things have become complicated. I don't have—"

She cut him off. Didn't want to hear his excuses. "It's too late, Dad. Too much time has gone by."

"Please. I want to make things right."

"Then do it for Briana, Addie and Taylor. Leave me out of it."

"I can't. You're my daughter. I love you."

She closed her eyes against hot tears.

"Go home, Dad."

She turned on her heel and fled into the convention room.

By the time she reached the cottage, Nicole was

shaking. Never had she thought after that conversation with her father that it would be their last. Especially after she'd learned he was ill. Why had she been so stubborn? Allowed the abiding hurt to dictate her response? She'd never have a chance to make amends with him now. And by the glaring lack of an envelope for her, he had no final words to share with Nicole.

She supposed she deserved that.

Worn out, she opened the door to the cottage. Gus ran out, seeing his escape route. "Not now."

She chased him around the side of the house, not surprised that his destination was the Price home. But the two-story was closed tight, indicating no one was home. She was glad, sure she'd never be able to make pleasant conversation if Ethan or Holly were outside.

"Let's go home."

They trooped into her yard when the back door to the Craftsman house on the other side of her cottage opened. An older woman stepped out, a basket in her arm as she headed toward a garden. Gus bounded over to make friends.

"Sorry," Nicole said as Gus danced around the woman's legs.

"Isn't he a darling?"

"More like trouble," she muttered.

The woman smiled at Nicole. "You don't remember me, do you?"

Shorter than Nicole, the woman sported tight white curls, stark against her light brown skin. Her dress was comfortably worn, her shoes sensible. But it was the sparkle in her eyes and the wide smile that brought recognition. "You're Kimmy's grandmother. Miss Celeste."

"As I live and breathe."

"I thought your house seemed familiar."

The woman's affectionate gaze took in her home. "You and Kimmy hung out here a time or two when you were in high school."

"Wow. It's been forever. How is Kimmy?"

"Married. Lives outside of Chicago."

"Her parents?"

"Living in Atlanta."

"And you?"

"On my own now. My husband passed away years ago."

"I'm sorry."

Celeste shrugged her shoulders in a world-weary gesture.

"Your mama drops by with goodies from her store. She's a delight."

After reliving the wretched memories of her father, Nicole's heart softened at the mention of her mother. "Won't get any argument from me."

"Heard you're home for the holiday lollapalooza."

Nicole hadn't heard of the photo shoot being referred to in those terms, but she went along with it.

"That's correct."

"You're going to need my help."

Unprepared for that statement, Nicole said, "Excuse me?"

"You don't think you can get the job done alone."

"I—"

"We'll talk about it later. Right now, you need to get to your mama's house for dinner."

How did she…? What just happened?

She waved. "Go. Go."

Gus barked, nudging Nicole's leg. With a shake of her head, she said goodbye and led Gus to the Jeep. She gave him a hug before she boosted him into the SUV, happy she'd have him along for what would undoubtedly be an uncomfortable reunion with her family. Conversation about their father's final gift was sure to be the highlight. Did she have it in her to participate?

As she backed out of the driveway, she noticed a dark sedan pulling up in the drive next door. Ethan got out, then helped Holly out of the back seat. The little girl saw them and waved. Gus—hanging his head out the window—woofed in return. And when Nicole glimpsed Ethan's calm features and the small smile he sent her, she wished she was spending the evening with the handsome doctor and his adorable daughter, not the emotional tempest awaiting her.

Fifteen minutes later, she parked in her mother's driveway. One car was in front of hers, two on the road. If she was at the end of the line, she hoped that made escaping easier.

"It's now or never," she told Gus as she let him out of the passenger side of the Jeep and they made their way up the walk to the front door.

Memories crowded her mind as she passed the

riot of blooming flowers emitting a sweet fragrance. The low ranch house where she'd grown up was always lit up to the hilt on Christmas, and covered in fake cobwebs on Halloween. She fondly recalled her mother tending her flower gardens in the spring, creating a colorful wonderland that continued all summer long. As she viewed the myriad of colors, she guessed her mother's passion remained. Mental images of racing around the property with Briana and Addie, playing football or soccer in the large, sloping front yard with the neighborhood kids, made her heart ache.

And finally, the impact of the night her father had left for good.

She swallowed hard. While the house looked the same on the outside, inside—and the complicated emotions that came with it—was another matter completely.

The front screen door opened. "You're the last one," her mother admonished.

"Sorry, Mom. Had to corral Gus before heading over."

Gus loped up the walkway, then the steps, and greeted her mother.

"You're such a pretty boy," her mother cooed.

"You don't mind that I brought him, do you?"

"No. Jacob and Cami will be thrilled."

Right, the eight-year-old nephew she'd rarely seen since he was born and Briana's adopted four-year-old daughter, both of whom she'd only recently interacted with at her father's funeral. As she thought it, she realized how awful that sounded.

Voices sounded from the kitchen. Making her way down the hallway, the conversation halted just as she entered the room. Taylor sat in the family room off the kitchen, phone in hand, separated from the others. On purpose? Also, when had her mother decided to include Taylor as part of the inner circle?

Including you?

Yeah, she wasn't going there.

Addie was setting the long farmhouse table with colorful dinnerware while Briana finished slicing cucumbers to toss into a salad.

Nicole cleared her throat. "Hi."

All three turned to her. For a long uncomfortable moment, no one spoke.

"Can you get the dressing from the fridge?" Briana finally asked, like it was an everyday occurrence for Nicole to stop by for dinner.

Taking the normalcy of the request as a win, Nicole said, "Sure."

Gus went to the back door, whining to go out. Nicole took a peek outside the screen door to find the children in the grassy yard. Jacob was throwing a baseball in the air and catching it in his glove, while Cami was twirling in circles as she sang an off-key song. Addie joined her.

"Is your dog good with kids?"

"Gus adores them."

"Then Jacob will love him."

"Don't forget Cami," Briana called out.

Nicole opened the door and Gus bounded outside. Jacob's mouth gaped open, then a huge smile took over his face. They approached each other much the way Gus had done with Holly before Gus lifted his paws to rest on Jacob's shoulders. The little boy laughed, his glasses askew. Soon, Cami was petting Gus, and if his doggy smile was any indication, he was in heaven.

Addie clasped her hands over her heart. "Isn't that the most darling thing you've ever seen?"

Briana walked over to peer over their shoulders. "I keep telling you to get a dog."

"I'm not home enough. It wouldn't be fair to an animal."

Guilt rose in Nicole, reminding her that part of her dilemma about the work promotion was Gus.

"Mr. Darcy is home alone."

"Making everyone safer," Addie said under her breath.

"Hey!"

Addie turned to Briana with one eyebrow raised. "Which he prefers. We all know how he is with visitors."

Nicole hid the smile that came from her sister's tart response. "How would that be?"

"Difficult," Addie said, while Briana replied, "Picky," the answers coming at the same time.

"I really want to meet him," Nicole said, earning surprised glances from her siblings.

Their mother returned from the front of the

house, placing her phone on the counter. "Sorry, business."

"That's why you have a manager, Mom," Briana reminded her.

"Some things have to be taken care of personally." She opened the oven door and removed the pan with already browned and sliced roasted chicken. "Dinner will be ready once the kids wash up."

Addie called the children to come inside and wash their hands. Taylor took a bowl of rice from the counter to place on the table while Briana added the salad. Nicole grabbed the salad dressings and a pitcher of iced tea from the refrigerator and filled the glasses. They all sat around the table like so many times before, when they were one happy unit.

"Everyone dig in," their mother commanded.

Plates and bowls were passed. Silence ensued. So much for a boisterous family meal.

"So," Mom said, filling in the lag in the conversation. "How was your meeting with Royce?"

"He showed us the building Dad left us," Briana said. "We need to decide our next move."

"You'll keep it, won't you?"

The sisters exchanged glances.

"Oh, please," their mother huffed. "You girls aren't going to pass up this inheritance, are you?"

"It's not that simple," Nicole said.

"Yes, it is." Mom's gaze zoomed to Addie. "What about your fitness center?"

"About that," Nicole said. "Are you seriously considering opening a gym?"

Instead of answering, Addie admonished Jacob, who was shoveling food in his mouth as fast as he could. "Slow down."

The boy stopped, then adjusted his pace.

"And to answer you, I'm thinking about it."

"Now, you don't have to dream," Briana added. "You have the biggest obstacle out of the way, a vacant building. You can do what you want with it."

"With funds to get it up to code," their mother said as she speared a piece of chicken.

All eyes flew to her.

"What?"

"How do you know?" Nicole sputtered.

"Your father told me."

Silence fell over the room.

"Can I have some more rice," Jacob asked, innocently breaking the shocked tension.

Her mother passed the bowl. "In the last few years, your father and I spoke. It's no big deal."

"Why didn't you tell us?" Briana asked as she cut up the chicken on her daughter's plate.

"Because I knew you'd make a fuss. Which you're doing right now." Her mom turned to Addie. "So?"

"We haven't walked through it yet," Addie reminded her.

"Why not?" their mother asked.

When no one answered, Nicole spoke up. "Mr. Stevens suggested we come to an agreement about what to do with the building first."

Mom eyed them. "It seems pretty straightforward to me."

Again, silence fell. She set down her fork. "You girls need to discuss this."

Briana spoke up. "It would solve Addie's problems."

"If I'm ready to take the plunge."

"You are, you just need a push."

Addie tilted her head toward her son. "Is the timing right? I have a steady job right now. And it's just the two of us."

"The timing is never right," Taylor said, speaking for the first time in a quiet tone. "You have to jump in with fingers crossed and a silent prayer on your lips."

Addie seemed to consider their half sister.

"I always dreamed of owning Tessa's clothing store," Taylor continued. "If I weighed the risks over what I could accomplish, I might never have gone for it."

"She is right," Briana said, surprising Nicole.

"There's always the current market value to consider if we want to sell," Nicole ventured.

"I don't know," Briana hedged. "Dad must have wanted us to use it to some capacity."

Nicole pushed her food around on her plate. "Does anyone else have a need for the building besides Addie?"

"No," everyone replied.

"Then let's do the walk-through," Nicole suggested. "If anything, it might help Addie decide if she wants to move forward. Mr. Stevens said the structure is sound, but if it's as run-down as the outside, we may want to pass."

After debating a few more pros and cons, the sisters decided to meet again for a walk-through of the building. They appointed Briana as the point person with the attorney.

"See," their mother said, resuming her meal. "That wasn't so difficult."

"Now, can we have dessert?" Jacob asked, bringing a much-needed round of laughter to the table.

Their mom rose to remove a chocolate-and-vanilla-pudding pie from the refrigerator.

"My favorite," Cami proclaimed.

"Really? Who knew?" Mom said, her smile bright as she aimed it at her granddaughter.

"You did, Grandma."

"So I did."

The remainder of the dinner passed quickly after that.

"Mom, we gotta go," Jacob said. "Baseball sign-up starts soon."

"Sorry," Addie said as she gathered her purse. "I hate to leave you all with the cleanup."

"Says the one who always got out of dish duty when we were kids," Briana said.

"Some of us have great timing," Addie said, giving her mother a kiss on the cheek and then ushering Jacob out the front door.

"I should leave too," Taylor said, smoothing her fashionable skirt as she rose from the table. "I'm knee-deep in inventory."

"Go ahead," their mother said. "I'll walk you to the door." She grabbed Cami's hand. The little girl skipped beside her grandmother.

Before leaving, Taylor's gaze collided with Nicole's. She didn't know what to say. Taylor nodded and left the room with their mother.

Nicole turned to Briana. "When did Taylor start coming to family dinners?"

"When she moved back to town. Mom insisted."

"Mom has always had a big heart."

Briana lifted a shoulder in a quick shrug. "She also insists that Taylor needs us."

Nicole wasn't sure about that, but since this had been her first family dinner since she'd lived at home, it wasn't her place to comment.

The two started cleaning the table.

"Did you name Cami after Grandma?"

"Yes. Camilla. But she's so cute, she's Cami."

Nicole couldn't disagree.

"Are you sure you don't care what we do with the building?" Briana asked.

"Why would I? I won't be here."

"As usual."

Nicole placed the dirty dishes in the sink. "Something you want to say?"

Briana seemed torn for a moment, then said, "It's not like you care."

Heat washed over Nicole's skin. "I never said that."

"No, but your absence speaks volumes."

Nicole rubbed the pounding that started in her temples. "I've had my reasons."

"So you've said."

Nicole dropped her hands to her sides, frustrated. "Maybe if I'd been Dad's favorite, things would be different."

Briana gasped. "That's not fair."

"Oh, come on, we both know it's true."

Briana wrapped her arms around her waist, making the tension in Nicole curl tighter.

"Why don't we ever try to end this?" Briana asked quietly.

Nicole sighed. Her sister was right. She needed to do better going forward. She started to tell Briana that when her sister spoke first.

"As for the building, maybe our joint decision is important."

"To whom?" Nicole asked.

"Our family. Mainly Addie."

"If she decides she wants it, then I'll agree."

Briana's voice rose. "With no opinions?"

"Like you want my opinion," Nicole returned, heat in her answer.

The two stared each other down, then their mother walked into the room. The woman took in the tense stance of her daughters, then steered Cami into the family room, where toys would distract her. "Girls," she said when she returned, disappointment lacing her tone.

Nicole stepped back. "Where is Gus?"

"Napping in the living room."

"I need to get him home for dinner."

"So soon?"

"Yes. Thanks, Mom." She fished her keys out of her pocket and went to collect her dog. Safely outside, she inhaled great gulps of air, surprised that her hands were shaking.

The first dinner with her family in years and she'd managed to make things worse. If only she'd left with the others, maybe she wouldn't be so crushed by her argument with Briana.

"I have to work on being less defensive," she told Gus as he walked beside her. "Or things will never change."

Gus waited for her to lift him into the passenger seat when they got to the car. She rubbed his head. "Always stay the same," she murmured.

He licked her cheek and that's when the tears started. She indulged for a few seconds, then brushed her wet cheeks and got in behind the wheel.

As she navigated the streets to the cottage, she realized that no one had made mention of the letters from their father. To shield their mom? Because it was obvious Nicole hadn't received one? Which produced another round of guilt and hurt, making Nicole wonder if returning to her hometown because she was curious was worth the pain.

CHAPTER FIVE

ETHAN ACCEPTED A glass of iced tea from his host. He and Holly had arrived at the Donovan house a short time ago, ready for a dinner featuring Faith's chili and grilled hot dogs. Holly and the children were running around the big backyard, working off energy after a long day of school. The laughter was pure joy to Ethan's ears.

"The kids are going to wear themselves out," Roan Donovan commented before drinking from his glass.

"Between being outside and having a good meal, Holly should be in bed early tonight."

"Do you have plans?"

Ethan started. "No. Just a quiet Wednesday night."

"Huh." Roan watched the kids play. "What do you think about life in Golden?"

Good question. He'd been so busy acclimating Holly and trying to get the legal paperwork for the clinic straightened out, he hadn't taken any time to analyze or form an opinion.

"Having never lived in a small town before, there have been some adjustments to make, but this place suits us. Holly is happy and that's all that matters to me."

Roan chuckled. "Adjustments. A perfect word to attribute to moving to Golden."

"You had problems when you arrived?"

"No. I had a group of matchmakers with a bull's-eye on my back." He smiled. "Worked out pretty well, if I do say so myself."

Ethan only heard one word. "Did you say 'match-makers'?"

"I did." Roan chuckled. "Best group around for miles."

Swallowing hard, Ethan asked, "And how do I stay off their radar?"

"You don't."

Ethan had enough on his plate. The last thing he needed was to worry about being steered toward romance.

Roan changed the subject. "How is the practice going?"

Ethan thought back to the conversation with his lawyer earlier today. They'd finally gotten some of the paperwork on the sale, but the previous owner had not included the contract of sale, like he'd been asked. Which meant the waiting game continued.

"Things are good. It was easy to take over the day-to-day duties, like seeing patients and the like. Getting the pet day care up and running took a little more finagling, but we're at full capacity now."

Roan called out a warning for the children to be careful as they ran around with Rocky, their golden retriever. Hearing Holly's laughter made Ethan's heart light. After that period when she'd been anxious and insecure after the divorce, it was encouraging to see her playing with the children. She stopped to give Rocky a hardy pet before taking chase with the others.

He smothered a sigh. As he'd predicted, Holly was indeed asking about getting a pet. Before long, Ethan was going to have to take the plunge.

"I wanted to thank you for suggesting the obedience classes for Rocky," Roan said as he scraped the grill to prepare for the hot dogs. "He's doing great, despite Emmie trying to undermine my commands."

Ethan grinned. Emmie was a force of nature, so he wasn't surprised by the news.

"Have you thought about bringing Emmie along when you take the class? If she's included, and understands why the commands are important, she might not make the process complicated."

"That's a good idea. She's calmed down significantly since Faith and I got married and we combined our families, but she still has moments when she acts out."

"Probably more the age than Emmie being troubled." Ethan held out his glass toward his daughter. "When we first arrived, Holly was clingy. Now, she's a lot more confident."

"She and Emmie have been hanging out," Roan said in a wry tone.

"And that means?"

"My daughter has enough confidence for her entire class at school. Maybe it's contagious."

Ethan considered the statement. Compared to the little girl who'd been quiet and withdrawn after her mother left, he was happy to see Holly's personality forming in a positive direction.

"Maybe they'll be good influences on each other," he suggested.

"Who is an influence?" Faith asked as she joined them, the baby in her arms.

"Emmie," Roan replied. "For Holly."

Faith shook her head, her dark blond hair swirling around her shoulders. "Can you imagine the trouble those two are going to get into in the future?"

Roan's face paled.

Ethan patted him on the shoulder. "You're a police officer. Surely, the thought of wrangling teenage girls doesn't scare you."

"Not with Kaylie. Although she's the older of the two, she's always been even-keeled, even at thirteen. I've always said Emmie is seven going on twenty-five."

Faith beamed at her husband. "Then it's a good thing you married me so I can keep everyone in this family in line. Boys and girls."

"Kaylie, Emmie, Lacey and you," Roan said, counting out on his fingers, "versus John, Finn and me. Doesn't seem even."

"If we had another baby, it might."

Roan circled an arm around her waist and tugged her close. "I'm not opposed."

"Neither am I."

As they shared a kiss, Ethan turned away. He enjoyed the banter between the loving couple, but deep down, couldn't deny the envy. This is what he'd hoped for when he and April had married. What he'd seen portrayed by his parents, who'd been married forty years and were still going strong. His disappointment over the failed marriage had cut deep—more, he realized now, because he didn't measure up to his parents' example.

In the beginning years of the marriage, he and April had fun together, but as time went on and they began working in their respective careers, the vibe changed. He'd tried to make their life together what she wanted, but was never able to reach the right chord with her. When Holly was born, he was more excited than April, which made him sad. She was missing out on a relationship with their amazing daughter.

"I'm glad Finn is the newest addition to our family." Faith spoke softly to the baby in her arms, her expression filled with love. Finn stretched, reaching a tiny hand in Roan's direction. The big man gently took hold of his son's hand and pressed a kiss.

"Thanks for bringing dessert," Faith told Ethan as she shifted the position of her son.

"I stopped by Linda's General Store to pick up brownies. When I smelled the apple pie, I couldn't resist that either."

"At least I know they're homemade," she teased.

"I can cook, but baking is beyond me," Ethan admitted.

"Better than I'm doing," Roan said under his breath.

"I tried to let him cook when we first got married," Faith said. "But honestly, it's just easier if I take care of the meals. When it comes to grilling though, he's the best."

Roan's chest puffed out.

The sliding glass door slid open. "Roan is grilling?"

Ethan turned to find the police chief making his way in their direction.

"Hot dogs, Brady." Faith hugged him. "To go with my chili."

Not the least bit embarrassed at dropping in unannounced, the chief's grin grew. "I heard. Why do you think I'm here?"

Faith turned to Roan.

Roan held his hands out in defense. "Hey, I didn't tell him. He must have overheard me when I was talking to you on the phone."

Brady sent an unrepentant grin at Ethan. "The squad room isn't huge. I hear everything."

Roan nodded at Faith. "See."

"You're all welcome," Faith said. "The more the merrier."

"Was that pie on the counter from Linda's General Store?" Brady asked. "It smells amazing."

"Yes. Ethan's treat," she said.

He held up his hand to high-five. Ethan hesitated,

then slapped his hand against Brady's. "Best desserts in Golden."

"Did you see Linda?" Faith asked Brady. "She must be thrilled that Nicole is home."

At the mention of his neighbor's name, Ethan's attention peaked. "I didn't know Linda and Nicole knew each other."

"That's right, there's no way you would." Faith shifted the baby again. "Nicole doesn't come home much, so when she does, her mom is very happy."

Linda was Nicole's mother? He still had much to learn about the residents of Golden.

"I told her she should stick around this time," Brady added.

"Doubtful," Faith said, handing Finn over to Roan. "Why don't you take him. I have to get the cornbread into the oven."

Faith went back into the house once the baby was safely cradled in Roan's arms.

"You're a natural," Ethan teased.

"I can even change a diaper," Roan boasted, his smile filled with pride.

Ethan held up his glass in salute.

Roan sniffed. "Which I need to do right now. Excuse me."

Brady shivered. "Better him than me."

"You'll change your tune if you ever have kids," Roan countered.

"No time soon."

Since they'd already started talking about Nicole, Ethan asked. "You ran into Nicole?"

"Yes. She and Gus were at the courthouse."

"Let me guess. You suggested the day care?"

"I did. She seems a little like a fish out of water with that dog."

"She's learning."

Brady shook his head with a laugh. "She never was one to shrink from a challenge."

He'd already figured that out. Although now that he thought about it, her usual smile was missing when she drove by his house earlier. Had something happened on the job?

"I'm not surprised she took on the decorating project," Brady said. "But to willingly come back to Golden? That was a surprise."

"Did something happen to make her wary?"

"No one thing. There was a bunch of drama after her folks got divorced. Nicole had a hard time with the whole situation."

He had gotten that impression when he and Nicole talked at the storage unit. As much as he wanted to know more about her, one, he didn't want to pry into her personal business, and two, she'd be leaving after completing the job.

His phone rang, drawing him from his thoughts. He pulled the device from his pocket.

"Dr. Price," he answered.

"It's the answering service, Dr. Price. You have an emergency headed to the office. A large dog was injured and is being transported to the clinic by its owner."

"I'll be right there."

He ended the call.

"Problem?" Brady asked.

"I need to get to the clinic. Save me some of that chili."

"Can't make any promises," Brady said over his shoulder as he beelined toward the children, who screamed with pleasure.

Ethan hurried inside to find Faith and explain. "Would you mind letting Holly stay here? I'll pick her up on the way home."

"Of course. I'll even make sure to save some dinner for you."

"Thanks. And sorry for rushing off."

"Don't worry about it." She shooed him off. "Go."

He went back outside and jogged to Holly. "Emergency at the clinic, princess. You're going to stay for dinner. I'll pick you up on the way home."

She raised her hands to place them on his cheeks. "Do good, Daddy."

He kissed the top of her head. "I will."

Over the next few hours, he tended to a border collie that had fallen into a large hole that had once been a well, but had caved in. Apparently, the owner, a local farmer, had been working to secure the opening so no one would accidentally fall in, but somehow the dog had taken a tumble. The farmer had removed the dog but wasn't sure of the extent of the injuries.

Once Ethan had done a thorough exam, he determined there were no broken bones. He cleaned the cuts sustained in the fall, stitching a few of the deeper wounds and suggested the owner keep a watch on an injured front paw. The animal would be fine after a short recovery. Once the dog was placed in the kennel to recuperate for the night, Ethan collected Holly from the Donovans and headed home.

She fell asleep on the drive. When they got home, as he was lifting her out of the car, he heard a bark. Gus scampered up to him with Nicole in hot pursuit.

"Sorry," she said, motioning for Gus to sit.

"It's okay." He addressed the dog. "As you can see, Holly can't play."

Nicole chuckled, then asked, "Late night?"

"Emergency at the clinic."

"Oh, well, we should let you go."

Before she could step away, Ethan blurted, "Want to come in for some coffee or tea?"

She pressed her lips together for a long moment. "You're sure it's not too late?"

"No. Let me get Holly down."

When he noticed her reservation, he said, "After an emergency, it takes me a while to unwind. You'd be doing me a favor by joining me."

Nicole seemed to hesitate, then shrugged. "Why not? I don't plan on sleeping anytime soon either."

He didn't ask why, just led the way to the front door.

Holly's eyes blinked open. "Nicole?"

"Hi, honey."

"Is Gus with you?"

He barked.

She tried to wiggle out of Ethan's arms. "Not tonight, Holly. It's bedtime."

She must have been exhausted because instead of arguing she sank back against him, snuggling close.

Once inside, he motioned his head to the back of the house. "Kitchen's that way."

Nicole nodded.

He took Holly upstairs, got her changed and into bed, then turned on the night-light.

Her sleepy voice stopped him before he could exit the room. "Daddy?"

"Yes?"

"Can Gus sleep over sometime?"

He grinned. His daughter was nothing if not tenacious. "How about we discuss that tomorrow?"

"Okay." With that, she rolled over on her side.

Leaving the door open a crack, Ethan went back downstairs to find Nicole turning on the stove to heat the kettle.

"Hope you don't mind. I found some tea bags in the pantry."

"You read my mind."

He took two cups from the mug tree on the counter. "Sugar?"

"No thanks."

Resting his lower back against the countertop, he observed his guest. "You and Gus are out late."

"We had dinner at my mom's house." She checked on Gus, who was sprawled out by the back door. It was almost as if he belonged here. "I was taking Gus out one last time for the night."

The water in the kettle began to boil, the bubbling loud in the dim, quiet kitchen.

"I found out tonight that your mom is none other than Linda of the general store."

Nicole's face lit up. "None other than."

"I stopped by to pick up dessert."

Confusion crossed her face. "For your emergency at the clinic?"

He chuckled. "I was supposed to have Faith Donovan's famous chili for dinner tonight until I got called away." He snapped his fingers. "Which I just remembered I left in the car."

"Go get it," Nicole urged.

By the time he ran outside and walked back into the kitchen, Nicole had the mugs filled with steaming water, the earthy fragrance emanating from the steeping tea bags. He placed the container in the refrigerator and asked, "Do you want to sit at the table or go into the living room?"

Nicole pulled out a chair. "Kitchen works."

He joined her as she viewed the room.

"Cozy."

He followed the direction of her gaze. The dark wood cabinets and light countertops, stainless-steel appliances and light yellow walls made for a homey kitchen. "I didn't do much. It was like this when we moved in."

Nicole took the end of the string and bobbed her tea bag in the water. "Was it hard? Moving on to a new life without your wife?"

Maybe he was beat or maybe he just wanted to

prolong this time with Nicole, so it didn't take Ethan long to answer.

"We'd parted ways emotionally before the divorce was final. I was relieved to find the clinic, and this house, and then make the move. Holly needs consistency."

"And you're hoping to find it in Golden?"

"I think we already have." He blew on the hot water, then sipped. "How about you?"

"Me?"

Was that panic in her eyes?

"What are you hoping to find in Golden?"

She lifted her shoulders. "Nothing more than a job well done."

"Even with your family here? Surely, you plan to visit with them?"

A distinctly uncomfortable grimace crossed her face.

Now, he was confused. "You don't want to see your family?"

"It's not that…"

She took a sip from her mug, stared out the window at the darkening sky, then turned to him. "My parents' divorce was far from amicable."

"Ah."

"It also affected me and my sisters in a bad way. Because of that, we don't really see eye-to-eye."

He thought about the bits and pieces he'd learned about Golden. "Don't your sisters live here?"

"They do. It's…" She waved her hand in the air between them. "Okay, I don't see them at all."

"Which makes being in Golden a problem."

"Bingo." She sighed. "Mom wants her family together and she's pushing for us to reconnect."

"Understandable."

"My father passed away recently, and we just found out he left us a building."

Ethan raised an eyebrow in question.

"Odd, I know."

"I'm sure he had his reasons."

"Apparently, he bought the building a few years ago. Not sure why. Maybe it had something to do with the divorce from his second wife. His hobby was searching for gold around here so he might have wanted a place to store it."

"Gold?"

"Golden was part of the Georgia gold-rush days back in the 1800s. A gold vein was discovered in the surrounding mountains. People came to prospect, some settled after the supply had dwindled and the town of Golden was established."

"Interesting."

She shrugged. "Tonight, my sisters and I discussed what we want to do with the building going forward. After a debate, we decided to do a walkthrough to see if we want to keep it. Addie would like to open a fitness center."

Ethan grinned. "I like that idea. I miss working out."

Nicole eyed his shoulders, then met his gaze. "Don't you work enough hours to keep you in shape?"

"It's a different kind of workout."

She wrapped her tea-bag string around one finger. "I agreed with the others so Addie can make her dream come true."

"Sounds positive."

"That conversation didn't take all night." She puffed out her breath. "We had to make small talk."

Ethan leaned back in the chair. "I realize I haven't known you very long, but that doesn't seem out of the realm of possibility for you."

She shifted her weight and leaned her elbows on the table. "It was…awkward. We were sitting in the kitchen we grew up in. The last place I talked to my dad before he left us." Her voice sounded tight. "Not the greatest memories."

"But you went because of your mom?"

Her gaze met his. A wealth of emotion glimmered there.

"She's the rock. I can't say no to her."

"Which means spending time with your sisters," he concluded.

"Yes."

Silence settled over the room. The refrigerator kicked on. A snore came from Gus's direction.

Ethan spoke first. "I guess the big question is, will you honor your mom's request?"

She threw up her hands. He loved how expressive she could be.

"Ethan, there's so much hurt there. Time has moved on. Where do we start?"

"It seems to me that taking the first step in the journey would solve some of your problems."

She smiled. "Who knew my new neighbor was going to share such pearls of wisdom."

"Hey, I'm not only a veterinarian."

Her lips quivered. "I'll remember that the next time I need good advice."

He took a sip of the cooling tea, then asked, "So, are you thinking about working things out with your sisters?"

"Depends on whether or not I decide to start the journey."

"You're missing the point."

She winked at him. "On purpose."

He chuckled but didn't push. He sensed that this was as far as she was willing to go in the conversation, and as much as he might regret it, he wanted another chance, on another day, to sit with her in his quiet kitchen discussing life.

Nicole drained her mug, then said, "We should get going."

They both rose. Ethan took her mug and placed it in the sink, deciding to go for broke.

"Holly would really like it if you and Gus came over for dinner sometime."

Surprise crossed her face. "Oh, I don't want to put you out."

"It's no trouble. And Holly can be insistent."

"In that case…"

"How about joining us for Friday night pizza? It's kind of a tradition."

She sent him a saucy grin. "Who can say no to pizza?"

"Not anyone I know."

"As long as I'm not running late at work, we'll be here."

They walked to the door. "Great, we'll see you at seven."

She snapped her fingers for Gus to join her, met Ethan's gaze for a long, charged moment, with the heat between them building, then ventured into the darkness. He watched until she was safely inside the cottage, then closed his front door and walked to the kitchen, wondering just how smart it would be to continue this interest in Nicole.

She might not be in town long, and he might have a rule about wanting permanence in his and Holly's life, but what could it hurt to enjoy time with Nicole while she was in Golden?

You'll be breaking your own rules.

He shook his head. "Afraid that's already happened," he muttered to the quiet room. After turning off the main-floor lights, he climbed the stairs to his empty bedroom.

CHAPTER SIX

LATE FRIDAY MORNING, the permit was ready. Armed with her list for the day and a collapsible wagon full of decorations, Nicole visited the store owners up and down Main Street. She'd fluffed branches of the artificial Christmas trees she'd removed from the storage unit to place outside the shops the day before. Today's plan included stringing lights and adding bows and garland to the bare trees. The magazine photographer, Mac Harding, would arrive on Monday, so she had to be ready with Main Street by then.

Gus, much to his displeasure, was at the day care. Nicole felt bad leaving him, but she'd be focused on her task, giving him ample opportunity to run off while her back was turned. Chasing a dog was not on the agenda.

It might be seventy-eight degrees outside, but she'd dressed as if it was the actual holiday. Green shorts, red-and-white-striped tank top and white sneakers, along with the elf hat she'd thrown into her luggage before leaving Savannah. If anyone found her getup odd, they didn't say so.

So far, she'd talked to three business owners, each one thrilled at Nicole's vision for making Golden a vacation destination to remember. But once she approached Golden Gifts, her steps slowed as she dreaded what might transpire inside.

Mrs. Olsen had been one of the more vocal residents gossiping about her parents' split, questioning how Nicole's father could claim his company held family values when he'd left his wife for another woman. Nicole thought it had more to do with Mrs. Olsen's son, who had worked for Connelly Electronics and hadn't relocated when the business grew and moved farther south to the bigger warehouse. Because of that, Mrs. Olsen had made Linda Connelly's life miserable at the time.

Her mom had been grieving the end of her marriage and didn't need the extra pressure. Mrs. Olsen and others who were angry with her father for taking his company elsewhere had piled on to her mom's misery. Rumors of another daughter added to the frenzy. Then her dad and his second family moved back to Golden, making Nicole's last year of high school, when Taylor enrolled, uncomfortable. At that age, who wanted their classmates to know about personal family foibles when the remarks were unkind?

Squaring her shoulders, Nicole marched into the gift shop. "Good morning, Mrs. Olsen."

A woman in her seventies, with a lined face and dark gray hair cut short, hobbled out from behind the sales counter. "Nicole Connelly. How nice to see you."

Nicole frowned. Mrs. Olsen seemed so much older. Her shoulders were stooped and her voice was raspy. Not the brash woman Nicole remembered.

She cleared her throat. "I wanted to let you know I'm decorating outside your store."

The woman leaned on a thick, wooden cane as she slowly shuffled toward Nicole. "I knew you'd be here after placing the tree out front yesterday. Tell me, what will you use for decorations?"

Okay, the shop owner's curiosity—like everyone else's in town—was probably due to the magazine article, not Nicole's return.

"I'm stringing lights today. Hopefully, I'll finish by dinner."

Disappointment creased Mrs. Olsen's face. "That's all? Just lights?"

Okay, here came the criticism.

"I'm going for a certain ambiance."

"Which is?"

Taking a chance, Nicole said, "Would you like to see what I'm aiming for?"

The woman's eyes lit up. "Oh, I would."

A little thrown off, Nicole pulled her phone from her back pocket and pulled up the picture she was using as her foundation. "Once I get the fake snow on the ground and in some of the windows, it'll resemble a Victorian village. Kind of like the miniature village we set up in the living room during Christmas when I was a kid."

Mrs. Olsen leaned closer to peer at the phone. Her floral perfume wafted from her in waves. "Pretty."

Nicole sensed a *but* coming.

"But…"

Bingo.

She pressed her lips together in patience.

"I was hoping to add my own little touch." Mrs. Olsen turned and tottered to the counter. As she did, Nicole took a surreptitious glance around the store. It appeared a bit run-down, dust collecting here and there. It couldn't be from neglect. Nicole remembered that the woman had taken great joy in her small business.

Mrs. Olsen reached behind the counter to remove a bag. She returned, holding it out to Nicole.

"I thought these plastic candy canes might look sweet on the tree. Like they did in the old days." Her wistful smile had Nicole longing for those days too. "My children always loved to place the canes on the store trees during the holidays."

The woman wasn't wrong—it would be cute—but none of the other stores would have added touches. When Nicole started to tell Mrs. Olsen this, she didn't miss the eager anticipation in the older woman's eyes. Nicole hated disappointing her, so she recalibrated.

"Tell you what. After the photographer has taken all the pictures the way I've planned, we can add the candy canes for after shots."

Mrs. Olsen's smile grew. "That would be lovely." She placed a shaky hand on Nicole's arm. "When

I heard you were coming home to supervise this magazine shoot, I told your mother she should be proud of you. We in Golden stick together. And even though you've been gone for a long time, you're still a part of the DNA of this town."

She'd spoken to Nicole's mother? Positively? Boy, times had changed.

"I won't be able to manage the shop for much longer," Mrs. Olsen continued, sadness overshadowing her smile. "None of my children are interested in taking over, so I may have to sell. Doing this event with the rest of the town will be my last real part of the community and I want to remember these days."

That explained the sad state of the shop.

A twinge of melancholy squeezed Nicole's heart at the thought of the shop owner closing the doors of her business for good. She clutched Mrs. Olsen's wrinkled hand for a brief moment. "I'll make sure we get pictures just for you."

Mrs. Olsen's lips quivered.

"Unless there's anything else, I need to get back to work."

"And if you need anything, anything at all," Mrs. Olsen said, "just ask."

"I will."

Nicole walked back outside and placed the bag of fake candy canes into the wagon, an idea forming in her head. Then, with a length of shiny gold garland draped around her neck, she began humming "The Twelve Days of Christmas" as she worked the light cord between the full branches.

"'Five golden rings...'" After plugging in the lights, she stepped back to view her handiwork. "Not bad."

"Only ten more to go," a perky voice from behind her said.

Nicole twirled around to find her neighbor, Celeste, standing on the sidewalk, her eagle eye critiquing Nicole's progress.

"Miss Celeste. What're you doing here?"

"I wouldn't be much of an assistant if I didn't show up to help," she admonished.

Nicole brushed the end of the garland from her leg where it prickled her skin. "My assistant?"

"Unofficial, of course." Celeste strode to the tree to straighten a bent branch. "Two pairs of eyes are always better than one."

"True, but I'm working alone."

"Something the volunteer committee would not agree with. You know we all pitch in around Golden."

Nicole did know that, but she'd hoped to fly solo, anyway.

"Aren't you busy?" she asked the older woman.

"Doing what?"

"I don't know. Planting your garden?"

"Already taken care of. I'm just waiting on my summer bounty."

"Maybe hanging out with a community group you belong to?"

Celeste tilted her head. "If I didn't know better, I'd think you were trying to get rid of me."

"Not at all," Nicole said quickly. Okay, she might have envisioned spending the afternoon alone executing her grand plan, but it didn't mean she wanted to hurt the woman's feelings.

The pleading in Celeste's eyes got to Nicole. "I really would like to work with you."

Holding in a sigh, Nicole realized there was no way to say no. And at the expectant expression on Miss Celeste's face, Nicole realized she didn't want her to leave.

"Fine. Since I've already set up the tree placements, I just need you to hand me the lights."

"I've very good at helping."

As opposed to my lack of delegating, Nicole thought as Celeste started wrapping garland around the branches. It wasn't exactly what Nicole had instructed, but soon they developed a rhythm, and the teamwork was just right.

The next hour flew by. Nicole had a great time catching up with Miss Celeste and other shop owners along Main Street. Some she knew from her childhood, others had recently moved to Golden to take advantage of increasing tourism. She found herself thinking she'd make time to go back and visit the new shops more closely before returning to Savannah. Maybe buy a few Christmas gifts early.

"I spoke to Kimmy yesterday," Celeste told her. "I hope you don't mind that I told her you said hello."

"Not at all," Nicole assured her as she repositioned a strand of lights on a branch.

"She was surprised you'd taken a job here."

Nicole shrugged. "I go where I'm needed."

"I was hoping Kimmy, and her family, would be able to visit while you're in town, but I'm afraid it won't work out. Her husband is busy with his career and the children keep my granddaughter on her toes."

Nicole ignored the old guilt making an unwelcome appearance. Losing contact with Kimmy had been selfish on Nicole's part, but running had been a stronger motivation than friendship at the time. Hearing about her friend made Nicole miss Kimmy and had her wondering what their lives would have been like had they remained close. "Maybe another time."

"Will there be another time?"

Nicole didn't have an answer. "Why do I feel like your question is meant to make a point?"

"About?"

She angled her gaze away from Celeste. "The way I just left town without even telling Kimmy goodbye."

"She understood."

Nicole turned, opened her mouth, but found she didn't know what to say.

"My dear, we all knew how you felt about your parents breaking up. Kimmy knew it touched you deeply. If I remember correctly, the two of you were growing apart by this time, anyway."

Nicole stared at the tips of her sneakers. "I was going to call her, but… I don't know, I guess I chickened out. We had all kinds of plans, like traveling and maybe attending college together, and I was bailing. Kimmy was sure to ask me to stay and I already had a job lined up away from here." She lifted her head to meet Celeste's gaze. "My mom didn't want me to leave and that was breaking my heart. I guess talking to Kimmy would have been a double whammy."

"There's no reason why you two can't connect now. You're both grown, both in different seasons of your life. Perhaps it would be nice to chat with an old friend."

Would it? The tension at home back then, the way her father blamed her for the final blowup with her mom, was all too much. Gossip had flown around town, making it unbearable to walk down the street without feeling judged. She'd needed to escape, needed to figure out how to deal with her family.

And have you?

No. That was the problem, Nicole was sure.

She'd run. Put Golden in her rearview mirror. Never dealt with the lingering hurt. Instead, she'd buried herself in work, becoming very good at her job.

But is that enough?

If she let it, coming home might finally answer that question. Was she secure enough to try?

"Take your time, Nicole. You might be surprised at how people's opinions change." Celeste smiled. "For the better. If you take a chance."

Could she? She thought back to her conversation with Mrs. Olsen, expecting the worst. But the old woman was excited about the prospect of her shop being in one of the photo layouts for the magazine. The merchants had been accommodating. So far, the job was moving along nicely. And most importantly, no one brought up the past.

Sure, there might be a hiccup or two before the job was complete, but she would handle it, like she did any dustup that occurred during a project.

Instead of answering, Nicole sent a wobbly nod to Celeste. She had a lot on her plate, so she'd take it all one day at a time.

They finished late in the afternoon. Traffic was getting heavy. Nicole checked her watch. "It's already time for dinner." Making sure she had all her belongings in her wagon, she said, "I need to get Gus."

Celeste nodded. "I'll meet you at the Jeep."

Nicole raised an eyebrow.

"After all this hard labor, you didn't think I was going to walk home, did you?"

"Of course not." Nicole started to walk away, then stopped. "Wait, don't you have a car?"

At Nicole's raised eyebrow, Celeste waved her hand in the air. "Long story."

"One I most definitely want to hear."

"Maybe, but I'd rather talk about today. I can't remember the last time I enjoyed an afternoon so much."

"Then you'll love what we decorate next."

Celeste sent her a satisfied smile, which—translated in Nicole's mind—meant that there was no way Nicole was going to stop Celeste from being her assistant.

Nicole grinned. "Okay, see you at the Jeep."

"And hurry along. We don't want dinner to get cold."

Nicole wondered whose dinner she was referring to. With Celeste, there was no telling.

ETHAN STOOD AT the sink rinsing foamy suds from drinking glasses before the upcoming dinner with their guest. A warm breeze wafted in through the open window in front of him. The same window where he'd gotten his first glimpse of Nicole.

Anticipation thrummed through him. From the radio came the steady beat of a popular country song. He tapped his foot along with the tempo. Holly was in the living room playing until Nicole and Gus arrived. She'd talked nonstop on the drive home from the clinic about how excited she was to have their neighbors over. Even though he couldn't get a word in edgewise, he'd wholeheartedly agreed.

His cell phone rang. He grabbed a nearby dish towel to dry his hands then took the call. "Dr. Price."

"Ethan, it's Dean Nixon. Sorry to call so late in the day."

"It's okay. Is there a problem?"

"I hope not."

Coming from his attorney, that didn't sound re-assuring. "What's up?"

"Dr. Andrews. He's digging his heels in again."

Ethan shook his head, perplexed. "I don't understand why. Initially, he went along with my business proposal for buying the practice. Why stall now?"

"Want my opinion?"

"Yes."

"I don't think he was ready to retire."

That was obvious.

Ethan stared out the window at his carefully manicured yard. Would all his hopes for a life in Golden be dashed if the sale fell through?

Dean cut into his thoughts. "But I have a solution."

"I'd be happy to hear it."

"Would you consider asking him to work at the clinic a few hours a week?"

The suggestion intrigued Ethan. "As my employee or a co-owner?"

"Employee. That'll make the entire process cleaner when he finally signs the papers."

"Would he be open to the idea? The patients love him and coming in a few hours a week might make retiring less daunting."

"That's what I thought."

"It couldn't hurt to run this by him."

"Great. I'll get the ball rolling and we'll go from there."

"Thanks, Dean. I owe you."

"Which I'm sure you'll be happy about when you get my bill."

With a chuckle, Ethan placed his phone on the counter and returned to the glasses in the sink, then out of the corner of his eye he noticed a streak go by. From his view, he saw Gus galloping toward the swing set, his leash dragging in the grass behind him. Then Nicole came into view, chasing after her wayward dog, who had a significant lead.

He couldn't tear his gaze from her, dressed in a floral sundress, the jaunty elf hat half-hanging off her head. Her outfit elicited a laugh. Nicole's antics made his heart light, and he couldn't recall when he'd been so charmed. A welcome reprieve after the stress that had ushered in the end of his marriage.

Finally, she stopped chasing the energetic dog. Placing her hands on her hips, she stared him down. Gus came back to sit in front of her, meeting her gaze without flinching. He wondered how long the standoff would last. When they didn't move, he dried his hands again, then walked out the back door and onto the wooden porch, stopping at the railing to rest his palms on the rough, flat surface.

Neither of his new neighbors twitched.

He decided action was needed and let out a low whistle. Gus jerked and then bounded over to him, rushing up the steps for a brisk rubdown. Not long after that, Holly came running through the house at a five-year-old's top speed, careening out the back door to see her new best friend. Shaking her head, Nicole worked her way over to the deck, then stood a few feet away while she peered up at Ethan.

"Really?" she asked. "I chased him around for what seemed like ages, working up a sweat, and all you have to do is whistle and he behaves?"

"I feel like my experience with animals gives me the upper hand," he told her with a straight face.

"I need an edge if I'm going to keep Gus in line." Her expression turned bleak. "I don't understand why he has to escape all the time."

Taking pity on her, Ethan walked down the steps to join her. "I would imagine there was some kind of issue with his previous owner. When animals exhibit behavioral problems, it's usually from an experience that happened in the early years of their life. The good thing you have going is that Gus isn't very old, and you can work with him."

"So, you have more ideas for dealing with him?"

"I have more than a few and I'd be happy to share them with you."

Their gazes locked. Nicole cheeks turned pink, but she didn't break the connection. He couldn't deny the satisfaction that came from knowing he had her full attention. And at the same time, he couldn't ignore the clutch in his gut. The early evening sun was warm enough without his temperature spiking as they exchanged heated glances.

A bark sounded from behind him. He twirled to find Holly having taken hold of Gus's leash and leading him around the backyard. She carried on a very detailed conversation with the animal, which brought a smile to Nicole's lips.

His gut clenched again. Honestly, Nicole couldn't have been any more attractive in that moment. The fact that his daughter delighted her made him crazy about this very confident woman.

"So," she said, her voice raspy. A result from the heat blazing between them? "Are we still on for dinner?"

"Yes. The pizza should be here any minute. I have drinks inside." He frowned at the eagerness on her pretty face, thinking he should have offered more. "I didn't have time to make a salad."

Her eyebrows rose. "You make salads?"

"Sure. Remember I'm a single parent taking care of my daughter. I insist she has daily greens whether she likes them or not."

Nicole chuckled. "My mom was always very fussy about what we ate when we were growing up. If she saw the collection of take-out menus I have at home, she'd be appalled."

"No cooking at all?"

"Rarely. I'm usually on the road, so I don't cook then. When I am home, I'm at the office late. After a long day it's just easier to order takeout."

"I've thought about taking cooking classes with Holly. I think it would be fun for both of us."

"Now, if I had someone to take a class with, maybe I would. But you know…" She shrugged her shoulders. "I live alone."

Which made Ethan wonder what her life was like. Was she happy being solo? Plenty of people were. Did she wish she had someone to talk to when she came home from work, like he did with Holly? But then, she had taken Gus in so she could talk to him, although Ethan doubted he was a very good conversationalist. As long as Nicole was in Golden, he'd try his best to include her in activities so that maybe when she went home, she'd remember her time here fondly.

When she went home.

He knew there was a shelf life for her time here and he wasn't about to change that, especially since his first priority was Holly, along with establishing the clinic.

The front doorbell rang. He locked his gaze with hers again, enjoying the color flushing her cheeks. "Our dinner. I'll be right back."

He hurried into the house, grabbed his wallet from the counter and went to the front door to collect the pizza. After tipping the delivery driver, he carried two large boxes containing steaming-hot pizzas into the kitchen. He lifted the lid to inhale the savory spices wafting from their dinner. About that time, Nicole walked through the door.

"Are you trying to sneak a piece?"

"No." He quickly closed the box top. "You'll laugh, but I love the scent of fresh pizza before anybody gets into it."

"Me too," she said. "But there's nothing that beats that first bite of all that gooey cheese and red sauce."

"You're a pizza aficionado?"

"Like I said, I eat out a lot."

He took plates from the cabinet then handed them to her. "Mind setting the table?"

"Not at all. You invited me for dinner, so I'm happy to return the favor."

They spent the next few minutes getting ready.

When Nicole went searching for silverware, they collided while Ethan carried the now dry glasses to the table.

"Sorry."

"My bad."

Their gazes met. Held. Nerves jumped inside him over the sparks arcing between them. Chris Stapleton crooned a romantic ballad on the radio and suddenly Ethan found himself tongue-tied.

Nicole's expression softened. Her sapphire-blue eyes sparkled and her tanned skin glowed. Her hair flowed around her lovely face, with strands tangled in the felt material of her elf hat. It was all he could do not to reach out and run the back of his finger over what he imagined was her soft cheek.

When Nicole blinked, Ethan shook himself. "I, ah, should call Holly."

It took a couple of minutes for his daughter to arrive, but when she did, Gus galloped right behind her, followed by their neighbor, Celeste, who was carrying a big bowl covered with plastic wrap. What was Holly's babysitter doing here?

The woman grinned at him as she handed over the bowl. "I never come to dinner empty-handed. Plus, I have all this first of spring produce from my garden, so I made a nice salad."

Had he missed something? "I didn't realize you were coming to dinner," he said as he took the bowl.

"I invited her," Holly announced. "We were talking the other day and I told her how Nicole was coming for Friday night pizza and that she should come too."

"So, that's what you were talking about," Nicole said to the older woman.

"Want to fill me in?" Ethan asked.

"After we finished setting up the Christmas trees around downtown, Miss Celeste said something about getting home so she wouldn't miss dinner."

Ethan grabbed salad tongs from a drawer as Holly lured Celeste's attention away by telling her a story about a new animal at the clinic. "She's helping you decorate?"

Nicole leaned close and lowered her voice. Her light scent—citrusy and uniquely Nicole—was more alluring than the pizza sauce. "Apparently I need an assistant."

"Celeste?"

"Hey, have you ever successfully told her no?"

He thought that over. "Never."

Nicole took the bowl from his hands to place it in the center of the table. "Forks?"

"Right." Ethan hurried to retrieve them from the drawer.

Nicole turned to Celeste. "I didn't realize when you referred to dinner you meant here."

Celeste took a seat at the table. "It's tiresome eating alone." She held out her arms and Holly hurried over to be enfolded in an embrace. "Thank you, my dear Holly, for including me."

Holly hugged her back, then spoke to her dad. "Can we eat now?"

"Of course."

Before long they were seated, taking slices of pizza and dishing out salad onto their plates. It was quiet for a few moments as they ate, but eventually the conversation picked up again.

"What is next on our agenda?" Celeste asked Nicole after dabbing her napkin against her lips.

"I have to pick up a few items I ordered, so I suppose tomorrow will be errand day."

"Then can Gus play with me?" Holly asked.

"Holly, you'll be with me tomorrow." Ethan explained to Nicole, "I work one Saturday morning a month."

"Daddy, I want to play with Gus."

"Actually, I was going to take him with me," Nicole said.

Holly crossed her arms over her chest. "Do I have to go to the clinic?"

A tightness squeezed Ethan's chest. This was the first time she didn't want to spend time with him. "But you love it there. You're behind on your picture making."

"Pictures?" Nicole asked.

"Holly started drawing pictures for the animals who stay overnight after surgery. Everyone loved them so much—we now tape them to the walls near the kennel beds."

"It makes them feel better," Holly explained.

Nicole smiled at Holly. "How sweet."

Holly shrugged. "I like to draw."

"And I'll bet your pictures make the pets happy."

Resting her tiny elbows on the table, Holly leaned in. "I don't like to see them hurting."

Nicole's gaze met his and he read the admiration in her eyes.

"She's drawn plenty of pictures for me," Celeste said. "I hang them on my refrigerator."

Nicole tilted her head. "What about me? Am I going to get a Holly original?"

"If you want one," Holly replied shyly.

"Are you kidding? Gus and I would love it."

"Maybe I can give it to you when you get home tomorrow."

Or…" Nicole turned a sly eye to Ethan. "Would you mind if Holly accompanied me on my errands?"

Holly jumped up. "Oh, Daddy, can I?"

That ache tore through him again. As much as he hated the pang of discomfort, he couldn't say no. Not when Holly was so eager to help Nicole. His daughter was smiling at Nicole as if she hung the moon.

Holly would love the outing, but would spending time together make it harder on his daughter when Nicole left Golden? He was getting way ahead of himself, but his daughter's excitement was contagious.

"I don't see how I can say no."

"You really can't," Nicole countered with a playful smile.

He met her amused gaze and once again Ethan wondered what would become of this growing attraction if he acted on it at all. Right now, he had no answer, but plenty of interest.

"I really want to go on an abenture," Holly told Celeste. The older woman listened with a serene smile on her face. And all Ethan could think was *I'm in way over my head.*

When dinner ended, he and Nicole cleaned up while Holly and Celeste went to the living room, so Holly could show off her new book. "You really don't mind taking her tomorrow?" he asked in a low tone.

"Not one little bit." Nicole placed the dishes in the sink to rinse. "Besides, you heard her, we're going on an abenture."

"To be fair, she says that when we go to the grocery store."

Nicole laughed, the sound lighthearted and musical to his ears. It touched him right down to the soles of his feet. That pesky heart rate spiked again.

"She has the heart of an adventurer," Nicole mused. "I can relate."

He wanted to relate to Nicole too.

After the dishes were put away, he, Nicole and Holly escorted Celeste home. Once she was safely inside her house, they walked back to Nicole's cottage, Gus trotting beside them.

"What time should I have Holly ready?' he asked.

The setting sun turned the color of Nicole's hair golden. "Eight? We can go out for breakfast first."

"Sounds good." He paused, unable to take his gaze from her. How long could he stand in the evening shadows making small talk before he had to take Holly home? "And what time will you return?"

"That's depends on how much we get done. Midafternoon, I would think."

He nodded.

A knowing grin tipped Nicole's lips. "You want to come with us, don't you?"

"Am I that obvious?"

"A little."

He shrugged, hiding just how much he wanted to tag along. "Duty calls."

"I wouldn't expect anything less from you."

"You make me sound...unadventurous."

"I figured since you're a doctor you're all about responsibility."

"I am. But I like to go rogue every once in a while."

Interest flashed in her eyes. "Hmm. I'd like to see that before I leave town."

Holly yawned. Ethan took her hand to head home but caught Nicole's gaze one last time for the night.

His voice husky, as he was leaving, Ethan said, "Be careful. You might just get what you ask for."

CHAPTER SEVEN

THE NEXT MORNING, Nicole was up early, ready to get the day started. The idea of spending time with Holly had her humming and dancing with Gus in the kitchen. When was the last time she felt this carefree?

"I'm not sure I want that answer," she told Gus, who twitched his neck as he danced sideways next to her.

She loved her job, loved traveling and seeing what she could accomplish. But she also couldn't deny the vague sense that she was missing out on something important in her life. Was moving to a management position the next logical step? Did she have to take that next step? Her boss seemed to think so, stating that her promotion was for the good of the company that had gotten Nicole to this place in her career. That meant her looming deadline was racing that much closer.

"Enough of that," she announced, then hurried to her bedroom to change. She'd see Ethan when she picked up Holly in—she read the clock on the nightstand—fifteen minutes. Flipping through her limited selection, she settled on a fluttery pink top, denim skirt and sandals. After applying makeup and styling her hair, she slapped the elf cap on her head.

"Might as well go all in."

She grabbed her backpack and connected Gus to his harness, then they stepped out into the sunshine. The temperature had risen, promising a beautiful day. The sun warmed her shoulders as she and Gus strolled across the grass connecting the properties. The front door opened. Ethan stepped out, coffee mug in hand, his eyes shining, his dark hair and beard gleaming in the sun. Her heart froze.

Oh, boy. There's a sight I wouldn't mind seeing every day.

The closer she got, the more the pit of her stomach swirled. She hadn't eaten breakfast yet, so that could be the cause. No, it was likely the smile on his face. The broad shoulders that filled out his dress shirt. The man she couldn't stop thinking about.

Definitely not on her list of expectations when she'd decided to return to Golden.

"Good morning." Ethan's husky voice sent shivers over her skin.

"Hi," she returned, her own voice breathless. Gus strained at the leash, wanting to get closer to Ethan.

Get in line.

"Holly's been awake since six."

She nodded toward the mug. "Second or third cup?"

He chuckled. "Second."

Commotion sounded from inside the house and

Holly appeared beside her father, dressed for the day in matching pink shorts and a top. "You're here."

"I am."

Holly rushed out to hug Gus. "Both of you. Today is going to be the best day ever."

A grin tugging at her lips, Nicole met Ethan's gaze after he turned his affectionate smile from his daughter to her. The color of his eyes deepened to a velvety brown and the heat level rose. Her throat was dry when she swallowed.

Gus wandered to Ethan, sniffing, then sat and gazed up at him.

"I think it's a girl's day, buddy."

Gus held out a paw.

"How about we hang together?"

"Wait," Nicole said. "I was planning on taking him along."

"When was the last time you took a five-year-old on an outing?"

"Never."

"Then I was going to suggest I take Gus to the clinic. This way you won't be running in multiple directions all day."

He was probably right. Holly had hopped down the walkway in front of the house, then pivoted and returned. Gus barked, then stood, as if to join the little girl.

"Hmm. You may be on to something," Nicole said.

"Trust me."

Ethan sipped from the mug, his words wrapping

around her heart. *Trust me.* Even though she hadn't known him for very long and didn't have faith in most people, she knew deep down he was trustworthy.

"Also," he added, "I know my daughter. You don't need additional distractions."

"Since you're her father, and have more kid experience than me, I'm going to follow your suggestion."

Ethan lifted a dark eyebrow. "Do you have *any* kid experience?"

Nicole thought about Jacob and Cami, both of whom she barely knew, and guilt crept into her chest. "Not really."

"Then you made the right choice."

Ethan reached out for the leash. When Nicole handed it over, their fingers brushed, and that jolt of electricity she'd experienced when she first met him flared between them again. She lingered, then withdrew her hand, taking a step back. Ethan's eyes were hooded now, but Nicole was sure he felt the charge between them. How could he not? Plus, she was secretly touched that he'd thought ahead when it came to Gus because she had not.

He cleared his throat, then said, "By the way, I strapped Holly's booster seat into your Jeep. The door was unlocked."

Words fled from Nicole's mind. His lingering gaze scorched her skin and made her lose all sense of…everything.

He sent Nicole one last long look before turning

his attention to her dog. "C'mon, Gus. It's you and me for the rest of the day."

"Take good care of him," Holly admonished her father as she took hold of Nicole's hand.

Nicole started, first from her musings about Ethan, and then at her surprise that Holly would make the gesture. But again, what did she know about kids? Today would probably be a crash course on the topic. She would try to decipher Ethan's gaze later when her runaway pulse wasn't wildly galloping out of control.

Gus went willingly to Ethan. Nicole smiled. "You have the magic touch."

"Good thing, otherwise, I wouldn't be very good at my job."

True, along with making her heart race and causing her to tingle. In her entire life, she'd never tingled. He was magic.

"Well, um, we should be back this afternoon. Probably after you've returned from the clinic."

Ethan tousled Gus's fur. "We'll be waiting, won't we, buddy?"

Gus barked and Nicole found that she wanted to get her errands done so she could return home to spend time with Ethan.

"Okay, then," she said to Holly. "First stop, breakfast."

"Goody. I waited for you, but my tummy is growling."

"Then we'd better make tracks." She turned to Ethan. "See you later."

"You bet."

His calm voice had her tummy whirling again. She awkwardly waved, then with the little girl's hand securely tucked into hers, they headed back to the cottage to get in the Jeep before driving to Main Street. Holly kept up a steady conversation as they went, telling Nicole about school and the animals at the clinic, yet all Nicole could wonder over was the fact that Holly trusted her. There was a lot of responsibility with that trust. Was she up for the job? She'd been alone for so long, with only herself to take care of, when was the last time someone had faith in her? Sure, at work, that went without saying. And since she'd taken Gus home. But another human? It was scary and awesome at the same time.

Before long, they were walking into A Touch Of Tabby café. A cacophony of loud conversation, cutlery clinking against stoneware and a waitress yelling an order to the chef assailed Nicole ears. The heavy scent of richly brewed coffee hung in the air. It was the environment of a well-loved establishment, transporting Nicole back in time. She waved at the owner, who in turn pointed them to an empty table. Nicole drew up short when she noticed Addie, Jacob and Cami seated at the neighboring table.

"Fancy meeting you here," she said, trying not to take umbrage at her sister's surprised glance that moved from Nicole, to Holly, and back again.

"You could say that," Addie said as Holly scooted onto the vinyl bench seat against the wall while Nicole sank into the opposite chair. "Something you want to tell me?"

"This is Ethan Price's daughter, Holly."

Addie frowned. "The new vet?"

"Yes. I'm renting the house next to his and we've all become friends."

One of Addie's eyebrows arched, but she remained silent.

"I have work errands to run. Holly is my assistant today."

"I thought Miss Celeste was your assistant?"

The remark made her draw back. "How did you know that?"

"Small town. Also, Mom told me."

Nicole nodded as she took a menu from the server and focused on Holly. "What would you like to eat?"

"Pancakes."

Nicole said to the teen waiting on their table, "Two pancake specials and orange juice."

"Coffee?"

Nicole thought about the day ahead and nodded.

"I'm going to help Nicole make Golden festival," Holly announced.

Nicole chuckled. "Festive."

"Right, festive."

The table was covered in white paper with a mason jar of crayons in the middle. Holly and Cami, already best friends, removed a few different colors and began to draw.

"How is the job going?" Addie asked. Even though it appeared she and Jacob were nearly finished with their meal, Nicole couldn't deny that her sister's interest warmed her heart.

"Right now, I'm in the process of decorating the downtown shops in a different holiday theme. I have big plans for the park, but that'll come after the first photos of downtown are taken."

"You do have the entire town talking."

Memories of the past, rumors that had swirled about her family, made Nicole uneasy. Addie must have noticed.

"In a good way," her sister insisted with a sigh. "I wasn't sure what to expect either when I first came back to town, but so far, so good. People are friendly."

Thinking about the reasons why Addie had returned, Nicole waited until Jacob was helping Holly with her drawing, then asked, "Did it take you and Jacob long to get into the groove of Golden life?"

A shadow passed over Addie's blue eyes. "It was tough at first, but he's doing well in school. We've both made friends and still have connections with people from when we lived in Atlanta."

"I'm glad to hear that."

Silence stretched out between them before Addie spoke.

"The floral arrangement you sent for Josh's memorial service was beautiful." She swallowed. "I was also glad you came to the church."

Nicole reached to place her hand over her sister's. "Of course, I'd be there."

They stayed in that position for a long moment.

Nicole squeezed Addie's hand, thankful when Addie squeezed back in return. It had been too long since Nicole had acted like a sister. She missed it.

Addie drew her hand back and straightened her shoulders. "We're going to be fine."

"I have no doubt."

"And now Briana has Cami. We try to get the kids together on a regular basis. In fact, Briana has a shift today so I'm watching Cami."

"How is that working out for Briana? Juggling being a police officer and a mom?"

Addie shrugged. "You know Briana. She handles it all."

The children debated whether or not to draw a dinosaur or a kitty.

"About the building," Addie said. "Don't make your decision on my account."

"Why not? I think having your own business is a wonderful endeavor. I'm Team Addie all the way."

The ghost of a smile flitted over Addie's lips. "Isn't that what we always said about each other. You, Briana and me?"

Nicole swallowed the lump in her throat. "Until things changed."

"Yeah."

The waitress returned with heaping plates of pancakes. Holly squealed in delight while Nicole's eyes grew wide. "That's a lot of food."

"Good thing you're running errands today." Addie rose. "And on that note, we're off to the park. There's a pop-up baseball game that Jacob wants in on."

Jacob slid from his seat, Cami right behind him, and stopped beside Nicole. "Will you come to one of my games this summer? We don't officially start until school is out."

At his request, Nicole blinked several times. "I, ah, would love to."

Cami clapped her little hands, her silky straight hair escaping her ponytail.

Addie stood. "I'll make sure you get his schedule."

"Thanks."

Addie placed her hand on Nicole's shoulder. "We are family."

Nicole swallowed the emotion lodging in her throat. "Yes, we are."

Her sibling, niece and nephew weaved through the tables on the way to the exit, saying good morning and wishing folks a good day.

Could this job in Golden be the path to becoming a family again? Going by the inkling of hope she felt and the myriad emotions running through her, Nicole could understand why her mother had been so adamant about Nicole staying in Golden for a month. Why she should make a solid effort to reconnect with her sisters.

Leaving that dilemma to another time, Nicole stared at the mound of pancakes. That's when she noticed Holly trying to pour syrup over her breakfast. The lid opened too wide, and a cascade of brown syrup rushed out. Nicole quickly leaned across the table to stop the overflow.

"Sorry," Holly said, her cheeks red.

"Hey, it's pancakes. We all get excited to eat them."

Taking Holly's fork and knife, Nicole cut the pancakes into bite-size pieces before adding syrup to her own plate and digging in.

"Daddy likes to come here," Holly informed her after swallowing a mouthful.

"Does he cook breakfast?"

"Yes. Usually eggs and toast. It's okay, but I like cereal."

"Me too. I'm usually on the run in the morning and don't make anything complicated."

"Maybe Daddy can make you breakfast one day."

Nicole wasn't commenting on that innocent suggestion.

"What are we hunting for today?" Holly asked around a mouthful of pancakes.

Reaching into her backpack, Nicole removed a slim book she'd gotten years ago that featured Victorian Christmas pictures and stories. She placed it on the table—out of reach of the syrup—and flipped through the pages.

Holly weighed in when Nicole closed the book. "It's pretty."

"Our job today is to find decorations like in the book."

Holly gave her a thumbs-up before finishing the last of the pancakes.

No wonder Ethan was crazy about his daughter—she was totally cute.

After their stomachs were full, Nicole took

Holly's hand and they walked to the Jeep. The year-round holiday-decoration supply store she'd discovered online was in Clarkston, the next town over. After twenty minutes on the winding mountain road, featuring scenic views of densely packed woods, rustic farms and a wide variety of pickup trucks, they pulled into the town. Not as beautiful as Golden, but then again, Nicole might be a bit biased.

She'd turned on the navigational app before leaving Golden, and soon the directions guided them to the designated street. Nicole pulled into a parking space in front of a house decked out for Christmas. Colorful lights framed the structure, with two decorated trees on the porch, and a sleigh in the yard with the name Christmas Days and More painted on the side.

Holly's eyes went wide. "It's so beautiful," she whispered.

Nicole had to admit, nostalgia swept over her at the sight.

"Let's go inside and see what we can find."

Once again, Holly took her hand. As Nicole pushed open the front door, a hearty "ho, ho, ho" greeted them. The older woman behind the counter looked up. Nicole had to stop short. Good grief, she was the image of Mrs. Claus, with her snow-white hair, rosy cheeks, thin gold, rectangular framed glasses, and a red dress.

"Welcome," the woman said in a musical voice.

Holly tugged Nicole to the counter. "Are you for real?" the little girl asked.

"I most certainly am."

Holly moved this way and that to peer around the store. "Where is Santa?"

"I'm afraid he's at the North Pole working with the elves."

Disappointment flashed over Holly's face until she laid eyes on a teddy-bear collection nearby. "Can I go over there?" she asked Nicole.

"Sure. Don't wander off."

"How may I help you, dear?" the store owner asked.

Nicole pulled the list from her backpack and the two discussed her needs. Nicole had decided to purchase electric candles to place in the store windows, find a few more swags of colorful autumn leaves to drape around shop doors and needed at least two dozen more dyed Easter eggs since there were more businesses in Golden than she remembered.

Every few minutes Nicole looked over her shoulder to find Holly admiring a ceramic Christmas village or a display of hand-painted Easter knick-knacks on shelves spanning an entire wall. Once she had her purchases on the counter, Nicole removed the business debit card from her wallet while Mrs. Claus went to the storeroom for one final item.

"You know," she said to Holly, "your dad is going to ask about everything you saw today. What will you tell him?"

She turned, her smile slipping when she didn't get a reply.

"Holly?"

Silence.

Panic welled in Nicole. She stuffed her wallet back in her bag and scoured the nearest area of the store. "Holly?"

No, no, no! How on earth had this happened? Holly was there one moment, and the next she was gone. After Ethan had entrusted Nicole with his daughter's safety.

Her ears roaring, she ran up one aisle then another calling Holly's name. Her heart painfully knocked against her ribs. What kind of adult loses the child they're responsible for?

After making the round a second time, her legs trembling and chest tight, Nicole finally came to a halt at the Halloween-costume section, almost missing the tiny feet that were visible behind a round clothing rack.

It took her three tries before she managed to eke out a word. "Holly?"

A head of curly brown hair peeked around the display.

Nicole's hand flew to her chest. Her nose stung with unshed tears of relief. "Thank goodness."

Holly made her way to Nicole. "What's wrong?"

"I was calling your name, and you didn't answer…" Her voice trickled off. How did parents not freak out on a regular basis? "Why didn't you answer?"

"Sorry. I didn't hear you. I was searching."

Not sure how to respond, Nicole asked, "Searching for what?"

Holly held up an elf hat similar to the one Nicole wore. "I want to be like you." She frowned at the cap in her hand. "This one is too big."

It was all Nicole could do not to drop to her knees and pull Holly into a firm embrace and never let her go.

Throat tight, she said, "Honey, all you have to do is ask."

"Really?"

Footsteps sounded behind her as Mrs. Claus joined them. "I see you found our Halloween costumes. Is there one you like?"

Nicole pointed to the red-striped hat in Holly's hand. "Do you have any children's costumes with these kids of caps?"

"I believe I do." The woman marched to the rack and removed a bagged costume on a hanger. She studied Holly, as if guessing her size, then checked the item before handing it to Nicole. "Only children who believe in Christmas get to be part of Santa's team."

Nicole's eyebrows rose when she saw it was a complete elf costume including cap, tunic, belt and tights in the size for a little girl.

Holly ran over. "Can I see?" When Nicole showed her a picture of the contents of the bag, Holly gasped. "A real, true elf uform."

"Of course," Mrs. Claus boasted. "Direct from the north pole."

"Oh, Nicole, can I try it on?" Holly vaulted up and down on her toes. "Can I?"

"I don't see why not," Mrs. Claus announced before Nicole could respond, leading them to a nearby fitting room. Nicole wasn't sure if she should be happy or miffed with the woman taking over. Once thing was certain—Mrs. Claus knew her market and how to sell to a captive audience.

Holly took Nicole's hand and dragged her inside.

"I'll meet you at the sales counter," Mrs. Claus said as she headed back to her post.

Holly was already toeing off her sneakers. "I always wanted to be an elf."

"You did?" Nicole asked as she helped Holly change. "Why?"

"They have a special job. All the kids in the world know that elves make the Christmas toys that make us happy."

"And you want to make toys?"

Holly struggled getting the tunic over her head until Nicole assisted her.

"No, silly. I want kids to be happy."

Nicole's heart melted. How could she possibly refuse Holly's request to try on the costume?

"And since my birthday is on Christmas, I think Santa would want me to be an elf."

As Holly tried to pull the tights over her legs, Nicole said, "Let me."

Soon, Holly was dressed in a green tunic with a wide red belt, a felt red hat with a black trim and black tights, every inch the elf she wished to be.

As she stood before the mirror, Holly exhaled an awed gush of air.

Nicole stood back, hand on her chin, as if taking it all in before giving her critique of the outfit. "I must say, I wasn't sure, but you could blend right in at Santa's Workshop."

Holly shrieked with delight.

"Can I get it, please, please, please, Nicole?"

Uncertain about what Ethan would do, Nicole hesitated.

"I have some birthday money saved up," Holly said. When Nicole still didn't respond, she came up with another tactic. "If it's not enough I can walk Gus for you."

"Hold on," Nicole said. "What will your dad think?"

"On my birthday, he calls me the birthday elf. He'll love this."

Would he? Nicole had no way of knowing. But one thing was sure, she couldn't let down Holly. Not when she acted like she'd been to the north pole and back.

"Okay. Let's pack it up and check out."

"Can I wear it home? Pretty please?"

They'd only known each other for a week and Holly had Nicole wrapped around her finger.

"Let's check with Mrs., er, Claus."

Holly ran from the room, leaving Nicole to collect her clothing. "Wait. Your shoes."

Holly turned, then dashed back. Nicole helped put on the sneakers, then Holly was off like a champion sprinter.

"Good grief," she muttered as she collected Holly's clothes. "You have to be in shape to wrangle kids."

As Nicole neared the counter, she heard the store owner respond to the girl. "Of course, you'll wear it home. Santa doesn't let just anyone out of the store dressed like you, but I can see that you're special."

Shaking her head over the sales pitch, Nicole paid for her items, placed Holly's clothes in a bag Mrs. Claus gave her and got them both into the Jeep, when her phone rang. She was surprised by the name of the photographer for the magazine spread on the caller ID.

"Hi, Mac."

"Hey, Nicole. Are you free?"

"Doing some errands for the photo shoots. What's up?"

"I'm in town."

"Now? I thought you were coming in on Monday?"

"Finished my last project early and took a flight to Atlanta. I have your production schedule, but while I was walking around town, I came across a perfect scene I want you to stage. Can you meet me?"

Nicole glanced at Holly, who was smoothing the skirt of the tunic.

"When?"

"Now?"

Her fingers tightened on the steering wheel. "I'm kinda—"

"I wouldn't bother you if I didn't need your input."

She confirmed the time on her watch. Ethan was

most likely still at the clinic. She could spare at least thirty minutes. "Where are you?"

"Outside Golden Gifts on Main Street."

"I'll be there soon."

She ended the call and met Holly's gaze in the rearview mirror. "Mind taking a side trip with me?"

Holly considered her question. "Can I show off my elf uform?"

Nicole smiled. Holly was one adept negotiator for a five-year-old. "Yes, you can."

Then they were off with all the purchases. Nicole parked off Main Street once they were in Golden. She and Holly headed toward the gift shop. Mac was already out front, a few women surrounding him.

"I see it didn't take long."

Mac lifted his head, his dark hair gleaming in the sun, his eyes filled with merriment.

"Long?"

Nicole nodded toward the small crowd. No matter where they went, it was the same. Women couldn't get enough of Mac Harding.

"What did you want me to see?" Nicole knew if she didn't ask, he'd hold court all day.

Mac excused himself from the group, then led Nicole and Holly to the window. As Nicole peered inside, she saw that a variety of toys had been placed on display. Toys that hadn't been there the other day. Mrs. Olsen must have made a change due to the photo shoot.

The collection worked perfectly. Nicole decided the tableau would be a great addition to her vision.

"Since I arrived early," Mac said, "I was strolling through the town when I saw this window. With the trees you've added, it's ideal. I wanted to get started."

"Why are you here early?"

"Scheduling conflict," Mac replied. "We need to ramp things up so I can leave in two weeks."

What? No! "We're supposed to work until the end of the month."

He shrugged in answer.

Her shoulders drooped. If Mac finished early, then that meant she would be finished ahead of schedule too.

A commotion caught her eye. Women were stopping to watch them. Despite his way with the ladies, Mac was a consummate professional. His mind was always three steps ahead, which was why Nicole loved working with him.

Mac's gaze fell to Holly, who was still holding Nicole's hand. "And who have we here?"

"Holly. My neighbor's daughter."

Mac tilted his head. "And chief elf of Golden?"

"I am," Holly said proudly.

Mac met Nicole's gaze. "She'd be terrific in the shot."

"I don't know." This wasn't something she'd discussed with Ethan, mainly because she didn't know the opportunity would arise. "I'd really need to check with her dad."

Mac nodded, even though his disappointment was evident.

Nicole answered Mac's staging questions while he removed his camera from the padded black bag. She noticed Holly getting restless and was thankful when her own mother walked down the sidewalk toward them.

"Hard at work?" her mom asked as she stopped.

"Sort of last-minute."

Her mother's attention focused on Mac. Color infused her cheeks. "He's cute. You'll be working with him?"

Nicole rolled her eyes. Didn't matter the age, Mac had an immediate effect. "I am." Holly pulled at her hand, giving Nicole an idea. "Mom, would you mind watching Holly for a minute while I finish up with Mac?"

"I'd love to." She smiled at Holly. "I was going for ice cream. Care to join me?"

Holly jumped up and down. "I love ice cream."

"Then we'll be fast friends."

Ice cream and an elf *uform* before lunch. What would Ethan think?

Her mother and Holly walked down Main Street, leaving Nicole with Mac. Immersed in the zone, he found different angles and lighting to enhance the shots. When he finished his impromptu session, he pulled the schedule she'd emailed him from his camera bag and they discussed the rest of this week. Her mother returned, Holly skipping beside her.

"I need to get back to the store," she said, giving Nicole a quick hug.

"Thanks for helping."

Her mother frowned. "If you lived here, I could help all the time."

"Mom…"

She waved a hand. "See you all later."

"What's that about?" Mac asked.

"My mom's campaign to get me to move back home."

Mac laughed. "Yeah, like that's gonna happen."

As he returned his camera to the bag, she wondered at his reaction. She'd always been adamant about not moving home, but since arriving, her heart was mellowing at the idea. Maybe not relocating here permanently, but at least not being a stranger.

"How come you don't live with your mom?" Holly asked.

Nicole shook off her thoughts. "Well, I don't live in Golden and I'm a grown-up, so I live alone."

"But you live next door."

"For a while. Until my job is finished."

A sad expression washed over Holly's face. "What's wrong?" Nicole asked.

Holly let out a big sigh. "I miss not having a mommy."

Nicole's heart sank. How awful to feel that way. There had been many times she'd felt like that about her dad, until she remembered why he wasn't in her life.

"I'm sure your mommy misses you."

Holly shrugged, breaking Nicole's heart even more.

"Maybe your dad—"

"No, you can't tell Daddy." Panic rang in Holly's voice, confusing Nicole.

"Why not?"

"It'll make him sad. I don't want him to be sad."

Nicole kneeled down to wrap Holly in her arms.

"Promise you won't tell him," Holly urgently whispered in Nicole's ear.

Nicole wasn't sure what to do with this information, but it was important to Holly. "I...okay. But if—"

"Daddy!"

Holly took off. Nicole turned to see Ethan and Gus headed in their direction.

Holly ran right into Ethan's arms. He swept her up and squeezed her tight, but when he gazed over Holly's shoulder at Nicole, there were questions in his eyes.

As Nicole rose, her stomach flipped at the intensity of his gaze. She placed her hand over her midsection.

"You okay?" Mac asked as he sauntered over to her.

"I'm in big trouble," she whispered.

CHAPTER EIGHT

"GOOD. YOU'RE BACK." Celeste waved as Linda walked up to the general store. She stood on the wide wooden porch, where white, oversize rocking chairs beckoned weary tourists.

"Is everything okay?" Linda asked as she climbed the steps.

"More like we need to check in."

"I just ran in to Nicole at Golden Gifts, working on the magazine project. She has Holly with her today."

"That little rascal wanted to run errands with Nicole."

Linda placed her hands on her hips. "And how would you know that?"

"I had dinner with Nicole at the Price house last night."

"Let's take a seat." Linda nodded to the chairs. "You're right, I need an update."

The women sank into the rockers as Celeste filled in Linda on the previous evening's activity.

An idea had been brewing in Celeste's head and she sought Linda to get her opinion. "What do you think about Dr. Price?"

Linda frowned. "What about him?"

"He's Nicole's neighbor."

"That's true."

"And they've spent time together."

"More than dinner last night?"

"He went with Nicole to do inventory at the storage unit. They've run in to each other at home and in town."

"Your point?"

"There's a spark."

Linda gaped. "Are you sure?"

Celeste grinned. "Definite spark."

"I'm surprised. Nicole's not really open to relationships."

"Maybe she hasn't met the right man."

Linda stared across the parking lot, lost in thought, before turning back to Celeste. "I took Holly for ice cream while Nicole was talking to the photographer she's working with. Holly didn't say anything about them all hanging out."

"Did she talk about Gus?"

"Incessantly."

"There you go."

Linda rubbed her forehead. "Nicole is leaving in three weeks. We can't fix the sister problem and hope she falls for Dr. Price in that short amount of time." She dropped her hand. "Do you think a friendship with him would give her incentive to stay?"

"Not sure, but I'll whisper in her ear."

Linda shook her head before meeting Celeste's gaze. "How is your plan to lure Nicole home going?"

"I've made myself her assistant and have asked her for rides to and from the job. I made sure to get myself invited to dinner. And I'll make sure to pop into the cottage when she's home and extoll the virtues of Golden."

Linda snorted. "She'd argue those virtues."

"Maybe, but if I keep her on her toes, she won't have time to focus on the negative."

"That's not half-bad."

"It's all the free time. I get great ideas when I'm sitting on my front porch watching the world go by."

"And on my end, I'll remind her how much I'd like to see her more often. How I want Nicole and her sisters to rebuild their relationships."

"Were any of her sisters around when you saw her?"

"No, but when I sat with Addie at Jacob's pop-up baseball game earlier today, she told me they ran into each other at breakfast."

"And?"

"That's all. It was a madhouse while the kids were finding out what teams they'd be on, so I really didn't get many details from her."

"But she didn't allude that it was a disaster?"

"No."

"Good start." Celeste rested her elbow on the armrest and rocked forward. "How did your dinner go with the girls? I didn't dare ask Nicole since we don't want her to know we're colluding."

"It was…strained. But they were all cordial until the end." Linda's troubled gaze met Celeste's. "When Addie and Taylor left, I walked them out to their cars. I came back into the kitchen afterward, hearing the tail end of Nicole and Briana's conversation voicing their differences of opinion."

"Hmm." Celeste tapped her finger against her handbag. "Over the building?"

Linda let out a resigned sigh. "More likely about their father."

"And since it's his gift that is bringing them together, he's a constant reminder to them."

"All the girls were profoundly hurt by their father's actions, each in their own way. I'm not sure how to fix this."

"But the girls did talk at dinner, right? They made an effort to get along?"

"They did."

"Then we have that to build on. Perhaps over time they can put their hurt over their father behind them and focus more on their relationship."

"That's what I hope for," Linda agreed.

They went quiet for a time, watching tourists and townsfolk as they went about their day.

"Celeste, are we dreaming that our plan will actually have an impact on Nicole, or are we doomed to failure?"

Celeste didn't like the defeat in Linda's tone.

"We're capable women. We make things happen. And besides, when love is involved, anything can happen."

"While I want to see all my girls settled, first and foremost, I want them to get back to where they were when life hadn't turned them upside down."

"Patience, Linda. You raised a tight-knit family and have added Taylor to the fold. In time, the girls will see how important each is to the other."

Linda squared her shoulders. "You're right. We can't expect change if we don't keep trying."

Celeste nodded. "Then that's what we focus on. And Dr. Price? He's an added bonus."

ETHAN HAD QUESTIONS. Lots of questions. Like, who was the guy hovering at Nicole's side and why was his daughter dressed up like an elf?

Mainly, who was that guy?

Nicole took a few steps toward him. "I thought we were going to meet at your house?"

"I was taking Gus for a walk and saw you. He couldn't get here fast enough."

Nicole reached down to rub Gus's head. "He is loyal."

When the dog saw Holly, he strained at the leash.

"Maybe not to me," she amended.

Ethan let the dog rush over to lick Holly. "Don't take it personally. You never know which human is going to be their favorite."

"I do feed him, so I have that going for me."

He chuckled.

"Are you working?" he asked.

"Sort of. My associate—"

The mystery man returned to Nicole's side.

"Did I hear my name?"

"No, Mac, you did not." She shook her head, then made introductions between the men.

"So, how do you know Nic?" Mac asked.

"She's my neighbor. You?"

"We've worked on multiple projects together." Mac inched closer.

Nicole sent him a warning scowl. "Mac is a great photographer."

He placed his arm around Nicole's shoulders. "Because you keep me in line."

She slipped out of his embrace. "Someone has to."

Mac winked at her. To his displeasure, Ethan felt his blood boil.

Nicole turned to Ethan. "He arrived early and wanted to get started. I stopped by to go over our schedule."

"Nic's got her act together."

Ethan got it. Mac called her Nic.

Mac's phone rang. He read the screen and said, "I need to take this."

She nodded, then turned to Ethan. "How about we take Holly and Gus to the park? They can run around for a while."

"Sounds good."

Nicole walked over to Mac to tell him she was leaving. Ethan didn't miss the protective vibes coming from the photographer. What did he think Ethan was going to do? Charm Nicole, then break her heart?

Or would it be the other way around?

The short stroll to Gold Dust Park was filled with Holly regaling him with her morning's exploits.

"I really, really wanted to be an elf," she said as she finished.

Ethan sent Nicole an amused glance.

She shrugged. "Your daughter is very persuasive."

Didn't he know it.

"Daddy, can I go play?"

"Stay where I can see you."

"I will," she called over her shoulder as she and Gus ran to a group of kids on the swings.

"Care to take a seat?" he asked, motioning to a nearby bench.

"Yes." Nicole removed her backpack and dropped it to the ground, then plopped down with a sigh. "I'm exhausted."

"Welcome to my world."

"I thought Gus was a handful, but keeping up with a little girl? Next level."

They sat quietly for a few moments, watching Holly and Gus race around the lush grass. Ethan couldn't remember if he and his ex-wife had ever been this comfortable together in silence. Yet with Nicole, it felt…right.

He spoke first. "So… Mac?"

Nicole kept her gaze on the activities going on around them. "Nothing there."

"He seems to think so."

"He'd be wrong."

Ethan wasn't going to analyze the relief pouring through him.

She sent him a sassy grin. "How was your morning, dear?"

He chuckled.

He'd go along with the not-so-subtle change in conversation. For now.

"We saw a few patients and I checked on the boarded animals."

"And the doggy day care was open?"

"Not on weekends."

She turned in her seat, surprise reflected in her memorable blue eyes. "And you took Gus, anyway?"

Ethan lifted his shoulders. "I knew Holly would keep you on your toes."

Nicole bit her lip. Looked like she wanted to say something, then thought better of it.

"I had paperwork to catch up on. The office was quiet, not that it helped."

She turned her face toward him again. "Quiet doesn't work for you?"

"No, the previous owner of the clinic not returning legal forms I need to file doesn't help."

Why had he gone there? Nicole didn't need to know his problems, but honestly, he wanted to hear her take on the situation. He might not have known her long, but she was sharp and seemed to really understand business. Hers, anyway.

"Dr. Andrews?" she queried.

"Yes. The sale hasn't officially gone through yet. He keeps dragging his feet."

"I remember him. He was always at town functions, talking about pet care." She scratched her ear. "Now that I think about it, that was his only topic of conversation."

"Hence his reluctance to give up control." Ethan ran a hand behind his neck and massaged the building tension. "We thought all the paperwork was in order. If I had known about this snag in advance…"

"You still would have come to Golden."

Surprised by her quick answer, he said, "You think?"

"It's clear you and Holly love it and you've settled in. And if Dr. Andrews started the process, doesn't he have some kind of obligation to finish?"

"Not until we get his signature. But my attorney is making headway."

"Not fast enough?"

"No. I've staked my future on the clinic, Nicole. Holly's too."

She reached over and took hold of his hand. The same flare of a spark that he'd felt the day he met her returned with a vengeance.

"It'll happen. You're more than capable of running the clinic and Dr. Andrews knows that."

When she slipped her hand from his, he couldn't explain the loss. "How can you be so sure? You've only seen me there once."

"I don't need to see more. Just the way you've talked about it is proof. And Holly is your greatest advocate, so there's that."

"Yeah, she is pretty awesome."

She got that funny expression on her face again. "What?"

Nicole went a little pale and blurted, "I lost Holly for about five minutes this morning."

"Come again?"

Her cheeks turned red. "We were at the store in Clarkston. I was placing an order with the owner and when I turned around, she was nowhere to be seen."

He blinked at her rapid-fire explanation.

"Since my daughter is running around with your dog, it appears you found her."

"I thought I was going to throw up when I called for her and she didn't answer."

He'd had that reaction a time or ten.

"Let me guess. She wandered off to an area of the store that caught her attention?"

"To be fair, the entire store got her attention."

"Where did you find her?"

"In the back of the store, admiring the elf costumes."

He rubbed his beard. "That explains her getup."

"She was mesmerized."

He grinned. "That happens on a regular basis."

"You mean she set me up?"

"Big-time."

Nicole stared at Holly, then a grudging smile crossed her lips. "I'm impressed."

A laugh escaped him.

"Tell me this. Was my daughter any help with your errands?"

"Actually, she was." Nicole reached over to her backpack and removed a glossy book the size of a magazine.

"What's that?"

Nicole handed it over. He flipped through the pages as she spoke.

"My theme for the Christmas staging came from this book."

He turned it back to the cover. "Victorian Christmas."

She angled on the bench to face him. "I bought that book on a field trip when I was ten years old. With my own money, I might add."

So, she'd always been enterprising.

"Where was the trip?"

"The Old Governor's Mansion before they moved to the current location in Atlanta. It's this wonderful example of Greek Revival architecture. The place was decorated for Christmas, and we thought it was the most beautiful place we'd ever set foot in. A huge tree in the foyer took up two stories. I wanted to decorate our tree at home just like the one in the mansion, but my mom wouldn't let me go overboard." Her delighted laugh reached out and grabbed his heart. "So, I smuggled some ornaments out of the house, bought gold garland with what was left of my allowance money and decorated a tree in our yard. I was so proud."

"And now Golden gets to benefit from that class trip."

"At a minimum, anyway."

He thought about that, then said, "Young Nicole would be sad about that."

She blinked rapidly, as if holding back tears. "That's why I have to do the job and get out."

One thing about Nicole, she'd been consistent in her honesty about leaving town when her job was over. Ethan might have hoped differently, but her words rang with certainty. Why did he have to like her so much? Her leaving would create a hole in his life. How could he have let that happen?

His voice was scratchy to his own ears when he said, "The people of Golden are lucky to have you."

Her response surprised him.

"Are they?"

NICOLE KEPT HER gaze on the kids running around the park.

"It seems like forever since Briana, Addie and I played with so much reckless abandon. We were always up to something, either in the woods or riding our bikes to this park. We were very close at one time."

"Being in Golden, decorating for the holidays, must bring back memories."

Something shifted in her. "I don't understand why I'm so nostalgic. It's not like I've celebrated Christmas, or any holiday in Golden, for many years. Maybe it's seeing my sisters again." She blew out a gusty sigh. "There's something about that time of year. Hope. Expectations. I guess I always felt that way before…"

"Before?" he prodded.

Should she tell him? When revealing the story would open wounds that had never properly healed? Or maybe she simply was tired of the burden she'd been carrying for what seemed like forever. And why tell Ethan, of all people?

She observed his handsome face. The compassion she saw shimmering there made her heart pound. She was off-the-charts attracted to this man. From the moment she met him, she supposed. His touch made her skin tingle. Being in his company just felt right. She didn't experience that with many people. Hadn't she been seeking him out ever since they met? Maybe that's why she wanted him to understand why she shied away from her family and Golden.

"You know how it feels to be disappointed by someone important to you?"

He nodded, his expression grave. "I do. When my ex-wife decided she didn't want to be part of our family."

She covered her heating face with her hands. Of course, he knew. Why did she phrase the question like that? She spread her fingers and peeked between them. "I'm so sorry. That was insensitive of me."

To her relief, he didn't seem offended.

"I think you asked the question because it's important to talk about who disappointed you."

Good grief. Was she that transparent? Obviously, since she asked the question.

She lowered her hands. "How are you so insightful?"

He shrugged. "It's my makeup, I guess."

More than that, he was a caring soul.

She took a deep breath and plunged into her story. "When I was younger, my dad had an affair and my parents ended up getting a divorce."

"I'm sorry. I wasn't aware."

"You must be the only one in Golden not in the know."

"I haven't lived here long. Plus, I don't get involved with gossip."

Which was a breath of fresh air given what she'd experienced after her folks split. "I suppose you had your fair share after your divorce."

"I did, and it's not fun."

"No, it's not. That's part of the reason I left Golden."

"It must have been bad."

Her stomach twisted as she thought about the past.

"My dad had an affair after he moved his company down near Atlanta." She paused, organizing her thoughts. "I was little and don't remember it all, but he'd gotten a big contract and needed new warehouse space that wasn't available in Golden. At first, he'd commuted, but it took a lot of his time, so he got a place nearby to stay during the week. Eventually he became intimately involved with his administrative assistant." She barely kept from rolling her eyes. "Oldest story in the book.

"Anyway, my folks separated, but it was too much for them and they eventually divorced. My mother was heartbroken. And embarrassed. Then things got worse."

"How is that possible?"

She loved that he didn't want her story to get any uglier.

"After some time, my dad decided to move back to Golden, bringing his new wife, Paula, with him. That's when we discovered we had a half sister, Taylor."

"You didn't know?"

"No, my dad pretty much dove into his new life with Paula. There were a lot of years of radio silence and since they didn't live close, we hadn't heard the news. Or, he kept it a secret, which is more likely."

"How old were you by then?"

"Sixteen."

"Wow, talk about surprises." He seemed to dwell on that information for a moment. "And him coming back to the town where you lived stirred up family issues."

"Especially when our lives became tangled up with Taylor's."

His eyes went wide. "Okay, that does make things officially worse."

"You have no idea." She jumped up and began to pace in front of the bench. "They bought a house, and we had to go to school with her. Addie was only a grade ahead of Taylor, and they became rivals. Paula didn't help, parading around town like she owned the world, making her daughter sound like she was more important to our dad than we were. Let me tell you, kids are mean when they learn your family isn't like theirs."

"But you coped?"

"We had to." She stopped, stared down at her sandals. "Eventually, Dad and Paula ended up divorcing too. It was a mess."

"So, you left town to get away from the talk?"

"Not exactly."

His eyebrows lowered. "There's more?"

She plopped back down on the bench seat.

"Before the divorce, my dad had been excellent at keeping his secret, although Paula was pressuring him to divorce my mom. Probably because of Taylor.

"One weekend when I was ten, he took me to his office. I overheard my dad and Paula arguing. Something about telling my mom. It really bothered me, so when my dad brought me home, I asked my mom if something was wrong. When she asked why, I told her what I'd heard. She went pale and said she'd take care of it. Trusting everyone, I went to my room, thinking whatever was going on was a misunderstanding. When she started questioning my dad, the truth about his relationship with Paula finally came out."

Her chest constricted so tightly; she didn't think she could get the words out. When she spoke again, it was just above a whisper.

"A little while later, I went to the kitchen. My dad

turned on me, told me it was my fault my mom was upset. I had no idea what he was talking about. He was furious about getting caught, I now realize, only at the time I thought I had done something wrong. It wasn't until after he left that we learned the truth about his affair. I felt like I'd blown up my parents' marriage by telling my mom what I'd heard. My relationship with my dad was ruined after that."

Her chest rapidly rose and fell, and Ethan gently placed a hand on her shoulder. "Breathe."

Slowly her pulse and her breathing regulated. She didn't realize she'd shifted toward Ethan's warm body until she raised her head. He wrapped his arm around her shoulder tighter and suddenly he was close. Very close. So much so that she could see the gold flecks in his brown eyes.

"Take it easy," he told her in a calm, steady voice.

She nodded, sagging fully against him. He tucked her into his chest. His breath brushed her ear when he spoke.

"It wasn't your fault. You were a kid. Your dad should have known better than to blame you for his indiscretion."

She closed her eyes, soaking in his earthy scent and strength. "But it happened all the same."

Ethan's warm embrace lulled her into a sense of safety. After a time, she reluctantly moved away and faced him. "In my head I know that's logical, but my heart breaks every time I think about how it all but destroyed my mother. If I'd kept my mouth shut, maybe my family wouldn't have been torn apart."

He leveled her with a steady gaze. "The truth would have come out. It always does."

Still, the guilt simmered. "Doesn't change the fact that I don't like being around anything that reminds me of that time. Nostalgia or not."

"You still carry the scars."

She ran a shaky hand over her face. "I guess I do. It's why I don't like coming back to Golden."

He was silent for a beat, never taking his gaze from her. "Can I make a suggestion?"

"After I dumped this on you?" she said, then hiccupped.

A slight smile tipped his lips. "Hey, I'm a good listener."

"And I'm good at keeping things bottled up."

"Except for today." He brushed a strand of her hair from her cheek. "You know you don't have to go it alone."

Her heart raced as his finger traveled along her skin. Was he saying that he was happy to be a part of…this? It boggled her mind because he was right—she was always alone. Her choice, but now that she was sitting with him, it made her wonder what she was missing out on by imposing her own solitude.

What was he talking about? Oh, right, his suggestion. "Go ahead."

"Your mother seems very happy with her life. When I go into Linda's General Store, she's always cheerful. Greeting customers. Fussing over Holly. I'd wager to say she's moved on from the pain she experienced."

She let that sink in. "And you're saying I haven't?"

"Only you can answer that question."

And it was a question she'd been dodging for years. He was right, her mother had moved on. Taken a chance and made something of the store. Now, it was a tourist destination, as well as a place where locals shopped. She might not have found a significant other to love, but she had her family and the community, who had apparently rallied around her after years of making the Connellys feel like outsiders. If she could put it all in the past, shouldn't Nicole?

Ethan continued, "Your dad blaming you for what he did stinks, but now you're a successful woman with an interesting job. You may not think so, but from what I've observed, you're a strong person, otherwise you wouldn't have come back to Golden for this project. You could have made an excuse to stay away, but you came, anyway. Now, you get to spend time with your mom and sisters, rebuilding your family."

It was true. Deep down she wanted to catch up given all the years she'd been gone.

"Maybe it's time to let go," he concluded.

A gentle breeze tousled her hair. She brushed a strand from her eyes. Her heart clutched tight. "My dad tried to apologize. I shot him down at every turn, and now he's gone." Her eyes stung. "How do I live with that?"

Ethan squeezed her shoulder. "Forgive yourself. And him. That's the path to moving forward."

Her vision went blurry with tears. "Is that what you did?"

He didn't remove his hand. "Eventually."

Her shoulders lifted with her ragged breath. "I guess I have some decisions to make."

She swiped at her damp eyes as Holly and Gus came running toward them.

"Daddy, can we go home and have lunch? My belly is growling, and Gus needs some food too."

Nicole's eyes locked on Ethan's, and she noticed his forehead lined with worry. She nodded, telegraphing that she'd be okay. When Gus nudged her knee with his nose, she leaned over to pet him. "You're hungry, buddy?"

His tail swished back and forth in answer. She stood, steadfast Ethan beside her.

"Want to have lunch with us?" he asked as he took Holly's hand and they walked to the park exit.

"Maybe another day. I need some time alone."

After switching out the booster seat from her car so Ethan could drive his daughter home, she said, "Thanks."

"Anytime."

While it sounded like a nice promise, would she take him up on the offer for lunch on another day? After revealing so much of herself today?

Nicole watched them leave—Ethan's long, sure strides, Holly skipping beside him. He was turning into a good friend. But her reaction to him was more than just friendly. She valued his opinion and went out of her way to see him. She longed for just a simple touch. And how he held her gaze at times, it made her shiver in anticipation.

So, friend? Yes. But could there be more? She was only in Golden for a short time, then she had to decide about her move within the company. Perhaps the real question was, should she pursue anything deeper with Ethan? Because the clock was ticking down.

She groaned.

Gus nudged her hand. "Right. Home."

Gus scurried to the driver's side of the Jeep. After Nicole opened the door and lifted him inside, she slid into the seat and rested her forehead on the steering wheel. Gus whined.

She lifted her head and stared at him.

"Are you as confused as I am?"

Gus cocked his head.

"Probably not."

She stared the engine and drove, unsure what steps to take next.

CHAPTER NINE

THE NEXT FEW days went by in a blur. Nicole kept Mac on schedule, meeting him at the sites she'd already staged so he could capture the best shots with his high-end camera. She had to admit that while she hadn't asked for an assistant, Celeste worked wonders, running interference with the women who wanted to disrupt Mac's focus, and being the go-between with the shopkeepers. She'd even gotten an elf cap for Celeste. The older woman was thrilled to be part of Nicole's team, she said, and wore it every time they worked, informing all who would listen that she had an important job.

In the time she'd been here, the townsfolk thanked Nicole for what she was doing—her job—and others asked her if she could include their old farmhouse or rental vacation cabin in the woods in the photo spread. Seems word of the magazine article had people curious not only about the content, but also about Nicole herself. How had she been doing? Where was she living now? Even Mrs. Allen, who'd referred to her as a hoodlum after the driveway incident and claimed that Nicole was following the bad example of her father, stopped to tell Nicole how much she enjoyed seeing the early Christmas decorations. It boggled her mind. But also made her wonder if folks in Golden had mellowed over the years. She guessed the Connelly family drama wasn't a big deal any longer.

Early Wednesday morning, Nicole, Mac and Celeste stood outside Tessa's clothing store. The wagon was filled with baskets and flowers, ready to be scattered outside the store. The sidewalk was damp, giving the scene a fresh, springtime feeling. Mac started snapping away while Celeste handed Nicole the baskets.

Nicole hoped the current owner didn't come out to visit like the other shop owners had when she'd been working. What would Nicole say to her?

"Shall we start?" Celeste prompted when Nicole found herself staring at the store window that featured tastefully dressed mannequins. Her half sister was nothing if not trendy.

After placing the baskets in position, Nicole then arranged the extra flowers Celeste handed her. She was so caught up in the task, she didn't realize that Taylor stood just outside the shop door. When she straightened, Nicole met Taylor's gaze. Her sister appeared hesitant, which made Nicole want to hug her instead of ignoring her like she had when they were kids.

Where had that notion come from?

"I wasn't sure if you'd stop by," Taylor said, brushing her thick auburn hair behind one ear. She played with a silver hoop earring that reflected the morning sunlight. Even this early she was fashionably dressed in a soft pink designer dress.

"You're a part of Golden," Nicole quickly informed her. "I wouldn't leave you out."

A short-lived grin came and went from Taylor's lips. "Your decorating has created a buzz."

"Really?" Nicole hadn't heard that. "Good or bad?"

"Very good. It's all over the Golden merchants' social-media pages."

"Like I told Miss Celeste, I'm good at my job."

"And modest," Celeste replied wryly.

Taylor laughed. It stopped Nicole short. Had she ever heard her sister laugh? Since their father hadn't given them much to be happy about, she realized this was a first.

"Is there anything I can do?" Taylor asked, keeping a tentative distance between them.

"How about posting to your social media as I go along. It'll no doubt help with your customers and future tourists."

Taylor pulled her phone from her pocket. "I can do that."

Which she did, until Nicole stepped away to view her handiwork.

From inside the store, the phone rang. "I need to get that," Taylor said. Uncertainty shadowed her eyes. "I'll talk to you later."

Nicole replied cautiously. "Sure."

After Taylor disappeared, Celeste said, "She wants to be included, you know."

Yes, Nicole did know, but she wasn't here to fix what her father had broken. If someone thought she had a clue as to where to start, they'd be mistaken.

Just before noon, the team parted ways. Nicole went to her Jeep to restock the supplies needed for the next location. She dragged her wagon and stopped outside of city hall for a panoramic view of the historic building. The town maintenance workers had already hung a giant flag over the portico, the Stars and Stripes appearing so grand. She finished the location by draping red, white and blue bunting over the main door and twisting red, white and blue vinyl streamers to trim the windows. Finally, potted red geraniums lined the wide steps, giving the stately building a pop of color.

She took a step back, deciding that Mac should capture the scene both in the daylight and at night for maximum exposure.

The maintenance crew had also transported a picnic table from the park to place on the lawn outside the courthouse. Nicole decorated it with a red-and-white-checkered tablecloth, pitcher, cups and plates, so that it resembled a summer picnic, and added a pretty centerpiece of daisies in a glass vase. Another scene ready to be photographed.

As she packed up leftover supplies, Nicole smiled, thinking back on her busy morning so far. Celeste made working together fun. She enjoyed bouncing ideas back and forth, and having an extra hand. And in return, she didn't mind running errands with Celeste since her neighbor had lost her driver's license.

Visiting the grocery store and driving to the post office so Celeste could mail goodies to her great-grandchildren were adventures when she had someone to share it with.

As for Ethan, after her outburst at the park, she'd kept her distance. Mostly because she had a lot to think about. Ethan had been right to point out that Nicole had been a child when her father's affair had come out and she was not to blame for her mother learning the truth. Logically, it made sense, but the little girl inside still grappled with her part in the situation coming to light.

Also, staying away from Ethan meant she had more time to analyze her wild fascination with him. He'd listened when she poured out her heart, given her advice and never once passed judgment. How downright attractive was that? Extremely. And she wasn't clueless to see that the attraction went both ways. What did she do now?

For a woman who didn't get involved in serious relationships, she was confused about the direction of her heart.

She was at a crossroads; forgive the past and move on, or remain in this state of emotional limbo and estrangement from her family. Should she take a romantic chance with Ethan? But where would that leave them when she went back to Savannah and her promotion?

So far, she was straddling the fence on all counts, not making a firm decision one way or the other.

"What is wrong with you?" she muttered to herself as she placed plastic bins in her collapsible wagon. She'd never been this indecisive.

No time to probe her current state—she needed to get to Gold Dust Park to give Mac an update and get started on her afternoon project. She'd just begun to wheel the wagon away when her mother hurried up the sidewalk, a large bag from her general store in hand.

"Mom. What're you doing here?"

She held up the bag. "Delivering a take-out order to the department of records. It's Lizzy's birthday."

Nicole didn't know who Lizzy was, but said, "You have staff for this sort of thing."

"I do, but I love getting out of the store from time to time. I get to visit."

Nicole tilted her head. "Visit?"

Her mother wrinkled her nose.

"I know that look. What?"

"Things have changed in Golden since you left, Nicole. No one cares about what went on all those years ago."

Nicole's shoulders lifted in defense mode. "I didn't say they did."

"But you came back thinking everything would be the same, am I right?"

Yes. "No."

Her mother sent her a don't-sell-me-that frown.

"Okay, maybe."

"Honey, the Connellys are old news. Well, except for the awesome boost your project is giving the town."

"I will admit, I've had people stop to talk to me that weren't exactly friendly back in the day."

"Everything that happened with your father, relocating the company and people losing their jobs because they couldn't commute, is in the past. His former employees forgave him and when he opened another small business here, he rehired some of them."

Surprise almost made her speechless "Wait. Dad opened another business?"

"Yes he…" Her mother sighed. "When your father got that big contract, he had to move. There wasn't space in Golden and he needed to hire specialized employees. But five years ago, he sold Connelly Electronics and opened a different business. Tried to make up for the jobs that were lost when he moved the original company south."

"I didn't know this."

Red flooded her mom's cheeks. "You wouldn't talk to him."

Nicole slammed her hands on her hips. "And what he'd done, it didn't bother you? After all he'd put you through?"

"I forgave your father a long time ago. We were okay at the end."

Nicole's mouth gaped open. She recovered and asked, "Why didn't you tell me?"

"You never asked."

She tensed, the guilt of not speaking to her father before he died crashing down on her again.

"Nicole, your father and I sat down and hashed it

out. When he opened the warehouse away from here, he wanted to move. I was adamant we stay. I wasn't interested in the company. We started growing apart. Then that one contract grew into more. Your father was swamped, one thing led to another..."

"And he got involved with Paula."

Sadness clouded her mother's eyes. "For all that I was upset over what happened initially, I understood later. She was there for him when I wasn't. In a way, we both had a part in the breakup."

Nicole shook her head. "But all those nights you cried."

"I was shocked more than hurt. Then when the rumors about his daughter swirled around town, I was embarrassed. Over time, I pulled myself up and started searching for what I wanted and found the store. It afforded a way to be part of the community and I've made so many more friends. I'm content now."

Voice flat, Nicole said, "I'm happy for you, Mom."

"But you still don't understand."

"No, I don't."

Her mom put the bag on a step and pulled Nicole into a tight hug. Hot tears welled in Nicole's eyes.

"He knows what a mistake he made with you. And he didn't blame you for keeping him at arm's length. He figured that was his price to pay for being so ugly to you."

Nicole pulled back, wiping her eyes. "I was wrong too. I left town with a chip on my shoulder. Now, he's gone and neither of us can make amends."

"Would you, if you could?"

"I'd at least try," she answered truthfully.

Her mother placed her hands on Nicole's shoulders. "You can't hold on to the hurt forever. It's not healthy."

"I know." Her mother had forgiven her husband, and she was the one hurt even more by the man's actions. Shouldn't Nicole? "I can't ask Dad to forgive me for how I acted, but I can move forward if I choose to."

"Which is a decision you have to come to willingly," her mother said quietly. Then, with questions in her eyes, asked, "How did you come by this hardearned wisdom?"

"It wasn't mine."

"Who, then?"

Nicole glanced away. "Ethan."

"You talked about this with Ethan?"

"I had a meltdown, and he was sort of there to take the brunt."

"Huh."

"It's not a big deal."

"I beg to differ. You've always kept your emotions locked up. Even with your sisters."

Another pain lanced through her. "Did you know Dad left a letter each for Briana, Addie and Taylor with his lawyer?"

"Briana mentioned it."

Tears returned. "I didn't get one."

"Oh, honey." Her mother hugged her again.

Once Nicole felt steady on her feet, she stepped

back. "I guess I didn't deserve one because of the way I acted."

"I don't know what to tell you. I'm as much in the dark as you are."

Nicole's phone dinged. She pulled it from her shorts pocket and read the screen. A small smile curved her lips.

"Ethan?" her mother queried.

"What? No. It's Celeste." She returned the phone to her pocket. "I taught her how to use the functions on her phone. Now, she writes me long texts and uses emojis."

Her mother chuckled. "She's enjoying her time with you."

"She's lonely."

"I'm proud of you for including her."

"Like I had a choice." Nicole took hold of the wagon handle. "I need to get to the park. You should stop by later and see my newest brainstorm."

Her mom picked up her delivery bag. "I will and I might bring your sisters with me."

She didn't hesitate when she said, "Sounds good."

With a wave, Nicole took off, stopping at her Jeep to gather items to add to the wagon, then lugged it the couple of blocks to Main Street. Up the hill, she traveled to the park entrance. She rushed inside to find Celeste and Mac staring at a box, in the middle of a large cordoned-off area, the site for the next photo shoot, the permit in plain sight.

"I don't know what to do about this," Celeste said to Mac.

Mac glanced at his watch. "She should be here."

"I am here," Nicole announced, coming behind them. That's when she pointed to the box on the ground. "Great. My delivery arrived."

She dug in her work bag and removed a knife, then slit open the sides and opened the box.

Mac stared down at it. "It's a bubble tent?"

"Yep."

"I'm not gonna ask."

Celeste bent over to examine it more closely. "What has this got to do with anything?"

"You'll see. In the meantime, Mac, I need you to go to city hall and get some daylight shots. Tonight, you can go back when it's lit up. While you're gone, I'll stage this next scene for you."

"Are you sure you can handle this alone?"

Celeste cleared her throat.

"I mean, you go, ladies," he said, backpedaling.

"That's more like it," Celeste huffed.

He took off, leaving Nicole to find the best place to situate the tent. "Did Brady drop off the snow machine?"

Instead of having to rent a machine, she'd found out that the town had its own snowmaker they used during the holidays and had offered it to her.

"It's over there by the platform where they place the town Christmas tree every year."

Spying the black, portable machine about the size of her wagon, Nicole rubbed her hands together. "I'm going to drag the box over. Will you bring the wagon?"

"As long as you tell me what's going on."

Nicole winked at her assistant, her cap slipping to the side of her head. She straightened it and said, "Patience."

"Not my strong suit."

Nicole chuckled and hauled the bulky box the remaining feet to the platform. "This is a better location because we can hide the snowmaker behind the platform."

"For…"

"Just you watch and see."

Nicole took the contents from the box and spread out the pieces, then turned to the instructions. After reading through, she began the process of assembling the tent. A few folks stopped to watch and chatted with Celeste, but Nicole concentrated on her task. Before long she had the dome frame built, then came the see-through polyester to cover the structure.

"What do you think?" she asked Celeste when she'd finished.

"Still not getting it."

Nicole went to the wagon and removed a wooden rocking horse painted in Christmas colors, a few merrily wrapped boxes with big bows on top, a large teddy bear with a huge red ribbon and a baby doll in a stroller. She placed them all inside, positioning them around the surprisingly spacious tent that could fit four people with outdoor folding chairs, and returned to Celeste.

Her blank expression proved she still had no clue.

"Once I get the ol' snow machine going, it will be—"

"A snow globe!"

"That's right."

"What a darling idea."

Nicole had placed the opening flap of the tent in the back so once she got the machine up and running, she could shoot snow inside "the globe" for a shaken effect. Then she'd reposition the machine to shoot snow on the ground, creating a winter scene. An extension cord snaked around the platform to the permanent electrical outlet that city maintenance used, already plugged in.

Nicole studied the machine, then picked a setting and moved a dial to turn it on. It sputtered, then stopped. She tried again with the same results.

"Did Brady turn the machine on to try it when he dropped it off?"

"No, he just set it there and then he got a call and had to leave."

Nicole turned the machine off. "I wonder if it's broken?"

"I don't know, but here comes someone you can ask."

Nicole peeled her attention from the machine to see Ethan and Holly heading toward them. He held Holly's hand and she skipped beside him; daughter dressed in her elf costume, father in a pale blue button-down shirt, sleeves rolled up to his forearms, and navy slacks. Rising slowly, Nicole tried to regulate her heartbeat, then decided to face what she felt—she was happy to see Ethan, even if she shouldn't be. Truth? She couldn't resist the only man she'd ever poured her heart out to, the man who listened and saw her like no one else did.

He stopped beside her, his dark gaze holding hers. She swallowed hard, sure she was going to make a fool of herself if he moved any closer.

"What's going on?" he asked.

"We, that is, I'm trying to… Well, we…"

"The snow machine won't work," Celeste answered, translating for her.

She narrowed her eyes at Celeste.

"Let me take a look," he offered.

"You're mechanical?" Nicole asked.

"There's always something that needs tweaking at the clinic," he answered.

Nicole's heart squeezed. "My hero."

AFTER A HECTIC morning at the clinic, then sharing school lunch with Holly, the admiration in Nicole's eyes made his day.

"A healer and a mechanic. I'm impressed."

He grinned, then noticed the clear tent a few feet away.

"Snow globe?"

"How'd you guess?"

"You aren't the only one with mad skills."

Nicole's pleased laugh tugged at his heartstrings.

"So, you'll help a girl out?"

"My pleasure."

The flush on her cheeks made his blood rush.

"Daddy, can I go to the swings?"

"I'll take her," Celeste said. "You two fix the machine."

Ethan watched his little girl walk away with the older woman, the two of them wearing matching caps.

"You've started a trend."

Nicole's eyebrows rose. "Me?"

"Wearing elf caps in April." He took in Nicole's outfit, which would have been outlandish elsewhere; jaunty red cap, short-sleeved red T-shirt and denim shorts and sandals. "Haven't you noticed some of the merchants in town sporting red-and-green caps?"

"What can I say? I'm ushering in the holiday spirit."

"Well, thanks to that, Holly refuses to wear anything but the elf costume. Today she pitched a fit until I agreed to let her wear it for show-and-tell."

Nicole's lips quivered. "Sorry?"

He crossed his arms over his chest. "Really?"

"No." Nicole laughed. "Holly is a natural."

"And hopefully this is a phase."

"After all the decorating hoopla is over and I leave town, she'll get back to normal."

Which was going to be a problem. Holly had fallen in love with Gus. She talked nonstop about Nicole. He didn't want his daughter, let alone himself, to get any more attached to the woman who was in town temporarily. Thankfully, Nicole was in the dark about the direction of his thoughts.

"Let's get started." She led him to the snow machine. "It won't start."

"Is it plugged in?"

"Yes. Behind the platform."

Ethan got down on one knee and examined the machine. He checked the dials and the cord. All seemed to be connected properly. He tilted the maker on its side, noticing an opening for the snow liquid.

"I think I see the problem."

Nicole kneeled beside him. Her citrusy perfume reached his nose, making him extremely aware of the woman who already had dibs on his waking thoughts.

"Do you have the liquid?"

"Let me check." She scanned the area, then her gaze fell on the bag Brady had left with the machine. She reached over, tugged it to them and removed a jug. "This should help."

He poured the liquid inside and fired it up. Fake snow began shooting out.

Nicole laughed. "You did it."

"I'm pretty handy around the house." He winked at her. "Which makes me a good catch."

Her sapphire-blue eyes shimmered. "I had no doubt."

The machine whirred, releasing flakes all around them. They were crouched beside the platform, hidden from the park, away from prying eyes. Snow swirled in the bright sunshine and eighty-degree temperature. It created a magical wonderland only he and Nicole were part of, unique and unexpected, much like his reaction to Nicole since her arrival in Golden. Was there going to be trouble down the road? Oh, yeah, but he was going for it, anyway.

The charged air had nothing to do with snowflakes falling around them, or children laughing, or even the idea of an early winter. No, it had everything to do with the beautiful woman whose mouth was inches from his.

And despite his fears of her eventually leaving, he leaned in to capture her waiting lips.

He brushed over the softness, once, twice, until she scooted closer. He reached over to cup the back of her head with his hand, his fingers tangling in her lush hair. Her hands landed on his shoulders, squeezing as she held on. The machine grumbled, but he could hear her surprise as the kiss deepened. Angling his mouth, he soundly kissed her like he'd never kissed before, his heart aching with a tenderness for this special woman.

Not sure how much time had gone by, he suddenly heard Holly calling him. He shook his head, breaking the trance just as Nicole seemed to realize where they were. Their gazes met and held.

Holly raced around the corner. "Snow!"

Ethan straightened, holding his hand out to Nicole. The jolt that occurred whenever they touched returned. As soon as she was upright, she removed her hand from his.

"Daddy, you made it work."

He cleared his throat. "I did."

Holly rushed to Nicole. "What's next?"

"We make a human snow globe."

Nicole grabbed the hose and connected it to another outlet on the back of the machine. She aimed it around the tent, covering the ground, then toward the open flap of the tent, and snow began to circulate inside.

Holly squealed with delight while Gus jumped and barked in excitement as both tried to catch the flakes.

Ethan watched the scene with a joy he hadn't felt since the divorce. His heart shifted. Life went on. People changed. His gaze fell on Nicole, her eyes as wide as a child's on Christmas morning. She'd walked into his life and turned it upside down.

Her attention turned to something behind Ethan. He glanced over his shoulder to see Mac the photographer barreling down on them.

"You started without me?" the photographer said, reprimanding her.

"Just getting the equipment set up," Nicole assured him.

He set his hands on his hips. "A snow globe?"

Nicole bit her bottom lip. "Yep."

"Brilliant. We can do a Christmas shot, then make it a winter wonderland scene." Mac's lips curved into a smile and, noticing Ethan, he walked over. "Any chance you'd allow me to photograph your daughter inside the snow globe? Or she and Gus playing outdoors?" Nicole appeared at his side. "You don't have to agree if you aren't comfortable. There are other kids in the park we can recruit for the shoot."

"Hey, man," Mac said. "Don't mean to cause trouble, but I gotta say, they're both naturals."

Ethan had to admit he was right. "Let me ask Holly."

He caught up with his daughter and lowered himself to her height. "How would you like to be in some pictures with Gus?"

Holly's mouth gaped open. "Really?"

"Only if you want."

"I do." She went on tiptoes to kiss his cheek. "See, I told you I had to wear my elf uform today."

He barked out a rough laugh, then watched his daughter rush to Nicole, who started to explain what she needed.

"Go into the tent and stop at each toy, like you can't believe Santa left them for you."

"I can do that."

Before long, Holly was in the tent, not even having to playact her excitement. Mac moved around, capturing the unfolding scene from different angles. Soon, Holly was back outside, playing in the falling snow with Gus. A crowd had gathered to watch the photo shoot in progress.

"She's a natural," Nicole said, echoing Mac's earlier words.

Ethan frowned. "That's what I'm afraid of."

Nicole sent him a curious look, but just then, the snowfall began to wane. She turned off the machine and asked, "Mac, did you get everything?"

He gave her a thumbs-up. "That and more."

"Great." Nicole walked over to Holly and gave her a hug. "You did a good job."

"Will Santa be happy with me?"

"I can't speak for him, but Mac and I are happy, so that counts."

Holly beamed.

"And you," Nicole said as Gus nudged his way into the hug. She rubbed his nose. "You did good too." Gus wagged his tail.

While Mac scanned the photos on the LCD panel of his camera, Holly and Gus ran around. Nicole made her way back to Ethan's side.

"You okay, Dad?"

"Yeah. Holly's happy, so that's all that matters."

"You don't seem sure."

He waved his hand. Now was not the time to launch into an account of what caused the breakdown with his ex-wife and why he was so protective of Holly.

"How about dinner and an explanation?"

"Has anyone ever told you that you're very persistent?"

She sent him a feisty grin. "Many times. That's what makes me good at my job."

He hesitated. "It's not something I talk about."

She pointed to herself. "I hear that. Although, I did kind of spill all my drama on you."

"That you did."

He wanted to reach out and brush his thumb over her soft skin, but there were too many people around and he wasn't sure where this attraction was going to land.

"If you want to—" Her cell phone rang, interrupting the moment. She pulled the device from her pocket. "I need to take this."

He nodded as she moved a few feet away. "The project is going great…" He couldn't hear the rest of the conversation, but her forehead wrinkled. After a few moments, she moved back toward Ethan. "I'm working on it," she said and hung up.

"Problem?"

"Corporate checking on my progress. And the promotion I told you about."

Like he'd forgotten, as much as he wanted to. Her decision would take her from Golden and return her to her previous world. And he'd be here in Golden, planting roots, getting involved with the community and making a solid home for his daughter.

He swallowed hard. "Thanks for this afternoon, but I need to get Holly home. I can tell she's staring to lose steam."

"Okay. Again, thanks for everything."

"I'm glad I could help."

She paused. "Do you want to get dinner later?"

"Probably not. Holly had a long day at school on top of all this. I want to get her settled down."

Disappointment glimmered in Nicole's eyes, making him feel like a heel. "Of course. Holly comes first."

"She does," he said, his tone firm. If he wasn't

careful, all his strategically crafted plans would go up in smoke. "Another time."

Nicole nodded, but some of her eagerness dimmed.

With a nod, he went to collect Holly. His diagnosis was correct—she was so tired she didn't even make a fuss when he told her they were going home.

"Can we have grilled cheese for dinner?"

"Sure thing."

"Can Nicole and Gus come over?"

"Not tonight, princess. How about we eat and watch a movie."

"Can I pick?"

"You can."

When she lagged, he swooped her into his arms to carry her the rest of the way to the car. Holly rested her head on his shoulder.

"I'm glad Nicole and Gus live next door. They're my friends."

"They are, but don't forget, they'll be leaving when Nicole's job is finished."

She moved her head to gaze into his eyes. "Maybe they could stay. If you and Nicole became better friends."

Was that a possibility? He wanted it to be, but Nicole had made no secret of the fact that she didn't want to remain in Golden. And he wouldn't uproot Holly.

So where did that leave them?

CHAPTER TEN

"NICOLE, DID YOU hear me?"

Nicole blinked before focusing on Addie. "Sorry. My mind was elsewhere."

"The decorations?" Briana asked, before sipping on what appeared to be a tropical drink if the tiny, pink umbrella was any indication.

"Yes. Decorations," she hedged, raising her voice above the conversation swirling around them.

A touch of heat lingered in the warm spring night. The scent of blooming flowers perfumed the atmosphere, along with savory scents coming from the kitchen.

Nicole and her sisters had met up earlier with Royce Stevens to do a walk-through of the Sinclair building. Afterward, they'd mutually decided to head to The Perch, a local restaurant and hangout located on the river. The Friday-night crowd was lively, a guitarist was scheduled to play soon and they each had a drink in front of them, as if it might make the uncomfortable gathering less awkward.

Nicole hadn't been thinking about decorations— more like she'd been wondering why she hadn't heard from Ethan in the past few days. There'd been something up with him when he and Holly left the park after the snow-globe photo shoot, but she couldn't put her finger on what it was. He'd so easily refused her offer for dinner, but why? They'd been having a good time. And that kiss… Could it have been the kiss? Had the sparks not tilted his world like they had hers?

She'd been on the lookout for him, which was lame. She'd never been this seriously interested in a guy and the one time she was, she couldn't read him.

"What do you have left to do?" Taylor asked in her reserved tone, so different from when they were younger. She recalled her mother talking about Taylor going through a bad divorce, but Nicole hadn't asked for the details. Noticing the shadows in Taylor's eyes, remorse crept over Nicole for not showing interest.

The sisters had invited their mother to the restaurant, but she'd bailed, using babysitting as her excuse. Probably by design, but Nicole had willingly gone along, dressing in a cute green-and-white-checked sundress and wedge sandals. Her sisters had all elected to wear dressy outfits too, as if they were out to impress each other. Perhaps at this point in their relationship that's exactly what they were doing.

"Let's see. I think some shots at Crestview Farm. Then Mac and I will go over the proofs and decide if there are retakes needed."

She hadn't told anyone that the timeline for the project had been cut back a week because of Mac's change of schedule. Honestly, she didn't want to dwell on it.

"Speaking of Mac…" Briana wiggled her eyebrows.

"We just work together. Nothing more."

"He is dreamy," Taylor added.

"You and every other woman in Golden seems to think so. Truth be told, he doesn't really date much."

Briana set her drink glass on the table. "That's a shame."

"We're here to make a decision," Nicole reminded her sister. "Not go all gaga over Mac."

Addie grinned. "Every time we go by the trees on Main Street, Jacob tells me he's started his Christmas list for this year."

"You've really taken a liking to that elf cap," Briana observed, barely hiding her smile.

Nicole took a sip from her fruity drink then said, "Seems I can't go anywhere without someone commenting on it."

"You and Miss Celeste." Addie gazed over the open deck that overlooked the river, where they were seated. "Is she going to pop up here?"

Nicole shushed her. "If you say her name, she might."

"It's nice that you're spending time with her," Briana commented.

Her defenses reared. "Why wouldn't I?"

Briana raised a hand, palm out. "Hey, I didn't mean

anything by that. I go on lots of senior checks for the job. Usually, they just want someone to talk to."

Nicole gazed at her older sister. She bit her lip. Were they going to walk on eggshells all night?

Nicole picked up her glass, took another sip, then decided to go for broke. "Okay, enough with the soft touch."

Briana placed a hand over her heart. "Us?"

Nicole chuckled. "What are we going to do with the building?" She turned to Addie. "Do you still want to open a fitness center?"

Addie grabbed the end of her blond braid and worried it between her fingers. "I really do. And with the money Dad left, we can bring the neglected building back to life."

Taylor stared into her drink, then said, "I think I should bow out."

Nicole exchanged glances with Briana and Addie, both of her sisters' surprised expression matching hers.

When no one spoke, Nicole decided to take the lead. "You're dad's daughter too, Taylor. This is what he left us, and we should respect that."

Briana raised an eyebrow.

"So, yeah, I'm dealing with stuff," Nicole said. "Bottom line? Dad's actions affected us all. Not one of us has a monopoly on the pain he caused."

Addie reached over and patted Nicole's arm. "Good for you."

While resolving her issues was still a work in

progress, Nicole wasn't up to going into details right now. Perhaps another time.

"Besides," Nicole said, "Mom has pulled you into the family fold."

Tears shimmered in Taylor's hazel eyes, so much like their father's. "And you'll never know how much I appreciate it."

"Mom wants us to bury old grudges," Nicole continued. "What do you say we give it a try?"

"I agree," Briana said. "Mom's right. We all need to forgive and move on."

Addie stared out over the crowd, not adding her input. Nicole remembered that since she and Taylor were close in age, there'd been problems in high school. Maybe Addie wasn't ready to work on her own issues?

"For Mom," Addie said softly.

Nicole nodded decisively. "Then I vote we keep the building. Allow Addie to open her fitness center if she decides it's feasible." She met her sisters' gaze. "Briana? Taylor?"

"I'm in," Briana agreed.

"Me too," Taylor answered.

Nicole held up her glass. "Then let's toast to closing the deal."

The four clinked glasses before setting them on the table again.

A small smile tipped Briana's lips. "Remember the time Mom made us make that silly pledge?"

Addie's forehead wrinkled. "The one where we

all had to pile our hands on top of each other and swear we'd always have each other's backs?"

"That's the one."

Memories of that afternoon engulfed Nicole. "We were arguing over something—"

"Who got to ride shotgun," Briana interjected.

Nicole laughed. "She made us all get in the back seat while she lectured us on what it meant to be a family."

Addie groaned. "And then she stopped at the park and made us recite the pledge in the parking lot."

"But it worked." Nicole nodded. "We ended up getting along for the rest of the day."

"She's a smart lady, our mom." Briana lifted her hand to hover flat over the table. "What do you say? For old time's sake."

Addie giggled but placed her hand over Briana's.

Nicole followed suit, turning to Taylor. "You're our sister, so you have to recite the pledge, or it won't take."

When had she turned into the mature sister, rooting for them as a team?

With a bit of hesitancy, Taylor laid her hand over Nicole's.

"Do you recall what she made us say?" Addie asked as their hands hovered over the table.

"Something about a small-town sisterhood," Briana answered.

"Then here's to being sisters," Nicole said.

They pumped up and down three times before laughing and pulling their hands back.

"Thank you for including me," Taylor said.

"You're welcome," the other three sisters said in unison.

Nicole gazed at Briana and Addie. "We haven't done that in a long time."

Briana sent her a frown. "If you hang around, we could do it more often."

Instead of getting drawn into that conversation, mainly because she didn't know what to say, Nicole jumped up and grabbed her cross-body bag. "On that note, I'm going to the ladies' room."

Waving to a few people, she navigated the indoor dining area toward the restroom. Once inside the small space, she rested her palms on the counter and stared at her reflection in the mirror. Did her sisters want her to stay? An impossible idea, wasn't it? Reconnecting seemed a lot less doable if she had distance between them. It wasn't exactly what their mom requested, since she wanted all her girls in Golden, but Nicole wasn't sure she could make her mother's dreams come true.

Even if she wanted to stay, she had to give an answer about the promotion at work. That would play in to whatever decision she ultimately made about Golden. When she figured out what she wanted, which currently was a big, fat "no clue," she might have some peace.

She blinked. Blue eyes gazed back at her. "You really are clueless."

About the promotion and Ethan.

Her mind had been laser-focused on both, but if

she was examining the level of importance more closely, thoughts of Ethan outdid those of the promotion. The life goals she'd imagined when she'd landed in Golden had been quickly replaced with deep brown eyes and a ready smile. He was a man who would be steady through any storm.

She straightened as the door opened. In walked Sharon, the former head cheerleader from high school. She stopped short when she saw Nicole. Bracing herself for snark, Nicole hid an involuntary flinch.

"Nicole. I'm glad I bumped into you." The tall, leggy blonde moved into the small space. "I was going to stop by your table before we left."

"That's, um, nice."

Sharon placed her small bag on the counter. "A few years ago, when you worked at Lila's Parties, you planned a birthday party for my nephew. My sister-in-law raved over it."

"Thanks."

Sharon warmed to the conversation. "Anyway, my son turns five soon and I was wondering if I could pick your brain for some good party ideas. I don't have a creative bone in my body." She held up her hand as if to stall Nicole's response. "I know you aren't in town for very long, but I would really love to hear what you think." A rueful smile curved her lips. "I looked up your company's website. You handle really huge events."

"We do." When was the last time Nicole had

thrown a child's birthday party? When she worked for Lila, which felt like ages ago.

"I'd pay you, of course," Sharon added when Nicole was silent for so long.

"That's not necessary. We can meet for coffee before I leave if you'd like."

As if she was holding her breath, Sharon exhaled and let out a little squeal. "You don't know how much this means to me." She raised her arm as if victorious. "Todd says I work too much."

"Todd?"

"My husband."

She hadn't married the quarterback she'd dated all through high school?

"I can see you're wondering. No, Brad and I broke up the summer after we graduated from Golden High. I met Todd in college. He's an accountant and I work for the Mastersons in their finance department. So…" She shrugged. "Good with money but not parties."

"Then I'd be happy to come up with some themes."

"Thank you." Nicole pulled out her phone and they exchanged numbers.

Sharon placed her phone back in her bag. "I don't mean to keep you. Since you're only in town for a short while, you probably want to be with your sisters."

"I'll talk to you soon."

Nicole left the restroom, mulling over the conversation as she weaved through the tables to her own. "That was weird," she said as she slid into her seat.

"What's weird?" Briana asked.

"I ran in to Sharon…" She frowned. "I didn't ask what her last name is now."

"Briscoe," Taylor said.

"Anyway, she wants to brainstorm ideas for her son's birthday party."

"Why is that weird?" Addie stared at her. "You're good at what you do."

"I don't know." Nicole threw up her hands. "Since I've been in town, I've spoken to people I haven't seen in years."

"I'm going to regret asking," Briana said, deadpan, "but why is that a big deal?"

"Because a lot of those people are part of the reason I left."

"Things have changed," Addie said.

"I guess…" Nicole hedged. The bigger question was, had she?

"If you moved back to Golden you could discover there's more to the folks here than you remember," Briana said.

"I don't know."

"What about the promotion?" Taylor asked.

She'd mentioned the promotion during the walk-through as an excuse to not claim her part of the building.

"I need to give my boss an answer."

"Are you going to take it?" Addie asked.

Good question. Nicole still hadn't decided.

With a huff, she moved her gaze around the patio, anything to take her mind off decisions, leaving town and one handsome veterinarian. Before she entered back into the conversation, her eyes tangled with a pair of brown eyes she couldn't seem to get out of her mind.

And in those eyes, she saw the same question posed by her sisters.

Are you staying?

ETHAN HADN'T MEANT to eavesdrop. The Perch was packed and he and his attorney, Dean, had ended up on the deck, waiting in line to order drinks. After receiving the final paperwork for the clinic, they'd decided a celebration was in order. The place was hopping, and they'd moved outdoors for fresh air and a view of the river rushing by. He hadn't meant to stop by Nicole's table or hear the conversation.

Addie noticed them and called out, "Dean. Just the man we want to see."

As the sisters turned in unison, Nicole's gaze tangled with his. She might have thought she hid her emotion, but Ethan could see the confusion and embarrassment simmering there. He hadn't spoken to her since the park, mostly because he didn't know what to say. After that kiss, the one that still made him dizzy thinking about it, she probably expected more. And he'd let her down.

Dean started a conversation with the sisters, but Ethan only had eyes for Nicole. She rose, gravitating toward him.

"Hi," he greeted. "You and your sisters having a nice night out?"

"We did a walk-through of the Sinclair building then ended up here. I think everyone is ready to head home." She tilted her head. "You?"

"I got the final paperwork from Dr. Andrews."

A genuine smile touched her lips. "Then you're celebrating."

"We are."

Dean's phone rang. He held up a finger and stepped away.

Addie stood. "I need to get to Mom's and pick up Jacob."

"I need to check on the store," Taylor said as she rose, pulling the strap of her purse over her shoulder.

"I need to get Cami and...leave you guys alone." Briana winked at Nicole, who blushed.

The women took off, leaving him behind with his beautiful neighbor.

Ethan stuffed his hands in his pockets. "Something I said?"

Nicole puffed out a laugh.

Dean hurried over. "Sorry, man. I need to run."

"We just got here."

Dean noticed Nicole. "Why don't you stay and have a drink with Ethan. You'd be doing me a solid."

One of her eyebrows arched.

"Later," Dean said, slapping Ethan on the shoulder as he rushed off.

Their eyes met again until a stranger closed in on them. "Is this table empty now?"

"Sure," Nicole said, removing her bag from the tabletop.

They moved out of the way as a new group of revelers commandeered the table.

"Listen, if you need to get home, I'll understand," Ethan said.

Nicole shrugged. "We're both out for the night. Besides, you planned on celebrating. Can't do that alone."

Gratitude washed over him. "How about we find a quiet place?"

When she nodded, he led her back inside. They stopped to get drinks, then wandered to the dimly lit front terrace, which was significantly quieter than on the deck. The trees barely buffered the rush of the flowing river. The air carried the sweet fragrance of spring.

Ethan pulled out a chair for Nicole at a small table. After she sat, he took his place across from her. As she sipped her drink, he tried to come up with a conversation starter.

"I'm sorry I didn't get back to you about dinner," he said. "Things got away from me."

"Hey, you're a busy single dad."

"True, but I should have called."

"I've been busy too."

This was not going smoothly.

"I let you down. Not my intention."

"Don't worry about it, Ethan. Instead, tell me about the clinic."

He turned his glass around in circles on the tabletop. "I was getting worried that the sale might fall through, but Dean's idea of asking Dr. Andrews if he wanted to work part-time as an employee turned the corner. He wouldn't have the long hours or responsibilities that come with owning the clinic, and both he and his wife liked the suggestion when we ran it past them. We just came from signing the papers." He held up his glass. "I'm officially owner of Golden's vet clinic."

"Congrats," Nicole said as she tapped her glass against his.

"Thanks." He blew out the stress that had lived in him for weeks now. "When Dr. Andrews started having second thoughts, I was afraid I might have moved too soon. Holly is making friends and getting used to our lives here. I don't want to mess that up."

"How could you? You're a good dad, Ethan."

He was trying. "The signed paperwork goes a long way to relieving my worries."

She took a sip from her glass. "Do you mind if I ask what happened? Why your ex-wife doesn't want a life with her daughter?"

Ethan ran a hand over his beard. Not a topic he enjoyed discussing, but after Nicole had let her guard down about her father, filling her in was only fair.

"We met in college. I was finishing vet school. April was completing a degree in communications. On a spur we decided to get married."

"Sounds romantic."

"At first. Early in her career, April had been happy to work in the PR department at a small television station in the town where we were living. About six months in, she was asked to substitute for the on-air talent who'd called in sick for the early morning newscast. April loved it. She talked about the thrill of being in front of the camera for days. When another station showed interest and offered her a correspondent spot, we talked it over and decided to move. By that time, I was out of school and was able to find a position at a pet hospital."

"This was before Holly was born."

"It was. Over time and a few more moves to different cities." His shoulders rose on an inward breath. "April had stayed with me through vet school, so I felt like I should support her career. I didn't relish all the traveling, getting settled just to pick up to move elsewhere, but I wanted my wife to be happy. We ended up in Cleveland just after Holly was born. Because it was a larger market, April had more airtime—which it turned out she craved—but she wasn't moving up the ladder fast enough. Long hours at the studio caused problems in our marriage."

Ethan remembered those days. How frantic April had become to be noticed for a prime-time evening-news spot. "I didn't begrudge April her dreams—it was one of the things that had appealed to me when we met, until it took a toll on our relationship. As her career moved forward, she took on an air of desperation, wanting to be in front of the camera. She spent less time with Holly, lost interest in the marriage. When Holly started asking if Mommy loved her, that's when I knew we had to find a better work balance." He shook his head, sadness touching him again. "April refused to give up her ambition. Then a job opened in New York City, and she took it. Without telling me. No discussion about how it would affect our family. I didn't even know she'd applied."

Sympathy shone in Nicole's eyes. "I'm sorry."

"It was the last straw and the beginning of divorce proceedings. I have to admit, I felt like a failure."

"Why? It seems your wife changed the rules along the way."

He stared into his drink for a long moment. "My parents have this great marriage. I aspired to have the same." He met Nicole's gaze. "When it didn't work out, I felt like I'd let them down. Let Holly down by not fighting harder for her mother."

"It doesn't sound like you would have won that battle."

"No. April was dead set on moving on." Those final memories made his chest tighten, but he tamped down the mounting tension. In a quiet tone, he said, "I still want what my parents have."

He could read the conflict in Nicole's eyes but didn't push the issue. She'd been up front with him about her future work commitment. If she stayed, he wanted it to be on her terms, hoped it would be because she wanted to be with him, not because she was pressured.

"Anyway, I jumped at the idea of owning my own practice. Holly and I visited, loved the area and I could see my small family living in Golden. I even put an offer on a house that was for sale, the two-story dream home where we'd make a new life. I went through all the steps to buy the clinic and when

I thought the sale was a go, Holly and I had moved to Golden permanently. Until this latest hiccup put my plans in limbo. Thankfully, it all worked out."

Nicole toyed with her drink glass. "Living in one place is really important to you."

"It is. Holly is secure. And while she only talks to her mother infrequently, she knows I'll always put her first."

"Then you shouldn't second-guess your future, Ethan." A couple exited the building, music and loud conversation escaping through the open door with them. Nicole scooted her chair closer to his, intertwining her fingers with his. "You're a good dad. Holly adores you."

He picked up their joined hands, brushing a kiss over her soft skin. "Thank you."

While he appreciated the compliment, he really wanted to know if Nicole would ever consider being part of his future. Did he want to put himself in that scenario again? To love and lose? It wasn't fair to ask, not when she had a job to finish and a decision to make about the promotion. She might have spilled her heart to him about her father, but was that enough to make her comfortable about moving back to Golden? He wasn't sure if she'd gotten to that place yet. Which meant he'd have to risk his heart if he pursued this path.

Nicole leaned closer, her free hand cupping the side of his face. Her fingers brushed his beard, bringing a smile to her lips.

Her breath fanned his face when she asked, "How is it we end up in these serious conversations?"

"We get each other?" he ventured.

"I think that might be true."

She shifted a fraction until her lips met his. The kiss moved slowly, leisurely. If he'd been standing, the kiss, along with being this close to Nicole, would have knocked him off his feet. He applied pressure, thankful she accepted and matched his passion in return. The buzz of electricity flared between them. Would he ever get enough of her?

She reluctantly broke the kiss, her fingers trailing over his beard. "I didn't think anything could match that kiss in the park, but right now I'd have to question that claim."

"Should we try again?"

She giggled. "In front of the entire town?"

"It's not the entire town, but I get it. You don't want people to speculate when we aren't even sure where this is going."

Her smile faded. "Something like that."

But that didn't mean he was ready to give up.

"How about this." He sat back. "Holly and I are going boating on Golden Lake tomorrow. Why don't you join us. That is, if you don't have a photo shoot lined up."

"Mac had to go down to Atlanta, so I'm free."

"I'll take care of everything." His serious gaze locked with hers. "We can enjoy a day without either of our pasts intruding on us."

She bit her lower lip.

"You'll join us?"

She hesitated.

"No pressure."

Color crept into her cheeks. "No pressure."

"Then we'll pick you up at ten."

CHAPTER ELEVEN

NICOLE AWOKE TO a rough, wet tongue scraping across her cheek. She batted at the air and rolled over. The culprit whined. With a put-upon sigh, she grabbed her phone from the nightstand, groaning when she read eight-thirty. Until she remembered that it was lake day with Ethan and Holly. She shot up and scampered out of bed.

"You're the best alarm," she told Gus as she sprinted to the bathroom.

After a quick shower and dressing in lake clothes, a T-shirt and denim shorts over her bathing suit, she packed a bag with sunscreen, a towel and other water-related essentials, and hurried into the kitchen. She poured Gus a bowl of food, which he scarfed down in record time, allowing her a quick cup of coffee and the chance to gather the food she'd prepared to bring along on today's adventure.

Ethan had told her he'd take care of lunch, but she'd cut up vegetables and bought dip just in case. In her excitement she'd also baked a batch of chocolate-chip cookies.

"See, Mom," she muttered as she placed the cookies in a water-tight container. "I can do a few things in the kitchen."

She packed the other food and filled a bag for Gus, then set her hands on her hips.

"Did I forget anything?"

Gus sat at her feet and gazed up at her, head cocked. With a chuckle, she ruffled his fur. "I think we're good to go."

Gus woofed and Nicole collected her things. Soon they walked outside to a perfect spring morning, which improved even more when she spied the handsome man leaning against the railing of his front porch, one foot crossed over the other, as if waiting for her. She nearly tripped over her feet when Ethan sent her a wolfish smile. He might be a serious-minded professional most of the time, but if this was what he looked like when he went rogue, she was a goner. The nerves she'd been battling ever since he asked her to accompany him to the lake kicked in big-time.

As always when this heartfelt reaction to Ethan took control, Nicole had to admit that no other man had ever ensnared her heart this way. Sure, she'd never been against meeting guys, going on a few dates maybe, but it never stuck. She'd never longed for forever. With Ethan, however, she craved the myriad conflicting emotions he unearthed in her. Joy. Nervousness. Underlying excitement. Mostly, she desired the crackle of electricity that arced between them when they touched. And she most definitely wanted another kiss. Many, if she was honest.

If she stayed in Golden, she could have all this.

"Good morning," Ethan greeted huskily, sending a cascade of shivers over her skin. "You're early."

"I was ready to go," she told him, her voice unsteady.

He was dressed for a day on the lake, wearing a tan T-shirt that hugged his impressive chest, cargo shorts and boat shoes. He bent down to pet Gus, who had scurried to his side. Then he glanced over at her, and the smile widened. "Think you brought enough necessities for the day?"

She lifted the bags hanging from each arm. "I tried."

Climbing the steps, she noticed how her heart leapt when he tugged her flush against him. Leaning down, he brushed a kiss over her lips. It was all Nicole could do to contain the dreamy sigh longing to escape.

He pulled back and their gazes met. "Sleep well last night?"

Her toes curled in her shoes. "I did. You?"

"When I was enjoying visions of you."

She nearly melted into a puddle. "Are you always this charming first thing in the morning?"

"When I want to be." He dropped his head, lips lingering over hers. "With you it comes easy."

She reached up to caress his cheek, her fingers brushing over his soft beard. One bag hanging from her arm bumped him in the leg. "Sorry."

"Not a problem." Ethan took advantage of the

fact that she hadn't dropped her bags and cupped her face. Kissed her again.

Nicole savored the kiss, drew in his warmth. When he pulled back, his expression mysterious and trained only on her, she realized that Ethan held a special place in her locked heart that she hadn't allowed another man to breach. What was she going to do about it?

That was a question for another day because Holly picked that precise moment to rush outside. Nicole was grateful to see she was dressed in pink patterned shorts and a matching top, not her elf uform.

"You're here!" She danced over to Gus, who licked her face, eliciting a laugh from the little girl. Ethan wound his arm around Nicole's waist and tugged her close. The scene resembled a family photo, perfect and happy and not anything Nicole had bargained for when she'd been assigned the project to decorate Golden.

"Should we get going?" Ethan asked, his low tone close to her ear. She could feel his breath on her skin and this time she didn't hide her shivery reaction.

"Do we have to?"

He chuckled and slowly slid his hand from her, leaving her wanting more.

"Nicole, Daddy made a picnic and we're going to go in a boat."

Holly's excitement was contagious.

"I know. Your father told me."

"He's the best."

Nicole met Ethan's gaze. She didn't disagree.

They trooped into the house, gathered an insulated bag and a tote with towels, and headed out to the car. Before long, they were driving toward Golden Lake, Holly giving them a detailed rundown of the day.

Ethan shot Nicole a quick grin. "She's been talking about this nonstop."

"Why wouldn't she? It's going to be an epic day."

"Epic?"

"Why not? Go big or go home."

He chuckled. "I like your attitude."

If his kisses were any indication, he liked Nicole too.

Twenty minutes later they pulled up to the marina and parked. Ethan popped the trunk, and they removed the bags, carrying them to the office. He donned a pair of sleek sunglasses and walked ahead to meet a grizzly bear of a man stepping outside.

"Ready, Doc?"

"More than, Homer."

He tossed Ethan a set of keys. "Got the boat tied up fer ya."

"Thanks."

With Holly skipping ahead and Gus right beside her, their footsteps echoed on the wooden dock.

"You have a boat?" Nicole asked.

"No. A friend offered to let me use it whenever I want."

She slowed. "But you know how to drive it, right?"

He placed a warm hand on her shoulder. "I grew

up not far from a lake. My dad and I went fishing a lot when I was a kid."

She blew out a relieved breath. "Good, because I don't know the first thing about boats."

"That's why I'm in charge today. Your only job is to relax."

She frowned. "I don't think I know how to do that."

"It's not a request. You do a lot for others—today I'm taking care of you."

Normally, that statement would rub her the wrong way, but instead, she accepted the fact that she didn't have to worry about the outing. She didn't have to be in charge. Or alone. It was a new, and strange, experience.

The motorboat, about twenty-four feet long, all shiny metal and glossy paint, appeared brand-new. Ethan went aboard with all the ease of a man who said he could handle the boat, piquing Nicole's interest. What other hidden talents did this man possess? Father. Vet. Boatsman. She was suitably impressed.

Ethan helped Holly aboard and Gus jumped on behind her. He reached out to take Nicole's bags, then took her hand to help her board. The slight sway caused by the motion caught Nicole off guard. She stumbled into the boat.

Ethan placed his hands on her hips to stabilize her. "You'll get your sea legs soon enough."

She grabbed hold of a metal bar running along the side of the boat, miffed by her clumsiness. "If you say so."

With an easy assurance, Ethan stored the belongings in a lower cabin located at the front of the boat. Then he returned with two orange flotation vests. He handed one to Nicole and placed the other on Holly.

"You're not wearing one?"

"I can swim," he told her, fastening the buckles on Holly's vest.

"So can I."

He stopped to meet her gaze. "And if the boat takes a sharp turn and you fall overboard, can you regulate fast enough to surface and tread water?"

"I don't know. I've never been in that situation."

He pointed to her vest. "Please put it on."

"When you put it like that," she huffed. She was used to doing things on her own, but she could admit that she didn't know everything. She'd take Ethan's advice and not show that his concern pleased her.

She donned the vest, settling it over her shoulders and trying to match the clasps. When he finished with Holly, Ethan secured Gus's leash before making sure that Nicole's vest was situated properly. His grin of approval shouldn't have affected her, but it did.

"You two take a seat and we'll get started."

Ethan jumped onto the dock, his muscles bunching as he untied the ropes wrapped around the *T* hooks. The boat moved a bit, bumping back into the dock, giving Ethan time to leap back aboard.

At his command, Holly and Nicole took their seats on the cushions covering the two benches on either side of the craft. Ethan stepped into what she thought was called a wheelhouse and cranked the engine. The motor sputtered, then roused to life. At the sound, her pulse began to race.

Ethan carefully steered the boat into the lake, then slowly idled to the buoys. Nicole raised her face to the sun, letting the warmth caress her skin. Suddenly, the grumble of the engine increased and they moved faster. Her eyes flew open, and she tipped over, unprepared for the change in speed.

Holly grabbed hold of Gus and hugged him closely. Ethan, his legs spread to balance his weight, had firm control of the wheel. Once Nicole straightened, the wind fiercely tossed her hair and water splashed her face. She threw back her head and laughed out loud.

Ethan steered them toward the middle of the lake. With her hand shadowing her eyes, Nicole viewed Golden from a completely different perspective. Lake houses were perched along the shoreline. Docks ran out into the lake, some with boats anchored there, bobbing in the water. Tall trees gave shade to the land, making the scene spectacular.

Ethan drove from one end to the other, then steered back to the middle and lowered the throttle to slow down. The warm sunshine hovered over them. Holly jumped up, more than comfortable with the whole boat experience than Nicole, and unhooked Gus's leash.

"You're a pro," Nicole told her.

"Daddy and I go out a lot, don't we?" she asked.

Ethan turned off the engine, letting the boat drift, then faced them, his lips curved. "Sure do, princess."

This was a man who clearly loved his daughter. Spellbound, Nicole's chest tightened with an emotion she didn't dare name.

Clearing her suddenly lodged throat, Nicole asked, "Now what?"

"Hold that thought."

Ethan disappeared into the lower cabin before returning with three fishing rods. Attaching the bait he'd brought along, they all had their lines in the water, waiting for a bite.

"I had no idea we were fishing today," Nicole said as she felt a light vibration. She moved the rod, but the movement stopped.

"Figured I'd give you the entire experience."

"It's been forever. My dad used to take us fishing when we were kids."

"We love to fish," Holly said. "But we don't catch anything to keep."

Ethan leaned closer and spoke in a low voice against Nicole's ear. "I let them go."

She shivered. "Why am I not surprised?"

They kept at it for about an hour, with no success. Nicole's line tightened again but by the time she reeled it in, the only thing to come out of the water was the lure.

"I don't think this is our lucky day."

By this time, Holly had lost interest and was playing with Gus. Ethan collected the rods and stored them away.

"Now what?" she asked when Ethan returned.

"Lunch," Ethan and Holly said in unison.

Ethan retrieved the insulated bag and placed it on the dinette table near the back of the boat. He unpacked sandwiches, fruit and chips while Nicole retrieved the vegetables, cookies and Gus's kibble.

"Daddy, can I have a cookie?"

"You need to eat a sandwich first."

Holly wrinkled her nose. "I'd rather have a cookie," she grumbled, then turned her attention to feeding Gus.

Nicole tried to hide a smile.

"It's not funny," Ethan told her. "She has a mind of her own."

"As she should."

"Within reason. Like choosing healthy food and not dressing like an elf."

Nicole's face heated. "Sorry about that."

His dark eyebrows rose over the tops of his sunglasses. "Somehow I don't think you are."

She chuckled. "Guilty."

Under a cloudless sky, they ate lunch and chatted about Golden, Nicole's project and the veterinary clinic. Their bellies were full when Ethan decided to move location. He powered up the engine and they sped to the far end of the lake to a small sandy beach. Pulling as close as possible, he dropped the anchor.

"Yay!" Holly clapped. "We're going to the beach."

Nicole stared at the shore. "When did Golden Lake get a beach?"

"A few years ago, from what I understand," Ethan informed her. "Some of the residents nearby wanted it, so they petitioned the city."

"Huh," Nicole said. "This would have been a fun hangout when I was a kid."

"Oh, yeah? Where did you go instead?"

She counted down on her fingers. "Bailey's Point. The covered bridge out by Crestview Farm." She grinned. "The stables at Crestview Farm."

"Horses or a boy?"

"How'd you guess?"

He shrugged. "Easy. So, which was it?

"Both. But mostly a boy."

Ethan chuckled.

"How about you? Any misadventures with a girl from your youth?"

"Missy Cates."

"Really? Her name just flies off your lips?"

"She was my first girlfriend."

Nicole placed her hands on her hips.

He held his hands up in defense. "However, you far surpass her in the memorable-female category."

"Right answer."

He leaned over and brushed a kiss across her lips. She grabbed hold of his shirt and tugged him closer, standing on tiptoe to deepen the kiss. A boat zoomed by, creating a wake that rocked the boat. They parted company quickly and regained their balance.

Ethan smiled at her. "You okay?"

Her body warmed over his intense gaze. This attraction between them was moving into dangerous territory. She should be worried, right?

"As long as I'm the only female you're committing to memory."

"Oh, you are."

His confident grin made her heart leap.

ETHAN'S FINGERS LINGERED over Nicole's soft skin. Her pulse fluttered in her neck. He could get addicted to her. To this. Spending time with the woman who had seized his complete attention.

She gestured to the shore. "So, um, the beach?"

"You're going to get wet," he warned.

"That's okay."

Did she need the cold water to cool her down as much as he did?

"Holly," he called over his shoulder, never breaking eye contact with Nicole. He didn't miss her shiver and sent her what he hoped was a normal, levelheaded smile, which was far from what he was feeling.

Holly clambered up the steps from the cabin with towels and a bulky bag in her hands, then ran to the ladder at the back of the boat. "You first, Daddy."

He reluctantly left Nicole to toss his sunglasses on the console and take the items from his daughter. He kicked off his shoes and lowered himself into the water. His eyes went wide.

"Cold?" Nicole asked with amusement in her eyes.

"More so than I thought."

"Hold me, Daddy."

He reached for Holly. Gus vaulted over the side, his splash covering them. "Next."

He watched Nicole take a deep breath, knowing her well enough now to be certain that she wouldn't back down. Her breath hissed when she hit the water, but she waded with him to the shore. They all rushed to the deserted beach at the same time. Ethan placed Holly down and she proceeded to peel off her clothes to dash around in her bathing suit, she and Gus running at the lake edge where the water lapped the sand.

"Are we swimming?' Nicole asked.

"If you want to."

She flashed a grin. "If you are."

In response, Ethan removed his shirt. Nicole's appreciative gaze was enough reward, even if they didn't go into the lake just yet.

She removed her outer clothing, shivering as she folded her shorts and shirt.

After shaking out a towel, Ethan draped it over Nicole's shoulders.

"Thanks. It'll take me a minute to warm up."

He spread out another towel, sank down and patted the spot beside him. "Join me?"

She dropped next to him. "You should have warned me."

"About the beach or the water temperature?"

"Both."

"This is Holly's favorite part of our outings. She

loves to zip around the lake, then run on the sand. By the time we get home, she'll be sound asleep."

"She is a sweetheart."

"Can't deny that."

Nicole stared out over the water for a long time. He enjoyed just sitting with her, no expectations, nowhere to rush off to. Thinking back, he'd never had that with his ex. At the time, he'd accepted the daily rush as normal. Now, in this town that had opened its arms to both him and his daughter, he valued the slower lifestyle.

"Daddy!" Holly yelled as she rushed for them from a few feet away. "Can Gus and I dig?"

He pulled the bag toward him. "Find gold this time," he ordered, handing her a pail and small shovel.

"You're silly." She paused in front of Nicole. "If Gus is here all summer, we can go out on the boat every weekend."

Ethan noticed a slight crease on Nicole's forehead. Holly took off before Nicole could answer.

"Sorry about that. Holly's just excited to have Gus to play with."

"It's okay. I remember that feeling, wanting the summer to drag on forever. I think that's what made Golden magical when I was a kid."

"It still can be."

"So much has changed." Nicole shook her head. "But I can see why you like it. For your family."

"It's more about quality time with Holly than the

location." He paused. Locked gazes with her. "Although the view is pretty great."

Nicole tucked her legs beneath her. The towel slipped from her shoulders. Her eyes were luminous in the sun. She was never more lovely than right now, with her skin glowing and oblivious to her hair, tangled by the wind. She was so natural. One of a kind. And if she made the decision to leave, would they ever see a future together?

"In spite of my reluctance to spend time in Golden," she said, "I do understand why you want to start a new life here."

"In what way?" He wanted her opinion. On everything.

"Small-town life is special. At least it was, until our lives changed. But before that, my family was part of a much bigger picture. Each holiday was better than the last and we couldn't wait to outdo our neighbors with costumes or decorations the following year. We went on adventures with friends, spending all day exploring in the woods or racing around on our bikes. My sisters and I would climb under the covers together at night and tell stories, only to fall asleep together. I got into my fair share of trouble with youthful pranks, but nothing mean-spirited." She tucked her hair behind her ear. "I can see why you'd want that for Holly."

"Sounds like you have good memories to go along with the bad."

"I do, but are they enough to overshadow what I'd like to forget?"

He wanted to tell her they were. That if she took a chance, he was enough for her to come back to Golden. But she had to decide that without pressure on his part.

"Only you can come to that conclusion," he said.

She shifted, drawing her knees up to rest her chin on top. "You know how you wanted to make the clinic your own? Put your individual stamp on it?"

That had been his dream when he started vet school. Even with the detour of a failed marriage, he still wanted it. "I've already started making it my own."

"The doggy day care?"

"My idea."

"I like your certainty. That you have everything you need to be a success." Her smile didn't quite reach her eyes. "That's how I view the promotion at work. I've poured a great deal of time and energy into building my position in the company to get where I am today. How can I give that up?"

"What about Golden? Now that you've been back, seen your family, can you rethink your feelings about the place?"

She didn't answer, and instead stared at the water. The surface sparkled, the sun creating an illusion of brightness even though there were dark depths below. He'd made it out of the darkness and only wanted to live in the light now.

"I really don't know." She tugged the towel tighter over her shoulders. "I'm glad I'm talking to my sisters, but why would they trust me after I turned my back on them?"

"Because that's what family does." His gaze landed on Holly as she dug in the sand. There was nothing on earth that would cause doubts about his relationship with his daughter. Until Nicole came to that same conclusion about her family, he didn't think he could convince her otherwise.

"Maybe I've let too much time go by."

"You'll never know until you make the effort to try."

She blinked. Were there tears in her eyes? He wanted to hug her, but didn't think she'd welcome it. While she didn't mind his kisses when they were flirting, she could also be prickly about her belief system when it came to Golden.

"Does it make me a coward that I'm afraid to try?"

"No. It makes you human to admit you have reservations."

He didn't expect Nicole to suddenly change her deep-seated and valid perceptions overnight. The hurt from the past still ran deep for her. She'd only been in town for two weeks. He couldn't expect a lifetime of her running away to change, no matter how much he wanted it.

"How did we get on this serious topic? Today is about fun." She twisted around, searching for Holly and Gus.

Holly ran up to Nicole and took her hand, tugging at it. "Come see what I found by the water."

Nicole rose. "What is it?"

Holly beckoned with a wave as she hurried to the shoreline.

Before Ethan had a chance to warn her, they were at the water's edge. Holly walked into the lake, then turned and started to splash Nicole. On a surprised wheeze, Nicole waded into the water and returned fire. The shrieks and giggling had Ethan joining them. The two females shared a conspiratorial look and then turned as a team to ambush him.

"Hey, that's two against one."

An all-out war started. Even Gus joined in on the battle. Nicole had quickly gone from serious to lighthearted as she brazenly splashed him, a facet of her personality he admired. He didn't cut her any slack, chasing her in the knee-high water, aiming and hitting with his direct shots. He finally caught Nicole by wrapping his arms around her waist and twirling her around. Her feet skimmed the water, and she secured her hands over his, relaxing against him.

The laughter and water play continued until Holly's teeth began to chatter. Ethan lifted her from the water and carried her to the beach, wrapping her in a towel and briskly rubbing the terry cloth to warm her. He sat, grabbing a towel for himself, then Holly dropped into his lap.

"Can we go now, Daddy?"

"Tired of playing in the sand?"

"Gus and I want to go fast again."

"Is that what he told you?" Nicole teased.

"No, silly. I just know."

They gathered up the belongings and waded back to the boat. Once the life vests were buckled on and Gus had been secured, Ethan replaced his sunglasses, started the engine and took one last fast loop around the lake. The sun was just starting to drop in the sky when they made it back to the dock.

As they drew closer, Ethan lowered the throttle, then turned it off, letting the boat drift to the dock.

"Let me help," Nicole said as she placed one foot on the edge of the boat.

"Think you can tie us to the cleat?"

"Cleat?"

His lips quirked. "The hook in the dock."

"You could have said *hook*."

"Hey, if you're going to be a boater, you need to learn the lingo."

"Aye, aye, sir," she said, and saluted.

During the ride, she seemed to have gotten over the questions in her head. She was back to her perky self.

"I'll toss you the rope. Loop it around the cleat like a figure eight."

She jumped onto the planks. "Got it."

Once she was in position, he heaved a section of rope to her. She grabbed it like a pro. After she'd tied the bow, the boat lightly bumped into the dock. He tossed her rope from the stern and she twisted the rope securely.

Making sure he had everything, Ethan handed the bags to Nicole, who placed them on the dock.

He helped Holly off, then did one last run-through to make sure he hadn't left anything behind. He grabbed the keys and joined the small group.

"This was really amazing," Nicole said as she shouldered her bags. She turned to walk backward. "I've never been boating but—"

"Nicole, you really need to watch where you're—"

Before he could finish the warning, her ankle got tangled in rope piled on the dock. She tripped, her arms flailing in the air to stop her fall. Ethan raced forward, wrapping an arm around her waist to tug her upward.

She landed hard against his body. He held tight, his heart racing.

Their gazes met. He saw the heat reflected there and put a little distance between them.

Oh, boy, this was getting serious.

"Daddy, you can let go now. Nicole is safe."

His daughter's words shook him out of the spell Nicole had cast over him. He stepped back, slowly letting go of his beautiful neighbor. She might be safe, but Ethan's heart was not.

"Thanks," she said as she got her footing back. "I promise, I'm not usually this clumsy."

"I'd catch you anywhere," he unintentionally blurted.

Her eyes went wide, and she picked up her pace, hotfooting it farther up the dock.

"Too much," he muttered.

"Too much what, Daddy?"

He smiled down at Holly. "Too much activity today."

Holly frowned. "It's what we always do."

Not with Nicole, they didn't. He wanted more days just like this.

Holly ran off to join Nicole. Ethan returned the keys to the marina office. "Boat do okay?" Homer asked.

"Perfect."

"You sure?" The older man cocked his head. "You look like you got coldclocked after jumpin' a big wave and hittin' your head."

His head did feel fuzzy after holding Nicole, not that he was about to tell that to Homer.

"We're all good. Thanks again for getting the boat ready for us."

"Hey, you took care of Hondo when he got sick." A basset hound, probably as old as his owner, shuffled to the door. "I owe you."

Hondo barked.

"Glad you're staying in Golden," the old man said.

Ethan walked to the car, head spinning. He was staying. Nicole was not.

How was he supposed to deal with that?

CHAPTER TWELVE

SURE ENOUGH, Holly fell asleep on the drive home, Gus curled up in the seat beside her. Ethan took the long way home, driving on the curving mountain roads, giving his daughter extra time to nap. The leaves from the trees created a lush canopy over the pavement. Wildflowers bloomed at the road's edge, adding a burst of color amid the green grass. Through his open window, the earthy scent of warm earth invaded the sedan. As they passed dirt-road turnoffs, he recalled that many of the paths led to hiking trails ending in spectacular views with waterfalls. As if he had no control, his gaze moved to Nicole. She leaned back in the passenger seat, window down, hair tousled by the wind.

Ethan checked his daughter in the mirror. "Told you she'd be out like a light."

Nicole hid a yawn behind her hand.

"Too much today?"

"The opposite, actually. I can't remember the last time I enjoyed a day off from work this much." She grinned at him. "Of course, the company had a lot to do with it."

"Hope you don't get behind with the decorating."

"I shouldn't. I'll go over next week's staging and make some tweaks later tonight. Mac is on a tighter schedule than I originally anticipated, so I've had to change the location order for the photos."

"Does that happen often? Last-minute changes?"

"Not always. When I work at an event, say a trade show, the staging is decided months in advance. There are usually photographers taking pictures at the events, not for magazines, but instead marketing teams for the businesses attending. This job has made things a bit different."

"You learn to pivot."

"Good word. And, yes. Especially with Mac. He's in high demand."

There was a heavy pause. Mostly on his behalf. Ethan hadn't liked the way Mac acted as if he had some kind of romance with Nicole. It rankled, especially now that he and Nicole had shared kisses.

"And what about…" Ethan went for casual but was afraid it didn't come off that way. "You and Mac?"

She jerked her head toward him. "Firmly in the friend zone."

His hands tightened on the steering wheel. "He seems to think it's more."

Nicole pulled her leg up and wrapped an arm around it as she angled toward him. "He does it to bug me."

"And you're okay with that?"

"I'm used to it." She sighed. "Full disclosure. We

did go out when we first met. As much as he's a great guy, there was no spark."

Ethan's jaw tightened. "Not like the spark between us?"

He took the turn to drive down Main Street. Nicole reached over and patted his arm, her fingers trailing over his skin. "I'd never kiss you if I were interested in someone else. I know my career will make whatever we decide is going on between us difficult, but I'm not denying I feel something for you, Ethan."

"I'm definitely attracted to you, Nicole. I never expected this, but I can't say I'm disappointed."

"Will you be when I leave? Disappointed, that is?"

"You haven't made a secret of the fact that you'll be going back to Savannah."

She bit her lower lip. "But we can make it work?"

"Why don't we enjoy our time together and see where it leads us."

He wasn't sure she liked the answer but couldn't blame himself for being cautious. She had been up front about her reluctance to make a commitment to this town. He could respect that, but it wouldn't change the fact that he'd already planted his family roots deep in Golden's soil.

"Then I guess you should know the job will be completed earlier than I thought. Mac had a schedule change."

Her words sat like a heavy weight on his chest. "How much earlier?"

"The end of next week."

Next week? That didn't leave much time to see where this relationship was headed. If they could make things work. "I wanted to tell you sooner but…"

"Yeah," was all he could think to say while he contemplated the unwelcome news.

Once home, they quickly unpacked the bags before disturbing Holly. His daughter snuggled against him when he lifted her from her seat, but soon noticed Gus underfoot and wanted down.

"Can I play, Daddy?"

"Sure thing, princess."

With a squeal, she and Gus took off.

"Why princess?"

Ethan's face heated "I started calling her that after watching one of her princess movies."

"I think it's sweet."

He shrugged off the compliment but didn't miss Nicole's small smile.

After carrying the bags indoors, Nicole hovered near the door. "I guess I should get home."

"Would you like to have dinner with us?"

When she hesitated, he wondered if he'd overstepped, especially after her announcement about leaving sooner than planned. He was already on shaky emotional ground, but suddenly their limited time together seemed urgent. He should be careful, not only for himself, but also for Holly. But he really wanted her to say yes.

"Nothing fancy," he said. "Maybe cook something on the grill."

"I'd like that. But first, I need to take a shower."

He nodded. "Me too. I'll get Holly cleaned up and then we can meet for dinner."

Nicole grabbed her belongings. "Sounds good."

Ethan followed her outside. She whistled for Gus, waved to Holly and started to walk down the front steps of the house. She hadn't made it very far when Holly ran over.

"Can I tell you a secret?"

Oh, no. What was his daughter up to?

Nicole met his gaze then returned her attention to Holly. "Of course."

Holly motioned for Nicole to bend down. She kneeled beside Holly, who proceeded to whisper loudly into her ear. "Daddy likes you."

Ethan went still.

Nicole paused, then said with a scratchy tone, "How can you tell?"

"He's smiling a lot." Holly pulled back, her face serious. "I mean *a lot*."

His face heated for a second time.

"Maybe you can like him back?"

Holly," Ethan called from the stoop before this went any further.

"Coming."

Clearing her throat, Nicole stood. "I'll see you at dinner."

"Yay." Holly hugged her legs then ran to Ethan.

Nicole met his gaze, but he couldn't read her. Probably for the best.

He made sure Holly got a quick bath, then put on a movie while he jumped into the shower. Under the stream of hot water, he debated if he should include Nicole in the Price family dynamics.

"You're getting ahead of yourself."

Yes, his attraction to Nicole was off the charts, but would her lifestyle mesh with the life he'd started in Golden? Would she be running off to the next big job? He'd been there once and didn't want that again. But Nicole wasn't his ex. Maybe she could adapt to this lifestyle and still keep her promotion? He'd bring it up over dinner and see where they stood.

He quickly dressed in a short-sleeved shirt and jeans, and had just gone downstairs when his cell phone rang.

"Your phone, Daddy!" Holly yelled from the living room.

"Thanks, princess."

He headed toward the kitchen in the direction of the ringing device. Holly was going to firmly control his life once she got older.

He read the caller ID, concerned when he saw Jossie's name. She was on the rotation schedule to monitor the progress of the recovering animals at the clinic this weekend.

"Hey, Jossie. Everything okay?"

Her voice was thready when she answered. "I'm afraid not, Dr. Price."

"What's wrong?"

"You know the five-K race I entered that took place today? Well, I sprained my ankle. I'm at the urgent care right now, so I can't get to the animals at the clinic."

"Don't worry about it. I'll head over and assess them myself."

"I tried calling Sandra, but she didn't answer. I think she had plans."

"Like I said, I'll go over."

"I'm really sorry."

"Don't be. And we'll cover the schedule for you next week. Come back when you feel better."

Ethan could hear the tears in her voice.

"Thanks. I can't believe this happened."

"Take care of yourself, Jossie. Let me know if you need anything."

"I will."

Ethan knew Jossie had a big family who would rally around her. She was in good hands. Now, he had to rearrange the dinner plans.

He mentally ran through his babysitting contacts, stopping when he came to Mrs. Johnson. Did he want to bother her at the last minute? She was the closest. He stepped onto the back deck and saw her in her garden. Guess he'd go over and ask.

He crossed the properties, checking out Nicole's cottage as he passed. All was quiet, unlike the woman who'd created a whirlwind in his cautious life.

"Miss Celeste."

She looked up from her basket. "Dr. Price."

"I know this is last-minute, but I need to get to the clinic and wondered if you could watch Holly for me."

"Of course. Is there an emergency?"

"Afraid so."

"Oh, no, not another hurt animal."

"No, this time an injured employee. Jossie was in a five-K race today and sprained her ankle."

"Is it bad?"

"Bad enough that she can't see to the boarded animals. I need to run over to the clinic and make sure they're alright."

She picked up her basket and slowly walked toward him. He watched her closely, concerned by her halting gait and thinking she seemed a bit pale.

Ethan tilted his head. "Are you okay, Miss Celeste?"

Celeste waved away his concern. "I'm fine. Had a walk earlier and went a bit farther than usual." She motioned to her garden. "I came out to get some vegetables to add to my dinner. Once I get cooking, I'll be good as new."

"You're sure? I can see if Faith Donovan is available to watch Holly."

Celeste placed a hand on her hip. "You don't have to fret over me."

Ethan hid a grin at her annoyed tone. "No, but Nicole will have my hide if you're not up to shape to assist her."

"Now, that's the truth."

"Gus!" He heard Nicole shout behind him. He turned to find Gus running straight for Celeste, Nicole not far behind. She grinned, making his chest hitch. She'd chosen a blue-and-white-striped, sleeveless top, jeans and sandals to wear to dinner.

"Sorry," she said on a short breath. "He escaped again."

"It's fine," Celeste assured her. "He has a lot of energy and I enjoy his antics."

Ethan raised an eyebrow. "He certainly is a problem."

Nicole grinned. "The good kind." She glanced between them. "What's up?"

"I was telling Celeste that I needed to make sure your assistant is in tip-top shape."

Celeste straightened to stand taller, or as much as her height would allow. "You have nothing to worry about." She focused on Nicole. "Oh, and I have some ideas."

"Like?"

"Your mama's store. Did you still want to use that old sleigh from the storage unit?"

"We pretty much covered Christmas, so I don't know that we need it now."

"How about this? We pick flowers from my yard and some from your mama's, and we fill the sleigh up with them. It's perfect, since Linda loves her flowers and it'll be different than what you've already done."

"I love it."

He could almost see Nicole's mind go to work.

"And if we place the flowers just right, you might think they're on a wagon instead of a sleigh."

Celeste beamed.

"I'll add it to my notes later and figure out a time to get Mac there."

"If I recall, you have time Tuesday morning."

Nicole grinned. "You have a great memory."

"I'm taking the assistant job seriously."

"Told you," Ethan added.

"I may have to hire you when I go back to Savannah," Nicole teased.

A band of tension pressed against his chest, but Ethan tried to ignore it.

Celeste's pleasure dulled a tick. "Since I can't drive, you'd have to chauffeur me back and forth and the commute is much too long."

"It would be fun though," Nicole said.

Celeste placed her basket on the ground. "Are you going out? You're all dressed up."

Nicole smoothed her blouse. "Dinner with Ethan and Holly if it's still on."

"I'm afraid there's a change in plans."

"Oh?"

"I'm needed at the clinic." He explained the circumstances. "I was hoping you'd come with me."

"I...this is a surprise."

"I've seen you in action. I thought you might like another glimpse at what I do."

She grinned. "I'd love it."

"I can watch Gus too," Celeste informed them.

Nicole glanced at Ethan, then back to Celeste. "Thanks."

"Don't worry about dinner," Celeste told him. "I'll feed Holly."

"Are you sure?"

"My pleasure."

"I'll go get her and be right back." He turned on his heel and strode back to his house. His daughter was more than thrilled to spend time with Celeste.

"Ready?" Ethan asked Nicole when he returned with Holly. She nodded.

"'Bye, Daddy." Holly waved as she and Celeste walked toward the garden.

"You're sure you don't mind me tagging along?" Nicole asked when they were out of hearing distance.

Ethan stopped. "Do you not want to come?"

"I do. I'm curious about what transpires in the day of a vet."

He took hold of her hand and laced their fingers together. "And I want to show you."

She glanced down at their entwined fingers, then up at him. "Lead the way."

He led her to his car, reluctant to sever the physical contact between them. Holding her hand felt right even if their timing was wrong.

They made the short trip to town. When he unlocked the door to the clinic, barking came from another room. The place had a deserted air to it compared to the hubbub of a busy office day. The lights were off in most of the building, creating long shadows.

"Feeding time," he told her.

After walking down a hallway, they entered a big room with large recovery kennels lined up against a wall. Night-lights scattered around the room maintained a faint glow. Disinfectant permeated the air, along with the lesser scent of animals. The patients stirred in their spots.

"There are only a few pets boarded this weekend. Surgery patients from last week."

Nicole walked over to gaze at a small dog who was waiting expectantly.

"Poor baby," she crooned. "Are you doing okay?" She placed her fingers against the steel enclosure, smiling when the dog sniffed her fingers.

Ethan opened another door to check on a plump cat. "I need to examine them, then clean the area."

"Can I help?" She seemed as enthusiastic as he was. "I'd love to work with you."

They settled into a routine of sorts, Ethan examining each pet and Nicole cleaning out the cage if needed. Time flew, but he couldn't help but lose his heart to Nicole when he listened to her talking to the animals in her soothing tone. They immediately trusted her, even if they weren't feeling their best.

After closing one of the doors, she noticed Holly's pictures on the wall. "It's so sweet that you hang up Holly's drawings."

One sheet of paper featured a mismatched purple cat playing with an orange dog. Another had small brown blobs he thought might be kittens. Pride filled him. "She has real compassion for animals. I want to foster that trait."

Nicole wiped her hands on a disposable cloth. "I'd say it's working."

"She's got this way—"

A loud banging came from the direction of the reception area.

Nicole jumped. "What's that?"

A frown knitted Ethan's forehead. "Usually, people call the answering service with emergencies when the clinic is closed, not show up unannounced. Let me check."

He headed down a dim hallway to the reception area, Nicole on his heels. The banging at the door continued. He unlocked it and pushed it open.

Nicole gasped from behind him. "Briana?"

"I saw your car in the parking lot, Dr. Price, and took a chance you were here." Briana, in her police uniform, rushed inside, a small kitten with matted fur in her hands. "He's so skinny and lethargic. Someone must have dumped him." She held the orange kitten toward him. "Can you save him?"

WHEN ETHAN CUPPED his hands, Briana placed the tiny kitten there, her fingers hovering over the animal. Her sister was right, the kitten barely moved his head. The eyes were closed tight, but Nicole could see the slight rise and fall of his chest.

"I need to take him to the exam room," Ethan said.

Knowing she wasn't going to get Briana to leave,

she followed Nicole, and Nicole followed Ethan as he headed straight to the room to start his examination. "Nicole, can you get the lights?" he asked as he walked to the table. "The switch is on the wall by the door."

Seconds later, light flickered from the fluorescent bulbs above. "Briana, grab a clean towel from the counter."

Briana found the pile and took the top towel to place on the table.

He checked the kitten. "A boy."

Briana nodded.

Fascinated to see Ethan at work, Nicole watched as he carefully prodded the animal, searching for an obvious injury. When he didn't find anything, he gently probed the ribs. Then he lifted the kitten's sunken eyelids. There wasn't much of a response. He proceeded to check the gums, and lifted and dropped the skin at the kitten's neck. "The kitten is dehydrated. It would explain why he's not responding." He gently ran a hand over the dirty fur. "I'm going to start an IV. Watch him for a moment?"

"We will," Nicole assured him.

Ethan went about preparing the equipment he'd need, then returned to tend to the cat. The little guy let out a squeaky meow when he inserted the needle, but still didn't struggle. Once Ethan had the IV secure, he found a brush and began to clean the fur.

"How long before you know anything?" Briana asked with an unusually shaky voice.

Nicole placed an arm around her sister's waist

and pulled her close. Briana had always been sensitive to animals and underdogs.

"I'll keep him overnight. We should know better in the morning."

Briana rested her head on Nicole's shoulder. Nicole hugged her, happy to allow her sister to lean on her. Just like when they were kids.

"Nicole, why don't you take Briana to the break room while I look after my new patient. You'll find water bottles in the fridge."

Nicole pulled back to read her sister's face. "Okay?"

Briana nodded again.

"Thanks," Nicole told Ethan before leaving.

They walked in silence until reaching the break room.

"Want a bottle?" Nicole asked.

"Please."

She removed two bottles and passed one to Briana, noticing that her sister had pink streaks in her honey-blond hair. It reminded Nicole of when they were kids and Briana would change her hair color monthly.

"So, where did you find him?"

Briana blew out a long sigh. "I was at Taylor's store. I'd stopped in to say hi after a call at a neighboring business. When I was walking to my car, I thought I heard a noise. The kitten must have had just enough energy left in him to cry out for help."

"He's lucky it was you. No way would you have left him alone."

Briana swiped at the tears in her eyes. "I know I'm a soft touch."

"When it's important." Nicole laughed. "For a hard-nosed cop, you have a soft streak a mile wide."

"Tell anyone and I'll vehemently deny it." Briana stared at the door. "Think Dr. Price is okay?"

"I think he's a professional and wanted to take care of the kitten without us hovering."

Her sister sent her a wobbly smile. "I don't know what I thought I could do to help."

"You started the process, he'll finish."

After cracking the bottle seal, Briana removed the cap to take a sip of water.

"Do you talk to Taylor often?" Nicole prodded.

"Mostly when Mom has dinner."

"Hmm." This was moving into a touchy area, but Nicole had to ask. "How do you feel about that?"

Briana placed her bottle on the counter. "It's still awkward, but we're trying."

"I saw her when I was decorating outside her shop," Nicole said. "She offered to post pictures on the local merchants' social-media page and after that, I had a lot of interest from businesses asking to be featured in the magazine. More interest than when I first started, for sure."

Briana placed her palms on the counter behind her. "How is that going?"

"We're almost finished."

"Everyone is excited."

Nicole paused. "I'm amazed at the reception I

received. I wasn't sure how folks would respond to me since I've been gone for so long."

"People grow up, Nicole. Change for the better. Look at me. I'm a mom."

She wanted to argue that point—her standard reflex—but she couldn't since she'd seen the truth of those words with her own eyes.

"I'm surprised to see you with Dr. Price," Briana said, changing the subject. Probably for the best, although Nicole couldn't quite clarify her relationship with Ethan.

The boating trip confirmed two things. One, she liked being a part of Ethan and Holly's life. And two, the man had an impressive chest. Nicole loved how the lake water beaded in Ethan's beard and made his hair darker. His eyes had gleamed with happiness, and she'd dared to hope that she had something to do with his mood.

"We were together after he got the call to come to the clinic, so Ethan invited me along," she explained, leaving out the details of their day or their plans for dinner.

"He's quite attractive," Briana said, as if she wasn't curious about Nicole and Ethan hanging out together on the weekend.

"He is. And a nice guy, as well."

"So?" Nicole persisted.

"So what?"

"Are you going to make your move?"

Nicole sputtered out a laugh. "Make my move?"

"He's not going to be single for long."

Nicole didn't welcome that prediction. "I'm leaving, remember?"

"You don't have to."

"Briana, you of all people know how I feel about Golden. Besides, my life is in Savannah."

"Is it truly?"

Not especially. More like she was based there. But still, it was currently home.

"Golden is more concerned about becoming a premier travel destination than they are about old Connelly drama," Briana informed her in a heated tone. "If you stuck around, you'd see that."

"I feel like every time I turn around, something reminds me of Dad. Especially that building he left us."

"But there's plenty here to remind you of us. Growing up together. Being each other's best friends."

That was true. She'd told Ethan so. Why couldn't she admit that to her sister?

Instead, she went in a different direction. "I didn't get a letter from Dad."

Briana grabbed her bottle from the counter. "I noticed Mr. Stevens didn't hand you an envelope."

"I suppose I didn't deserve one. I never got to set things right with Dad before…"

His death still haunted her.

A long silence stretched between them.

"We all had our issues," Briana finally said.

Nicole didn't disagree.

She rolled her shoulders. "Did you read your letter?"

Briana shook her head, curls dancing around her face. "Not yet. I'm still working through our relationship."

"None of this is easy."

"It isn't, but it could be." Briana pushed away from the counter. "You don't have to move back here, but do you think we could all get together from time to time? Mom, Addie, me and you. Even Taylor. She was just as innocent as we were."

"What would we even say?"

"I don't know, but I feel like it could be the beginning of us healing."

"Even though I'm hurt that Dad didn't want to give me any last words?" Her voice caught. "Despite how much I would have told him otherwise?"

Briana crossed the room and pulled Nicole into a hug. She latched on, wanting to feel close to her sister again. Wished they'd all handled the past differently. Wondered why her father had deliberately not left her a letter.

Her mind twirled in circles.

Briana pulled back. "I don't know what to tell you, Nicole. Put all that we went through with Dad aside. Can't we rekindle the relationship of sisters who were once close? Add Taylor to our band. Move on from the things that held us back?"

"I want that," Nicole whispered.

"Then we have to try."

Footsteps echoed down the hallway and then Ethan appeared in the doorway. "Everything okay?"

Nicole wiped her eyes as Briana stepped away and asked, "How's the patient?"

"I can see a slight improvement in just starting the IV. Time will tell."

Briana crossed the room to hug Ethan. "Thanks, Doc."

His surprised gaze met Nicole's and her lips trembled.

"I need to get home." Briana stepped away. "Cami and Mr. Darcy are getting great big hugs whether they want them or not."

Holding back a smile, Nicole decided that Golden PD was lucky to have her sister working for them. Not only was Briana a good cop, but she was also an even better person.

Nicole walked with them to reception. Once Briana left and Ethan locked the door, he said, "Want to talk?"

"No, I'd rather eat." *Said the queen of denial.*

"I called Celeste. She fed Holly and they're playing cards, so we can grab a bite somewhere."

"You do realize Celeste is a card shark and is probably teaching Holly some form of poker game."

"Don't hedge your bets. Holly is already good with numbers."

They checked on the kitten, and the last of the recovering animals, then left the clinic, Ethan locking the door. "Any preferences?"

In the last of the setting sun, Nicole drank him in. His brown eyes held hers and gleamed in the fading light. He was solid, handsome and so much of what she never thought she needed.

All at once, the past and the unsure future collided. The ghost of her father still hovered, making her question herself. She wanted to be on the same page as Briana and get closer to her sisters. She wanted to think she might have a future with Ethan and Holly. But the clock was ticking down and she was no closer to knowing what she really wanted.

"Do you mind if we get takeout? I'm tired."

"Sure. It was a long day." He pulled out his phone. "How about sandwiches?"

"Sounds good." She gave him her order.

He placed an order at a local sub store, and they swung by to pick them up.

The sun was finally on the horizon when they pulled up in the driveway. Nicole sat for a moment in the car, admiring the house Ethan had transformed into a home for his daughter. He wouldn't leave Golden. She knew that. Why should he? Everything he wanted was here.

Except you?

Was it unfair to keep hanging around if Holly thought Nicole and Ethan might have a future? Nicole still hadn't decided about the promotion. Even if she didn't take it and remained in her current position, she'd still be traveling a great deal. Would a long-distance relationship last if they went that route? Ethan had already experienced upheaval with his ex-wife and decided he wanted permanency. Roots. Something she couldn't offer him.

Her stomach twisted. She had to make a choice. Two weeks ago, it had seemed so easy. Go to Golden, do the job, then get out. Now, after Ethan's stirring kisses and Holly's darling antics, she wasn't sure.

She hated being unsure. And she only had a week left in town.

How had she gotten herself into this situation? Probably because she couldn't help falling for the vet next door.

CHAPTER THIRTEEN

"WHAT DO YOU THINK?" Nicole asked Ethan early Sunday morning as they stood on the ground floor of the vacant Sinclair building.

Ethan shook off the fog that hadn't yet lifted. To say he'd been bewildered to find Nicole on his front steps, ringing his doorbell at what felt like the crack of dawn, was an understatement. Especially in light of the way they'd parted company the previous evening.

"All I know is that you were at my door when Holly and I were barely awake and asked me to come on a fact-finding mission with you."

"This is the mission."

"Good thing the Donovans are early risers and were happy to let Holly play at their house," he grumbled under his breath. He had no idea what her fact-finding mission entailed, but the thought of being alone with Nicole had him dressing himself and Holly in record time. Thankfully, the jeans and T-shirt he'd thrown on were acceptable enough to stand in the dusty building.

He turned slowly in a circle. The shabby exterior

needed work. Once fresh air circulated, the musty smell inside would dissipate. But in his view, the drywall needed to be painted, the windows needed thorough cleaning along with the floor being swept. There was no telling what surprises they'd find in the other sections of the building.

"Nicole, I'm not a building appraiser."

"No, but you're smart." She spread her arms out wide. "Wouldn't this make a great spot for a fitness center?"

He took a sip from the coffee cup Nicole had placed in his hand after a quick stop at Sit A Spell Coffee Shop. There'd been the usual waiting line since the place had the best coffee for miles around. Nicole had chatted with everyone when they asked about her project. Was she always this perky on the mornings when she wasn't centered on work?

After they'd left each other last night, he'd wondered what had made her withdraw. Sitting in his car while parked in the driveway, she hadn't wanted to talk about the conversation with her sister in the break room while he tended to the malnourished kitten. There had been a heaviness when he'd joined them and announced he was finished with the kitten, much like the tension in his car on the drive home. Her distracted expression had been pensive. Whatever had transpired between the sisters had set the mood for the remainder of the evening. He thought he'd get to spend more time with Nicole, but instead, she'd taken her sandwich and gone home.

Until she showed up ringing the doorbell this

morning. Thank goodness, he'd spoken to Sandra the night before and she was going to the clinic to feed the animals.

"How about we back up," he suggested. "First, why the interest in the building? You said you didn't care about it one way or another."

"That's true." She pantomimed rolling up sleeves, unnecessary since she was wearing a short-sleeved top with her jeans. "But this could be a game changer for my sister. Addie's always been risk adverse, so I know it will take her months before she lists all the pro and cons about opening a business. If I can give her a plan, she might take this opportunity more seriously."

"Did she ask you to check in to this?"

Her gaze wavered from his. "No. She doesn't know I'm here."

"Does anyone?"

Guilt crossed her face. "Yes. Mr. Stevens, my dad's attorney. I woke him up to get the key before coming to your house."

"You do know it's Sunday morning," he said in a dry tone. "Most folks don't stir early for…this."

Her chin jutted out. "He answered his phone. First mistake."

Ethan nearly groaned. "I probably don't want to know, but what was his second?"

"Agreeing to let me run by his house. Gus jumped on him and nearly dragged the bathrobe off the man."

"That explains why Gus is at home."

"I wasn't sure what kind of mischief he'd get into, even in an empty building." She planted her hands on her hips, looking all official. "Back to the original topic. Is this a good place for a gym?"

Ethan swallowed another gulp of coffee, shook out the cobwebs in his head and focused. "The location is very convenient for merchants and employees working in Golden. I'm assuming Addie wants to cater to the locals."

"That was my understanding. She's the manager at Mountain Spa Center, which is pretty far out for people who work downtown. This way, she can create specialty programs and be open hours before and after work."

"I know I'd like to come in early before the clinic day starts."

"And so would many others."

"Okay. Location in the pro column." Ethan walked around the large open area. "Think there's enough room?"

"I went on the internet last night to find pictures of gym layouts." Nicole's excitement ratcheted up again. "Addie may not be able to get as much equipment in here as the spa, but if she hires a professional, I think it could be done. She'll need locker rooms, even if they aren't fancy, which will have to be built out, but otherwise, it seems like enough space."

"I'm going to regret asking, but have you talked to Addie about this? Maybe she's already factored the square footage of the ground floor into her decision-making."

"I did call her last night and we chatted for about thirty minutes before Jacob interrupted. He said something about baseball, which I understand he's into, so she ended the call. But I got enough info from her to start a search."

She hurried over to the backpack she'd dropped by the door when they'd entered and removed a collection of papers along with a yellow notepad and pencil. "Here's what I printed out," she said as she handed him the stack. "I thought I'd sketch the available space so we could go from there."

"We?"

"I mean Addie, if she decides to go this route."

He had to admit, Nicole was all in on this mission. He studied the printed papers, impressed by the well-thought-out layouts she'd found. When finished, he walked across the room to peer over Nicole's shoulder. He leaned close enough that her hair tickled his cheek. The lemony scent he associated with her filled his senses as he watched her draw a likeness to the room. "You're talented."

Her pencil kept moving. "I sketch staging proposals before an event. I've gotten pretty good at sizing up space."

"This isn't a job though."

"I know." She focused on the paper, but her hand stilled. "But it's the least I can do for her."

Ethan stepped back and put his coffee cup on the floor. "Why do I sense there's something more going on? Does this sudden interest in solving your sister's dilemma have anything to do with the conversation you had with Briana last night?"

Nicole lowered the pad. Wouldn't meet his gaze. "What if it does?"

He crossed his arms over his chest. "You know you can tell me."

She puffed out her breath. "We were talking about acting like sisters. All of us. Someone needs to take the first step, so I thought doing this for Addie might break the ice."

"Or overstep."

She blinked. "I hadn't considered that."

Which made Nicole so special to him. She didn't see her involvement as unwanted or unnecessary. She simply wished to help her sister. She really had to stop being so remarkable or his heart would be a goner for sure.

"Instead of a grand gesture," he offered, "why not have a very real conversation."

"Because real conversations are hard."

He pulled her into his arms. "When was the last time you all sat down and really talked?"

"Dinner at Mom's house when I first came back to town."

He remembered that her reaction hadn't been positive afterward.

"Then again at the café and The Perch. But they were small conversations. Like we didn't want to get into anything too deep."

"Nothing before?"

She tensed. "We were young when my parents split. Plus upset, angry and not getting along. That was before Taylor came into the picture."

"You do realize that pushing Addie might backfire."

"But at least I'll have tried," she whispered.

He moved away mere inches, placing a small distance between them so he could read her face. She had that stubborn lift of her chin that he'd come to recognize, but he also spied a hint of vulnerability he sensed was at the core of this impromptu mission.

"Because you don't feel like you tried with your father?"

She closed her eyes. "Yes."

He kissed her forehead.

"I can't make it right with Dad, but I can at least try harder when it comes to my sisters. Being here, seeing them, I miss them, Ethan. More than I thought possible."

He drew her close again. "And since you're always keeping busy at work and taking the lead when it comes to projects, this is your way of making amends?"

Her gaze met his. "Am I being lame?"

"No. Very generous, in fact."

He cupped her face in his hands and angled his head.

"Are you going to kiss me again?" she asked.

"Oh, yes. I am."

He leaned in, pressing his lips to hers. The notebook and pencil clattered to the floor as she wound her arms around his neck. He swept her into his arms and held her tight, like he'd never let go. He couldn't get enough of her. And if this limited amount of time they had left was all she could give him, he'd take it. Precious moments like this would only be a memory after she left, but he wasn't going to turn away from the here and now.

She eventually broke the kiss and sent him a mischievous grin. "This isn't why I got you out of your house so early this morning."

"Really? I think this is a perfect way to start the day."

"Says the busy veterinarian who was hoping to sleep in on his day off?"

"Who needs sleep?" He placed a kiss on the end of her nose.

"Not people who have ideas."

She shimmied out of his embrace and picked up her notepad and pencil.

Ethan couldn't contain his grin. "Are you always like this when working on a project?"

"Worse."

"I find that hard to believe," he told her as he retrieved his coffee.

"Trust me. My staff turn off their phones when we're on location, this way I don't rush them ahead of our established meeting times. All I need is coffee and I'm good to go."

"Do you ever think your staff has a point?"

"Nope. Now, where were we?"

He exhaled a disappointed breath, much preferring kissing to conversation. "Evaluating how your sister is going to react."

Nicole clutched the notepad to her chest. "When we were kids, Addie always needed a push when it came to making a decision. Briana and I would be out the door and she was still debating the wisdom of whatever we were doing. I was shocked when she eloped with Josh. It was a very un-Addie thing to do."

Ethan recalled that Addie's husband had lost his life in the line of duty. "And yet you're still going to spring this on her?"

"I don't mean to be insensitive, especially in light of Josh's passing, but Addie needs a gentle nudge. She's sort of stuck, and this project would give her a goal." Nicole paused a moment, then said in a wry tone, "I was making lists for all of us when I was five years old."

"That, I believe."

Her shoulders lifted to her ears. "I know I'm a bit much."

"No way. You're just the right amount."

"Why, Ethan Price, I think that's the nicest thing anyone has ever said to me."

He chuckled. "And…?"

"And you are the kindest, most patient man I've ever met."

"I was kind of hoping for breathtakingly handsome and one-in-a-million catch, but I'll take what I can get."

She moved close and tapped the end of her pencil lightly on his chest. "You are, but I didn't want my compliments to go to your head."

"Too late."

She continued drawing. Ethan was content to watch her in her element. When she was finished, he asked, "What about upstairs?"

"We talked about maybe leasing the offices out. Make this a real multifunctional building."

"Think that's what your dad had in mind?"

Her smile dimmed. "I don't know what his intentions were."

"If you did, then you'd all come full circle?"

She put the pad away. "Not quite. Briana and I are making headway. If Addie doesn't think I'm butting in, we're good. I'm not sure about Taylor. I made sure that Mac took plenty of pictures when I staged the decorations at her storefront. Other than that, I'm not really sure how to approach her."

"You said she wanted to keep the building."

"Yes. Like me, she doesn't need it, but supports Addie." She waved her hand as if brushing something imaginary away. "Which is an entirely different can of worms. Their past is more tightly intertwined."

It was hard to keep track of all these Connelly family dynamics. "When do you have dinner with your family again?"

"Tonight. That's why I wanted to come here this morning. I have all day to make notes to back my case that Addie should take the plunge and do this.

It's easier to make a decision when you have all the facts in front of you."

"I'd love to be a fly on the wall when you tell her."

"How about I fill you in afterward. I may need someone to say 'I told you so.'"

"I wouldn't do that, but if it's a reason for you to stop by, I'll take it."

"Thanks, Ethan." She wrapped her arms around his waist. "It seems like the minute I arrived in Golden I've been intruding in your life."

He returned the gesture, savoring her warmth. "You've definitely added color."

"Like when I first chased Gus into your back-yard?"

"You and Gus have livened up our lives."

"So, you're saying you'll miss us when we're gone?"

His mood deflated. "More than I anticipated."

Her face softened. "Ethan, I don't want—"

The ring from his cell phone cut her off. "Hold on." They moved apart and he tugged the phone from his back pocket and met Nicole's gaze. "It's Faith."

Concern crossed her features.

"Faith, what's going on?"

"Sorry to bother you, Ethan, but Holly had a spill and she needs you."

NICOLE WAS FURIOUS with herself for dragging Ethan away from his daughter, especially when she read the fear on his face. Holly had been excited to see her friends, but from the little Ethan had relayed about Faith's call, it sounded as though Holly was hurt.

She locked up the building in a hurry, then jumped into Ethan's car. It didn't take long to reach the Donovan residence. There were two police cars in the driveway. One belonged to Roan Donovan, but what about the other vehicle?

"Is that Brady's police car?" Ethan asked in a stilted tone.

"Maybe he was just visiting."

At least that's what Nicole hoped. What if this was a horrible emergency?

As soon as the car stopped, they both ran to the front door. Roan already held it open. "It's okay," he told Ethan. "We have it under control."

Ethan didn't wait around for details and instead headed straight to his daughter, who sat on the floor in the living room.

"Daddy," she cried as Ethan lifted her into his arms.

"What happened, princess?"

Holly started crying. The other children started talking a mile a minute. Faith came in from the kitchen, the baby in her arms, Brady trailing her. It had been a long time since Nicole was in the middle of a family drama.

Faith whistled to get everyone's attention. "Holly fell when the kids were out front," she told Ethan. "She skinned her knee."

Holly shifted in Ethan's grasp, showing off her bandaged appendage. "It hurt, Daddy."

He kissed her head. "But you're okay otherwise?"

"Yes. Miss Faith made my boo-boo better."

When Ethan turned Holly so he could see her knee more clearly in the window light, she noticed Nicole.

"Daddy, put me down," she demanded.

He did as she ordered, and the little girl scrambled over to her. "Is Gus here?"

Nicole sank to Holly's height. "No, sweetie. He's at home."

"He would make my boo-boo better if I could see him."

Nicole had to press her lips together to keep from chuckling. Holly seemed to be milking the effect of her boo-boo. "You can see him in a little while."

That seemed to satisfy Holly. Soon, she joined the other children arguing over which movie to watch. They settled on a show featuring talking animals. Once they were enthralled, the adults drifted to the kitchen.

"Crisis averted," Brady said in his usual jovial tone.

Roan rolled his eyes at his boss. "Says the man who doesn't have children."

Ethan dropped down into a kitchen chair. "Your call took about five years off my life," he told Faith.

"Sorry. She was crying and nothing we did would calm her down. Trust me, I rocked my best mama skills, but Holly wasn't having any of it."

"I even offered her a piggyback ride," Roan said, clearly perplexed. "No one says no to those."

"She just wanted her dad," Faith pointed out, patting her husband's chest as she passed by. "Now, coffee everyone?"

Still feeling bad about taking Ethan away from his daughter, Nicole hovered in the doorway. She was an outsider. Yes, she'd grown up with Faith and Brady, but their lives had moved in different directions. Did she have anything in common with them anymore?

Brady waved her over. "Hey, Trouble, Get in here."

Ethan slanted her a questioning glance. "Trouble?"

Figures he'd pick up on that. "An old nickname," she said, glaring at Brady.

"Which apparently you haven't outgrown," Brady added.

"What does that mean?"

He hitched a thumb over his shoulder. "The crying five-year-old."

"What did I have to do with that?"

"She wanted your dog."

"Oh. Well, he's the real trouble and he's at home."

"Hopefully," Ethan muttered.

Brady tilted his head.

"He runs off," she explained.

Brady sent her a direct look over her choice of words.

"What is this? Pick-on-Nicole day?"

Her old friend conjured up a boyish grin. "Just like old times, right, Faith?"

Faith placed a tray of bakery goodies on the table. "All I remember is you bringing out the worst in us, Brady."

"Now, that sounds right," Roan said as he snatched a cherry pastry.

The teasing continued. Nicole noticed that Ethan seemed preoccupied. She made her way to his side, taking a seat beside him. "Are you okay?" she asked in a quiet tone.

"Yeah." He ran a hand through his hair. "My pulse has finally slowed down."

"I'm sorry."

"Why? You didn't cause Holly to get hurt."

"No, but if I hadn't decided to drag you out this morning, she would have been safe and unharmed."

"Things happen when you have children," he said. "And I like hanging out with you, so we're okay."

But all Nicole could think was, what if things hadn't turned out okay? What if Holly had been seriously hurt? It was bad enough when Nicole had lost Holly in the store—terrifying, really—but Holly had been fine. Today could have been so much worse.

"Daddy!" Holly called from the living room.

Ethan rose and went to her, leaving Faith to take his place beside Nicole.

"You look worse for wear."

Nicole hid a grimace. "The scare freaked me out."

"She's fine."

"But what if she wasn't?"

Faith settled the baby across her chest. "No good comes from getting hung up on worst-case scenarios. Trust me, this was a blip."

"Feels more like earthquake territory to me."

"Not around kids much?" Faith asked with a chuckle.

"How about not at all."

Faith studied her. "You really care about Ethan and Holly, don't you?"

"Isn't it obvious?"

"I haven't seen you in forever, Nicole," Faith said as a frown formed. "And when we did hang out together, we both were hiding from the pain of our family lives."

Nicole remembered. All the hurt and embarrassment had led her to hanging out with a group of kids that were real trouble, and not in the teasing way she'd just experienced with Brady. Thankfully, they'd all made it out, with Brady going into law enforcement and Faith raising her family. But what did Nicole have to show for the years she'd been gone? A barely furnished condo where she lived alone, her mother missing her and a spotty relationship with her sisters.

Seems Faith and Brady had overcome the past. To her displeasure, Nicole came to the conclusion that she had some catching up to do.

As the chaos wound down, the disquiet in the pit of Nicole's stomach grew. What was she thinking getting involved in Ethan's life? She was used to being alone. Traveling for her job. Going where she wanted when she wanted. Ethan didn't have that luxury. Nor did he want it if his devotion to his daughter was any indication. Golden was home to them now.

Nicole watched the group interact with the ease of friends who'd spent years in and out of each other's lives. She'd gotten close to a man who wouldn't just pick up and leave town. Would it be so awful to fall in love with a wonderful man like Ethan and live in Golden? Rekindle her relationship with her sisters? Belong to a group of friends who knew her past, but it didn't define who she was to them? Did she want all this? The drama? The pain? The happiness? The hope?

From deep down came a resounding yes.

CHAPTER FOURTEEN

"Do you think anything we've done has made a difference?" Celeste asked as she poured steaming water from a floral decorated teapot into Linda's matching cup. They'd met early Monday morning to compare notes because Nicole's time in Golden was running out fast.

Sunlight poured through the window, bathing the kitchen in bright light. In this room, Celeste had held countless conversations about love, life and happiness.

"I'm not sure. I love my daughter, but she's hard to read."

Celeste took a seat and hooked a finger around the cup handle. "True. Even when asked pointed questions."

Linda took a sip of the organic blend. "The girls were over for Sunday dinner last night. I was quite pleased that Nicole interacted with her sisters. She and Briana seem to have made strides in their relationship, Addie was surprised, but pleased by the research Nicole put together for the fitness center, and Taylor is still quiet when she's with us."

"Did Nicole say anything to give you hope?"

"She came armed with a plan to convince Addie that the fitness center is worth the risk. She also made sure to talk to Taylor about her shop and the merchants' social-media platforms. It was more conversation than I've heard in years."

"Nicole is making strides then."

"On the surface. They all seemed okay, but there are undercurrents I can't get a handle on."

"Let's focus on Nicole for right now."

Linda sat back in her chair. "I asked about the promotion—she changed the subject. I asked about Dr. Price—she told me how Briana brought an injured kitten to the clinic. I asked about Holly—she talked about Gus. I can't get a candid answer from her. I love her, but the way she redirects is very frustrating."

"She has mastered that art. Just like her father."

Linda's facial muscles went tight. "I'd advise you to keep that comparison to yourself."

"True. It wouldn't be well-received."

With a sigh, Linda said, "We've encouraged the townspeople to engage with her. You've gotten Nicole into situations with the Price family. I think we've done all we can do."

"There's still the love angle," Celeste went on, undeterred. "She's spent significant time with Dr. Price. A romance could change her mind."

"I honestly don't think she'd take the chance." Linda rested her elbows on the floral tablecloth. "If we're banking on love, then it has to root its way deep into Nicole's heart." Linda paused as if trying to come up with her next words. "I've no doubt of her capacity to love, but she's shut herself off from us for a long time. Do you think she can finally believe that she belongs?"

"She'll be leaving much too soon," Celeste muttered under her breath. She rose and paced the well-worn treads of the floor until she stopped, tapping her chin with one finger. "I have one last idea that might show Nicole that she's wanted here."

Interest gleamed in Linda's eyes. "What is it?"

"As we've been working around town, I've spoken on the sly to the merchants and others who have had photos taken for the magazine. I suggested a surprise party in the park to thank Nicole just before she leaves. She'll realize that all the folks are grateful for her hard work. By getting together to celebrate a job well done, she'll have to see that it's time to come home."

"Are you sure arranging a party isn't too much? You seem to be slow on your feet since you started working with Nicole."

Celeste discarded the notion with a flick of her wrist. "I've enjoyed getting out. One can only sit at home for so long."

"Still…"

"I'm fine," Celeste declared in a steely tone.

"Okay," Linda said. "I like the idea. But only if I can help you get the word out."

"Deal."

Linda stared out the window in the direction of the cottage next door. "Let's hope this works."

NICOLE'S FINAL DAYS in Golden were winding down. Late Thursday morning she sat outside Sit A Spell with Sharon Briscoe, drinking coffee and planning Sharon's son's birthday party. In a million years, Nicole would never have envisioned this scenario. Sharon had been part of the larger group of kids who'd made Nicole's life miserable in high school. Now, Sharon was gushing over Nicole's birthday-themed ideas.

Sitting with the stylish woman, Nicole was glad she'd dressed in a sundress for the meeting. She supposed that when she moved up to management and was in the office more, she'd have to start dressing more professionally. Maybe she could ask Taylor for some fashion tips since that wasn't Nicole's forte.

"I can't tell you how much this means to me," Sharon said as she picked up the cell phone she'd laid on the table. Now that the meeting was finished, she dropped it in her purse. "I wasn't sure you'd have enough time to fit me in before you left."

"Just because the staging is wrapping up doesn't mean I don't mind giving you a few pointers."

"A few? I have enough ideas for the next ten years of birthday parties."

Nicole chuckled. "Glad I could help."

"You know, we could use a good party planner in Golden." Her eyes twinkled. "Hint, hint."

"I appreciate the suggestion, but I have to get

back to Savannah." She still had to give her boss an answer concerning the promotion. Find out if he'd go for her expansion idea. Yet she wasn't in a hurry to drive home to her empty condo.

"Well, if you ever get homesick, you're welcome to set up shop here." Sharon stood. "It was good seeing you again, Nicole."

Nicole blinked. "Um, same."

Sharon waved and hurried off to her next destination.

Sitting back, Nicole watched Golden as it came to life this weekday morning. Tourists, shop owners and locals alike were busy either sightseeing, manning their stores, or running errands. There was electricity in the air that she'd never experienced before. Granted, when she was younger, she'd never been aware of town dynamics, but after having spent several weeks in the small mountain town, she couldn't deny that Golden was growing on her.

As she viewed Main Street, she noticed that some of the seasonal decorations remained outside the stores, even after the photographing had been completed. Most of the town's inventory had been returned to the storage unit, but the things that Nicole wasn't taking back to Savannah remained. A small smile took shape. Nicole had made a difference. Why did this job feel so different than the others?

The only dark cloud over the week came from not seeing Ethan often. They'd both been so busy, they hadn't carved out time to spend together. After the last day they'd spent with his friends—well, hers too—had he decided to step back? He had a community in Golden and she wasn't a part of it.

She missed him though. Missed the way he encouraged her to reveal her inner self. Missed his kisses. Just being with him, even if they were silent. Somehow, he'd managed to breach the barriers she'd erected around her heart.

Holly had been absent, as well. She'd had school functions to attend and sleepovers at the Donovan house if Ethan had an emergency at the clinic. Nicole had thought her last week in Golden would have included adventures with the Price family. As much as she hated the thought, maybe not seeing them would make it easier when the time came to go.

Her phone dinged. A text came from Mac, asking her to meet him for the last photo session before he left for his next project. Excited, she grabbed her bag and hurried down the sidewalk.

It didn't take long to reach Linda's General Store. Her mother stood on the wide porch talking to Mac. This, and the surprise she'd arranged for the shop owners, would be her lasting mark on Golden.

"Hi, Mom," she called out as she reached them.

"Nicole," she greeted, then craned her neck. "Where's Celeste?"

"My ever-present assistant decided to stay home today."

Worry pinched her mother's brow. "That doesn't seem like her, especially since this is the final photo session."

Nicole thought about that and said, "She seemed kind of tired, so I didn't argue with her. I'll check on her when I go home."

"And I'll give her a call," her mother said, side-tracked.

"I'm sure Celeste is fine," Nicole assured her mother.

"Anything I can do?" Mac asked, getting in on the conversation. "I have to admit, Celeste has grown on me."

"Mac was just telling me he's leaving us," her mother complained. Nicole held back an eye roll at the use of *us*.

"No one told me." Her mother leveled a narrow gaze at Nicole. "I suppose you'll be leaving too?"

"I was always going back to Savannah, Mom."

Her mother pouted. Seems Mac had worked his charm on the women of Golden, including her mother.

Mac winked at her mom. "But I did promise I'd be back."

"Don't forget."

"I won't."

Mac hopped down the steps to join Nicole. "The staging looks good."

"It does."

She'd gotten Brady to help her move the sleigh from the storage unit to just outside her mom's store. Between the local garden shop, her mother's yard and Celeste's gardens, the sleigh was overflowing with flowers of all types and colors. There were so many, the overflow had gone into pots and baskets on the ground, scattered around the sleigh.

"I wasn't sure I'd be able to pull it off."

Mac hitched his head toward the store. "Your mom is pleased."

Nicole agreed. Seeing her mother happy was all Nicole wanted.

"This special setup is for her. She's been so invested with this magazine feature."

"And she's your mom."

"There is that."

Mac started taking pictures from different angles. The camera clicked with each shot. Nicole stood back, conflicted about her feelings. This was the last official staging in Golden. Soon she'd be headed back to Savannah and her life there. Would it feel the same?

While Mac was working, Nicole's phone rang. Fishing it out of her backpack, she frowned when she read the screen.

"Mr. Sanders."

"Hello, Nicole. Did I catch you while you're working?"

"I'm at the final location with Mac."

"And then you'll be wrapping up?"

"I will."

"Then I'm glad I was able to reach you."

Nerves took flight in her stomach. The boss didn't usually call while she was on a project unless there was a problem.

"Is something wrong?"

"On the contrary. I wanted to personally inform you that I seriously considered your expansion idea. I'd like to speak to you about implementing the new division you proposed when you get back before introducing it to the board."

He saw the merit of her concept? Nicole was speechless.

"You'll still move up in management as part of your promotion, but I'll need you to flesh out the boutique idea with more precision and present it to the board. Then we can come to a final verdict."

"Wow. I don't know what to say."

"Say you'll be here bright and early on Monday ready to move in a new direction."

Still stunned, she said, "Thank you. I'll be there."

"I have to run."

"Of course. I'll see you next week, Mr. Sanders."

She ended the call, dumbstruck by the news.

"You look like you just lost your best friend," Mac remarked.

"What?"

"Your face. It isn't happy."

It wasn't? But this was what she'd dreamed of. Why she'd put in the long hours in the company. It was all falling into place.

"That was my boss. Remember I told you about the promotion?"

"Yeah. You're seriously going to take it?"

"I think I have to."

The way his eyebrows angled telegraphed his confusion.

"I also floated an expansion idea by him at our last meeting. He's interested."

Mac sent her his patented charming grin. "Hey, that's great."

"It is. I'll have to head back to Savannah right away and tweak the proposal before Monday.

"That isn't much time."

True, but she had to go for it. "I can do it. I've had tighter deadlines before."

He held out his fist and she raised hers for a bump. "Then congrats."

Over his shoulder, Nicole noticed her mother making her way toward them.

"I'd like to keep this quiet," she said into his ear.

A frown replaced his grin when he stepped back. "Why?"

"My mom was hoping I'd want to move back home."

He lifted one shoulder. "I don't see why you don't. Golden is great."

She tried not to show her shock. "You actually like it here?"

"I do." He turned his head and smiled at Nicole's mother as she stopped before them. In a louder voice he said, "After all, I promised Linda I'd be back."

Her mother playfully slapped his arm. "Oh, Mac. You're something else."

Something, that was for sure.

"Don't move from that spot. I have a care package for you since you'll be traveling."

Mac placed a hand on his chest. "Be still my heart."

Her mother giggled. Giggled!

As she walked away, Nicole said, "It's probably best you're on to your next job. I don't think the female population can survive much more of you."

Mac sent her a wink. "If I didn't know you so well, I'd think you were jealous."

"And you'd be wrong."

He placed his camera in the bag and casually asked, "The veterinarian?"

She tried to cover the truth as she said, "Why do you ask?"

"Just a vibe I'm getting from you two."

Vibe? Nicole was sure it was more than that.

"Dr. Price has a practice here and I have a job in Savannah. Long distance won't work for either of us."

"Shame. Happiness looks good on you."

Nicole's cheeks heated.

Mac chuckled. "I have the prints you ordered."

"Oh, Mac, thanks."

He removed a large yellow envelope from his bag. "You have a good eye. I would have picked the same photos as you did."

Mac had allowed her to peruse his computer after he'd downloaded the pictures he'd amassed from the last two weeks. After he highlighted the final picks being sent to the magazine, she'd ordered prints of very specific locations for very special people.

"After you trusted me with your catalog of photos, I had to choose the best."

He handed her the envelope. "Nice thing about digital. I can have the prints processed quickly."

"I can't thank you enough." She hugged the envelope to her chest.

He shrugged like it was no big deal.

"Also, the nature shots you took are amazing."

He frowned. "Those are just for me."

"I didn't mean to pry, but once I came across a few, I wanted to see more. Ever thought about doing your own thing? Getting away from the commercial end of photography?"

"Maybe someday. Right now, my schedule's too packed."

Her mom exited the store, carrying a big bag. She handed it to Mac. "For you."

He held up his score. "Did you empty out the store?"

"It's snacks and souvenirs of your time in Golden."

"This was very generous of you."

She shrugged. "This is Golden at its best."

A car pulled into the parking lot. "That's it for me, Nic. Headed to the airport." Mac gestured to the waiting SUV.

On impulse, Nicole gave him a hug. "It was an honor to work with you."

"Same. Let's do it again."

He embraced Nicole's mom, then stepped back to bestow upon them a huge smile. "Until we meet again."

"Do you have time to run inside and say good-bye to Alyssa?"

"No, ah… We said our goodbyes."

He gathered his camera bags and luggage and got into the rideshare that would take him to the airport. After one final wave, Nicole and her mom stood beside the sleigh of flowers. She inhaled the sweet aroma, savoring the scent of summer.

Her mom wiped away tears. "I'm going to miss that young man."

Nicole looped her arm through her mother's as they walked to the store. "And will Alyssa?"

Her mother met her curious gaze. "They started a friendship when he would come into the store. I think there was a bit of flirting going on between them, but my manager is tight-lipped."

"Interesting."

On the porch, they parted ways. Nicole claimed a rocking chair to sit and remove the prints from the envelope. She'd come up with this idea after the first day she'd spoken to Mrs. Olsen. The older woman had wanted a memento of the decorating in Golden—Nicole had sensed it. That's when she'd decided to ask Mac for any unused pictures to hand out as a gift to the businesses that had participated in the project. Each one had her smiling as she re-called what had transpired between the merchants, Celeste and Mac. How her staging was featured in each shot. Once she'd flipped through them all, she found one in particular and set it on top. This one deserved a special delivery.

She dashed inside to tell her mom she was leaving, then made her last stop for the day before heading home.

Just before arriving at Taylor's store, she stopped on the sidewalk. Since Nicole had been in town, a new sign had gone up over the store. Vintage to Modern. It was official, Taylor had become the newest owner of the only fancy clothing store in town.

Nicole opened the door. The scent of potpourri, along with the new fabric smell, tickled her nose as soon as she walked in. Clothing hung neatly on racks dispersed around the floor. Accessories were displayed on wall shelves. Glancing around the inviting entrance to the store, she spied her half sister behind the counter, an antique mahogany sideboard with the drawers facing the customer, pulled out with merchandise tucked inside each one. Taylor glanced up to greet her customer, her smile slipping when she saw it was Nicole.

"Hey," Nicole said as she walked across the sales floor. "Are you busy?"

Taylor's gaze moved around the empty store. "You just beat the rush."

Was that humor? Where were her customers? "Are you—"

Taylor cut her off, twisting the diamond earring in one earlobe. "I haven't gotten the word out that new management is open for business. It's been a bit slow."

Nicole hooked her thumb over her shoulder. "Nice sign out front."

Taylor lit up. "Thanks."

"I won't keep you long, but I have something for you." She took a photo from the envelope and handed it to Taylor.

Her half sister stared at it for a long moment. "It's my store," she said in a hushed voice.

The picture had been taken first thing in the morning. Nicole had set up flowers for a spring-time Easter visual. The sidewalk had been damp, and the light shone on the window to reveal the tasteful mannequins showing off some of Taylor's inventory. It was a perfect representation of fine taste and small-town charm. Best of all, in one corner, the camera had caught Nicole and Taylor in conversation.

"Mac let me scroll through the photos he'd taken so I could make copies for some of the folks around town. I saw this one and knew you had to have it."

Taylor met her gaze. "I don't know what to say."

Nicole pointed to the wall behind her. "Say you'll frame it. Instead of a dollar bill from your first sale that most stores display, you have a photo of the store when you first took over."

Taylor laid it down, running her finger over the edge of the print. "This was so...thoughtful."

"Which I haven't always been," Nicole admitted.

Taylor's head lifted and the sisters locked eyes. Nicole swallowed hard before continuing.

"When things got tough, we should have all banded together. I was the first to cut and run. It was my way of dealing with the pain of our dad's actions, but I caused others pain, as well."

Taylor's initial surprise faded, and she nodded. "None of us handled it well."

"I know my mom has wrapped you in the arms of our family and I want to say that going forward, I hope we can get to know each other better."

Hope gleamed in Taylor's eyes. "You're coming back to Golden?"

"Oh, no. I just mean, I won't be a stranger."

Taylor seemed disappointed. "I thought for sure you'd stay."

"Because of the building Dad left us?"

"No, I think you've given Addie a lot to think about when it comes to her fitness center, so we're all on the same page about that."

"Then what?"

"Dr. Price. You two have been spending lots of time together."

Nicole tried to downplay the truth. "We were, but I have to go back to the office."

"That's a shame. You two seem like a good match."

Nicole thought so, but also knew the obstacles to building a relationship would be difficult to over-come, especially now that her boss was interested in her boutique proposal.

"I will be back and all of us will meet at Mom's and put this shaky past behind us."

Taylor smiled. For once, it seemed genuine, not forced. "I look forward to it."

Nicole said goodbye, picked up Gus from doggy day care and drove home. The entire way her mind filled with thoughts of Ethan. Leaving him was going to be a lot harder than she'd imagined.

Once home, Nicole changed into a more comfortable pair of lounge pants and tank top, hoping for a quiet night. She'd start that proposal for Mr. Sanders, sort the prints she'd deliver to the merchants and others before she left, start packing...

The sound of barking stopped her thoughts. Familiar barking.

"Gus?"

She left the bedroom to find the living room empty. As she went into the kitchen, she found the back door wide open. "Not again."

The barking increased as she walked out to the patio. She saw Gus next door at Celeste's house.

"Gus, get back here!"

Instead of obeying, the barking grew more frantic. That's when she noticed Celeste slumped at the bottom of her back steps.

CHAPTER FIFTEEN

"CELESTE!" NICOLE CRIED out as she sprinted across the grass to reach her neighbor. Gus continued barking, putting Nicole's nerves on edge. She came to a clumsy stop and dropped to her knees in the grass before Celeste, relieved to find her neighbor conscious.

"Celeste, are you okay?"

"Just a bit lightheaded."

It was more than that. The color had leached out of her face.

"Let me call 911."

"No." Celeste reached out to stop Nicole, but her hand dropped as if the energy had drained from her. "I was coming to see you," she said, her voice thready.

"That doesn't matter right now." As Nicole patted her pants pockets, she realized her phone was in the cottage. Not knowing what else to do, she yelled, "Gus, get help."

The dog took off, running in the direction she'd hoped he go. Unsure if she should move Celeste, Nicole ran her hands over the woman's arms. "Did you fall?"

"No. I had to sit down." She fumbled for something in the pocket of her dress. "This is yours. The mail mixed it with mine."

As Celeste shoved the envelope toward her, Nicole took it, folded it in half and stuffed it in the pocket of her pants.

"Can you move?"

Celeste blinked at her a few times.

"Celeste, do you understand me?"

"Yes, I…"

The woman started to slump even lower onto her side.

What should Nicole do? She didn't want to leave her alone, but she didn't have her phone. Could she risk running into Celeste's house to use her landline?

If possible, Celeste grew even more pale. Nicole moved to the step and let Celeste lean on her. "What can I do?"

"Just let me rest. I'll be good as gold in a minute."

The weakness in her tone made Nicole even more nervous. "Can you make it inside?"

"Let me catch my breath."

Why would she need to catch her breath when she was merely sitting?

Deciding she needed to move, Nicole was in the process of lifting Celeste when the barking started again. She lifted her head to see Gus, Ethan and Holly running their way.

Relief overtook her. "Thank goodness."

"Nicole, what's going on?" Ethan asked as he crouched before them.

"Celeste is having trouble breathing,"

"I'll be fine," Celeste insisted again.

"I don't have my phone," Nicole told Ethan. He had his handy and dialed the emergency number. "Yes. There is a woman in need of medical attention." He rattled off the situation and address then hung up. "Help will be here soon."

"There's no need for all this fuss," Celeste muttered, her voice raspy. "I just needed to give Nicole her mail."

"Which will wait," Nicole reassured her. "We need to focus on you right now."

Ethan reached out to take Celeste's pulse. His face grew more serious when he met Nicole's gaze.

Not good.

"Should we bring her inside?" she asked Ethan.

"No. It's best to keep her calm and still until the paramedics arrive."

Nicole tightened her arm around Celeste as if by sheer force of her will, Celeste would be okay.

"You're a good girl…" She barely heard Celeste say it.

"Please, just hang in there," Nicole pleaded.

"Daddy," Holly called out, her arms around Gus, tears on her cheeks. She had to be terrified.

"It's okay, princess." Ethan's calm voice assured his daughter and Nicole. "I called for help."

In the distance, Nicole heard the faint wail of sirens. The group huddled around Celeste as the sound drew closer. Soon, there was the rumble of the ambulance engine. Ethan ran around to the front of the house to lead the paramedics to the patient.

Two men arrived carrying medical bags, which they placed on the ground. Nicole recognized one of them from high school. She was loath to move away from her friend until they insisted, needing to evaluate Celeste. As they went to work, Ethan took Nicole's hand, tugging her to him. He wrapped her in his embrace. She held on to him as she watched the scene play out before her.

Gus nudged Nicole's leg. Holly hovered near him. Bending down, Nicole went to pull her close, but Ethan beat her to it and lifted Holly. In his arms, she circled her father's neck with her small arms and hid her face in his neck. Nicole placed her arms around both of them.

"I didn't know what we were going to find when we came running." His gaze moved to Holly, indicating to Nicole that he was troubled that he'd made Holly upset.

"How could you?"

"When Gus was barking out of control, my first reaction was that something had happened to you. I went racing out the door. I should have thought…"

Nicole shook her head. She spoke her hope out loud. "Don't. Everyone will be fine."

One of the paramedics had radioed the hospital to give an update. Celeste was given oxygen, then moved to the gurney and wheeled to the driveway.

Nicole's heart ached as she followed, wondering what was to become of her friend.

Realizing they'd be taking Celeste to the hospital, Nicole ran inside to find her purse, then returned to join Ethan and Holly.

After Celeste was loaded, one of the paramedics came to them. "They'll get her started on fluids in the ambulance. I can't give you a timeline of how long she'll be in the ER."

Nicole handed him Celeste's purse. "Can we go to the hospital? Be there for her?"

"You aren't family, Nicole. They won't give you any updates." The paramedic frowned. "Speaking of family, didn't Mrs. Johnson's daughter move away?"

"To Atlanta."

"I'll inform the hospital so they can contact her."

With that, he and his partner placed their gear in the ambulance, climbed in the back with Celeste, closed the door and left. The trio stood in Celeste's front yard. Nicole didn't know what to do next.

Ethan lowered Holly to the ground and took Nicole by her shoulders. "You don't look so good yourself."

Nicole ran a shaky hand through her hair. "I'm... The shock of finding Celeste hasn't worn off yet."

"Let's go inside."

He led her to the cottage. They all trooped into the kitchen. She needed to keep busy, so she went to take a box of tea from the pantry. Ethan stopped her.

"Nope." He turned her in the direction of the living room. "Go take a seat. I'll make us some tea."

Suddenly sapped of energy now that the crisis had passed, she did as he instructed. When she reached the couch, she sank into the plush cushions. Gus followed, whining at her feet occasionally. She reached out to brush her listless fingers over his fur. Holly climbed onto the couch and cuddled beside her. Nicole wrapped her arm around Holly, feeling a slight tremble.

"Will Miss Celeste be okay?"

"The doctors are going to take good care of her," Nicole assured Holly as much as herself.

"She looked sad."

Stroking Holly's curls, Nicole said, "That's because she didn't feel good."

Holly huddled closer. "I want her to babysit me again."

"As soon as the doctors fix her up, I'm sure she'll be happy to watch you."

The whistle from the teapot sounded from the kitchen. Nicole held on to Holly. Moments later, Ethan appeared with two steaming mugs. He set them on the coffee table in front of Nicole.

"Daddy, I don't want tea."

"I have juice in the refrigerator," Nicole told him.

One dark eyebrow arched.

"I like juice," she huffed. It wasn't like she'd bought the jug just in case Holly came over and was thirsty.

With his outstretched hand, Ethan tugged Holly from the couch, and they went into the kitchen. Nicole reached out for the mug, held it between both hands, but didn't drink. Her stomach was swirling too much to take a swallow, but the warmth from the ceramic mug felt good.

Tears filled her eyes. She was anxious about Celeste and grateful to Ethan. He didn't have to stick around. Didn't have to rush their way when Gus's barking alerted him to the emergency. But he had. They'd dealt with the situation together. Which never happened to her because she'd always chosen to be alone.

Ethan and Holly walked back into the room. He stopped to place a kiss on the top of her daughter's head. Holly smiled at him.

The scene in front of her had Nicole's heart pounding. She rubbed the heel of her palm across her shirt.

Oh, no. Had she fallen in love with Ethan?

What did she do now?

Holly noticed Gus's toys in the corner and wanted to investigate. Ethan gave her the okay and lowered himself beside Nicole.

"Feeling any less shaky?"

"Not really." She set down the mug. Between her revelation about loving Ethan and worrying about Celeste, she would be shaky for more than a little while. "Any clue what's going on with Celeste?"

"I overheard the paramedics talking about her high blood pressure. Although, I don't know what that means, exactly." He took her hand. "I'm not an MD."

"I know, I just thought…"

"I get it. You want answers."

Her shoulders sagged. "Apparently, I'm going to have to wait to get them."

"Hospital protocol."

"Do you think we should go, anyway?"

"Why not give the doctors some time. We can go over later."

Her voice hitched. "I hate the idea of Celeste all alone."

"She isn't alone." He leaned closer. Their shoulders brushed. "The capable doctors and nurses are with her."

Nicole sighed. "You're right."

"What happened?" Ethan finally asked after they sat in the quiet for a long moment. The steady rhythm of his thumb brushing against her palm calmed her.

"I'd just come home from work and changed. My next stop was going to Celeste's house to check on her. My mom was worried because Celeste didn't come to the last photo shoot with me today. She was concerned when I told her Celeste was too tired to tag along."

Ethan's thumb stilled. "Remember the night we went to the clinic and Celeste watched Holly? She appeared worn out to me then. I asked if she was okay, and she convinced me she was fine."

Nicole shivered. "She tried to do the same when she was slumped against me on her back stairs."

"Is she always this stubborn?"

"Apparently so."

Nicole burrowed into his side. He dropped a kiss into her hair. His strength and warmth were all she needed right now. "Celeste was all worried about some piece of my mail that got mixed in with hers. Like that matters."

Ethan shifted toward her. "You know she cares about you, right?"

Nicole lifted her head. Her eyes met his. "I know. And darn it, she lured me into a friendship by steadily insisting that I needed her help. But honestly, I enjoyed every minute with her. Running errands. Talking. She's one special lady."

"She is."

"And I think she misses her family, so I was happy to step in."

With her head resting on Ethan's shoulder, Nicole closed her eyes. The past hour had been earth-shattering, first with Celeste's emergency and then the shock of just how deep her feelings for Ethan had become.

"Daddy, look."

Nicole opened her eyes when Holly skipped over with one of Gus's toys in her hand. "It's like a prize from my birthday party last year."

Not surprisingly, the toy was a stuffed elf. Nicole had picked it up just before she'd started her holiday-related project.

"It does."

"Can we have a party again this year?"

Nicole marveled at how quickly children could snap back to normal. Holly had been worried, but her father's presence told her everything would be okay, and she could be a kid again.

Ethan smiled. "You bet, princess. It's a while off though."

"I know." She moved the toy around in her hands, then her gaze moved to Nicole.

"You'll be here for my birthday and Christmas, won't you?"

Which was many months away. Before Nicole could answer, Holly jumped up and down.

"Oooh, you can plan my party!"

Nicole sat up. Her heart melted. She didn't think when she said, "I'd love that."

His lips tightening in the corners, Ethan sent Nicole a warning.

"It'll be special," Holly said. "Like having a real mommy."

A HEAVY SILENCE fell over the room. Holly turned her attention back to Gus, but Ethan's gut clenched like he'd just been kicked in the stomach. Nicole worried her lower lip between her teeth. Just as he'd predicted, Holly was way too attached to Nicole. Just as he was.

Admit it, you're in love with Nicole.

He ran a hand down his face, expelling a long breath at the revelation. Nicole squeezed his arm. He rose, heading to the kitchen. He wasn't surprised when she followed.

"I'm sorry. I didn't think she'd react that way."

He turned on her, panic morphing into anger in

his chest. "What did you expect? You've become important to her, Nicole. To both of us."

"Ethan. I—"

"Is this the part where you tell me it's been nice knowing me, but you have to get back to your real life?"

"That's not fair."

"Isn't it?" He locked his gaze to hers. "Have you made a decision about the promotion?"

"It's complicated."

How could he have blindly thought Nicole would change her mind. That she'd stick around. Choose him over her life elsewhere.

"It's really not. Either you're staying or leaving."

She opened her mouth, but no words came out.

His heart sank when he read the reticence in her eyes. "I guess you've made your decision."

"No. I have to tie things up before…"

"Before what? Deciding we're good enough for you?"

"Ethan! Of course, you are. Probably too good for me."

He began to pace the kitchen. Needed to keep moving to keep the pain sliding through his body at bay. "I never should have let things go this far. I won't let you break Holly's heart." He stopped. Spun to her. "I let her mother do that once. Never again."

"That's why I want to have a clean plate before I commit."

"Commit? Really?" He almost wanted to laugh out loud. Would have if his heart hadn't been shattered. "Because from where I'm standing, you're simply running."

She reared back like his words had struck a bull's-eye.

He ran a hand over his mouth and chin. "Let's be honest. I'm in love with you, Nicole. You're not ready. And I refuse to be a placeholder in another woman's life while you figure out what you want. I've already done that, have the scars inside to prove it. I can't…no, I won't do it again."

A heavy pall settled over them. All the light and cheeriness had been sucked out of the kitchen. Ethan wasn't sure he could breathe.

"I was always honest about going back to Savannah," Nicole said quietly.

"You were. And I ignored the signs. That's on me."

"Ethan…"

He straightened his shoulders. "Holly!" he called.

Nicole's eyes went wide. "You're leaving?"

"Yes, before you can, so I don't have to explain to Holly why you're gone."

Holly jogged into the kitchen, a bright smile on her adorable face, no clue to the undercurrents eddying around them.

"It's time to go home, princess."

"Aw, Daddy, I want to play."

"Playtime is over. Say goodbye to Nicole."

Holly rushed over to hug Nicole's legs. Nicole's hand ruffled through Holly's hair, hesitating as if knowing this was the last time.

"Wait," Nicole said. She disengaged from Holly

and hurried into the living room. Seconds passed before she returned. She handed a picture to Ethan. "I asked Mac to print some special shots for me."

In the photo, Holly was dressed in her elf costume, playing with Gus. The camera also caught Nicole in the background, her hands clasped over her heart.

His heart stuttered.

"I thought you might like this to remember the fun we had."

Ethan stared at the picture for a long time, both his chest and head pounding. This rejection hurt worse than when his ex-wife had left him. At least that had been the end and they both knew it. This, with Nicole, had only been the beginning.

Or so he'd hoped.

He tried to speak but had no voice. He cleared his dry throat. "Thank you."

Holly took his hand. Ethan met Nicole's gaze one last time, then left the cottage for good.

CHAPTER SIXTEEN

NICOLE WATCHED ETHAN and Holly walk across the lawn back to their house, the tears in her eyes making their progress blurry. On a choked sob, she closed the door and returned to the living room, falling facedown on the couch.

Gus came up to her, licking the only visible part of her face. She rolled over and stared at the ceiling. "I blew it, Gus."

Why hadn't she told Ethan that she wanted to stay?

Because you were always going to leave.

So, why did she feel like she'd just been run over by a tanker truck?

Bigger question, why hadn't she told Ethan she loved him?

You're afraid.

To her everlasting shame, she was. Were the actions of her father always going to haunt her? Ethan was nothing like him, yet still she hesitated. Could she be honest enough to admit she'd used her job as an excuse not to plunge into a relationship? What was wrong with her?

Coming back to Golden had not been what she'd anticipated. What were the odds of meeting Ethan and Holly, only to fall for them? She never figured in a friendship with Celeste, or the fact that she'd reach out to her sisters for a fresh start. All this had happened in less than a month, yet her fallback position was to flee.

As she pushed her legs off the couch to sit up, something crumpled under her. She reached into her pocket to find the forgotten envelope Celeste had decided was so important that she had to deliver it despite her ill health. She pulled it out and with a disgusted click of her tongue, tossed it on the table. Until she noticed the handwriting.

Nicole reached for the letter, curiosity rising in her. When she read the distinctive cursive on the envelope, her stomach dropped. She continued to stare. How was this possible?

She clutched the envelope, afraid of what was inside.

With shaking fingers, Nicole unsealed the flap and removed a single sheet of paper. Her eyes grew hot when she read the first line:

To my dear Nicole,

She dropped the letter onto her lap, her pulse racing. Was this a letter from her dad, like those he'd given to her sisters? A letter she didn't think she deserved.

Nicole hesitated. Did she want to know what was

inside? If so, she had to read it quickly, like removing a bandage from a wound.

Nicole picked up the letter and started again.

To my dear Nicole,

You're probably surprised that this letter came to you through the mail. By now, you will have discovered that the letters I left for your sisters were hand-delivered. Not trusting that you would take the envelope, I instructed my lawyer to mail it to you after you received the inheritance.

So, if you have decided to take a chance and read my final words, the first thing I want to tell you is that I love you.

Nicole squeezed her eyes shut. Tears escaped, streaming down her cheeks. She stayed like that for a long moment, then sniffled before she continued.

I have always loved you, but unfortunately, I let my selfishness and the circumstances I created blind me to the very gifts I had in my life. You were right to be angry with me. I took the easy way, blaming you for what I'd done. I earned your disdain. But once I'd realized what I'd lost, that's when I came to you for forgiveness. I'm not angry that you didn't give it. It was a longshot, but I had hoped to make peace with you before leaving this world. Now, I can only hope that you find it within yourself to forgive me and allow that forgiveness to remove the bitterness of my actions from your heart.

You have become a beautiful woman, Nicole. A success. I'm so proud of you. I won't see what the future brings you, but I believe it will be filled with happiness and love. I only wish I could be part of it.

I don't deserve a last request, but I'm going to ask, anyway. Please reunite with your sisters. Don't let the sisterhood die. You need each other, and Taylor needs you all. I'm hoping the gift of the Sinclair building will be the first step toward that end.

I love you, Nicole. Be good to yourself and live life like there's no tomorrow. You were always in my heart,
Dad

Nicole dropped the letter, racking sobs erupting from her chest.

Her father had reached out. Had included her in his final act. She didn't deserve his love after the way she'd shut him out, but he'd given it to her, anyway.

It took a long time before she ran out of tears and palmed the moisture from her face. Gus trotted over to lay his chin on her knee. She buried her face in his fur, taking solace from his presence.

As her father's words sunk deep within her, what they meant to her, peace settled over her.

"I forgive you, Dad," she whispered, understanding that she truly meant it.

A lightness she hadn't experienced in years spread over her. She smiled, recalling all the good times she'd shared with her father when she was young. That was the man who had written the final letter.

She dropped her head back to peer up at the ceiling. "Thank you."

Smoothing out the paper, she folded it and returned it to the envelope. What did she do now? She could rush next door and ask Ethan for another chance, but unless she made a firm commitment to him, what was the point? Did she stick around and be the girl next door, or go back to the life where she was alone?

She stared at her father's handwriting.

In her heart, she'd always known he loved her. She'd let the pain become an excuse to keep him away. To keep messy emotions away. Now, she felt like she had her father's blessing to move on with her life and not hold back.

You know what to do.

She eyed her cell phone on the coffee table and picked it up.

"I ASKED YOU to come by this morning because I have something to say to you," Nicole told her sisters. They stood outside the Sinclair building on Saturday morning, in a small circle, with varying expressions of curiosity, uncertainty and amusement on their faces.

"I know we've discussed keeping this building. Addie, it's up to you if you want to go forward with the fitness center. I think you should, but no pressure."

Addie frowned. "Where is my sister and what have you done with her?"

"I've had an epiphany."

Briana chuckled. "What brought that on?"

Nicole paused, then placed a hand over the back pocket of her jeans, where she'd tucked her father's final words to her. "I received a letter from Dad, after all."

Her sisters exchanged uneasy glances.

"Mine came in the mail, which is another story, but the bottom line is, we should work through our differences and make something of Dad's gift to us."

Briana blew out a whistle. "Wow. Okay."

"I forgave him. I needed to end my stubbornness for good concerning him."

Taylor's eyes shimmered in the bright sunlight. "I'm happy for you."

Nicole eyed her sisters. "You all read your letters, right?"

Addie's gaze shifted to the building. Briana stared down at her brightly painted toenails peeking out of her sandals. Taylor adjusted the purse strap on her shoulder.

"Look," Nicole said, reading the mood, "I can't tell you what to do, but reading the letter was cathartic. It could help you too."

No one responded.

Nicole slammed her hands on her hips. "Fine, I'll change the subject. I was thinking—"

Addie held up her hand to stop her. "Before you go on, you all should know that I've already started investigating opening the fitness center. A friend from Atlanta has been my sounding board and with his help, I think I can swing it."

"*His* help?" Nicole echoed.

"Yes. But that's not the point. The point is that I agree with all of you. We should keep the building."

Nicole grinned. "That's good because I have plans of my own that involve sharing the building."

"I thought you didn't need it," Taylor said.

"I didn't. Until I quit my job."

Addie's jaw dropped. "You did what?"

"I want to use the building too."

Briana crossed her arms over her chest. "Explain."

"I declined the promotion. Before I left, I had floated an idea about starting a boutique-party division within the company. Then I decided, wait, why don't I do it right here in Golden? Since I've been back, people have been asking for my expertise and I've been excited to share. I always loved the smaller, more intimate events when I worked for Lila. Now, I can go back to my roots. And I still have contacts in the area. So, I'd like to use one of the upstairs offices to open my own event-planning business."

"I'm not complaining," Briana said, "but what made you change your mind?"

Taylor grinned. "A certain veterinarian?"

Nicole's face heated. "Yes."

Addie clapped and cheered, "I knew it!"

"Yes, well, I'm in love with him and he loves me, but I blew it between us."

"So, moving to town does what?" Briana asked.

"Shows him I'm not going to run. I'm here for the long haul, just like he is. We can plant roots, grow a family." She stopped and blinked back hot tears. "If he'll listen."

"He will," tenderhearted Addie assured her.

Briana reached out her hand, palm down, in the middle of the circle. "I'm in."

After a prolonged beat, Addie placed her hand over Briana's. "Me too."

Nicole placed her hand on top. "Taylor?"

The fourth hesitated, but finally reached out and added her hand to the pile. "We are the Connelly sisters, after all."

They said in unison, "Here's to being sisters," and pumped up and down three times before drawing their hands back.

"Okay," Nicole said, having one area of her life resolved. "Now, I have a man to convince that I love him."

"Wait," Addie said. "Before you do, can you stop by the park first? Mom needs us for something."

"Okay, but it has to be quick. I don't want to give Ethan any more time than necessary to decide I'm a flight risk."

They walked down the sidewalk toward the park.

As they drew closer, Addie paused. Nicole almost bumped into her. "Are you okay?"

"Yes, I'm…"

She followed Addie's wide-eyed gaze to a tall man with ash-blond hair and broad shoulders headed in their direction. He looked familiar to Nicole, but she couldn't place him.

"Nolan," Addie whispered under her breath.

"Nolan Travers?" Briana asked. "The baseball player?"

"Yes, the one and only."

"Why is he here?" Taylor asked.

Addie smoothed her hair. "He's, um…"

"Let me guess," Nicole said. "Your Atlanta sounding board?"

Addie groaned.

"He's cute," Briana commented.

Taylor giggled.

"Yeah. He has that effect on women," Addie said with resignation.

"Maybe, but he sure seems focused on you," Nicole said as she linked arms with Briana and Taylor. "I think our sister needs a little private time."

They greeted Nolan in passing, then entered the park. To Nicole's surprise, there were lots of people gathered there. When they saw her, they all yelled, "Surprise!"

"What is this?" Nicole asked Briana out of the corner of her mouth.

"Celeste planned this going-away party for you.

To have everyone thank you for all the work you put into making the magazine photo shoot happen."

"But I'm not going away."

"Well, she didn't know it at the time."

Thankfully, Celeste had only spent one night in the hospital. When Nicole had gone to visit her, she'd learned that a cardiologist had diagnosed an irregular heartbeat and started her on medication. In time, she'd be good as new. Her daughter had driven up from Atlanta to stay with Celeste until she was back on her feet.

Nicole's mother walked over, her arm hooked with Celeste's, big smiles on both faces.

"We wanted to celebrate before you left," her mother said. "You put a lot of time and effort into your job and the town appreciates it."

She blinked. "I was all around town yesterday delivering pictures and no one said a word." In the crowd, she recognized Mrs. Olsen from Golden Gifts leaning on her cane, Dot from the permit department furiously waving in her direction and even her old nemesis, Mrs. Allen, with a reluctant smile on her face. Brady stood with his police officers, arms crossed over his chest, sending her a wink. Holly played with the Donovan kids while Faith watched over them. All the people she'd connected with while in Golden.

"They were sworn to secrecy," Celeste said in a mock whisper.

Her mother beamed. "And everyone was talking about how nice it was of you to give them prints from the photo shoot before you left. To commemorate your weeks here. They realize not all the photos will make it into the magazine, but now they have a piece of the buzz you brought to town."

Nicole placed a hand over her heart. She had no idea what her gift had meant to these people. "I don't know what to say."

Briana elbowed her. "Tell her the news."

With a cheeky grin, Nicole announced, "I'm staying."

Her mother yelped and covered her mouth with her hands.

"Not the reaction I expected."

"I'm thrilled." Her mother exchanged a glance with Celeste.

Nicole didn't miss the gesture. "What was that look all about?"

"Love" was Celeste's vague answer.

Her mother pulled Nicole into a tight embrace.

"I can't breathe," she hissed.

"Sorry." Her mom dropped her arms. "I'm just so happy. I want all the details. Why? When will you be here for good? Where will you live?"

Over her mother's shoulder, Nicole glimpsed Ethan. He stood on the sidelines, arms crossed, face expressionless. At least she wouldn't have far to go to grovel.

"I promise I'll explain it all, but right now, I have to talk to Ethan."

As she walked away, she heard her mother's loud whisper. "Is he why she's staying?"

He was. Forever and always.

Nicole waved to the crowd as she strode toward Ethan, said a loud thanks and told them to have a good time. Holly streaked by in her elf uform, Gus at her feet. Seeing the two together cemented Nicole's decision for good. By the time she reached Ethan, serious lines had formed on his forehead.

"Can we talk?" she asked.

He stared over her head. "I think we said it all."

"Actually, we didn't." She exhaled a long breath. "Come with me."

She dragged him behind the bronze park statue. Her hearty yank had Ethan frowning. "At least now we might have some privacy."

"Nicole, I won't change my mind. You've made your decision."

She rubbed her hands together as nerves fluttered in her. "I have, but you don't know what it is."

"Sure, I do." He shook his head like he knew her answer. "You're taking the promotion."

She tilted her head. "Are you positive?"

Uncertainty crept into his eyes. "That's what I thought."

Moving closer, she stopped just short of touching him. "When you left my cottage, that's what I thought, as well. But after a letter and discussion with my sisters, I realize I belong in Golden. I always have."

When he didn't say anything, she panicked. "The bottom line is, I've fallen in love with you, Ethan. With all my heart. I'm not running ever again. I'm opening my own business right here. I can see a future in Golden, with you and Holly." She stopped. Bit her lip, then said, "That is, if you still love me?"

Without hesitation, he reached out and tugged her into his embrace. "Like I could ever stop. I've envisioned long, miserable years of missing you. Now, we both get our dreams."

His lips descended on hers. She savored the warmth, her toes tingling when she realized she'd have a lifetime of kisses from this man.

He pulled back. Rested his forehead against hers. "You're sure?" he asked.

"One hundred percent."

He kissed her again. But not for long, because Holly ran around the corner to catch them. "Daddy, are you kissing Nicole?"

Nicole turned but Ethan kept her locked in his arms. "I am, princess."

"Yay."

"Yay, indeed."

"Does that mean Gus is staying?"

"He is," Nicole and Ethan answered in unison.

"Told you," Holly said as she skipped away. Nicole heard Gus's bark and pulled out of Ethan's embrace.

"Okay, here's the deal. I rented a U-Haul truck to move my belongings from Savannah. How do you feel about a road trip?"

A dazzling smile lit Ethan's face. His eyes sparkled with happiness. "I'm all for a road trip if it ends with you coming home."

Nicole took Ethan's hand to lead him to friends and family, ready to share their good news. "Home. I like the sound of that."

* * * * *

For more great romances set in Golden, Georgia, from author Tara Randel, visit www.Harlequin.com today!